Sea
of
Moonlight

Seduced BY Moonlight

Janice Sims

ARABESQUE®

SEDUCED BY MOONLIGHT

ISBN-13: 978-0-373-83112-8
ISBN-10: 0-373-83112-9

www.kimanipress.com

Printed in U.S.A.

This book is dedicated to my sister, Lillie Elaine Nattiel, who is a nurse, and to her sisters and brothers in uniform everywhere!

Acknowledgments

Thanks to my editor Evette Porter for being
so wonderful to work with. And thanks also to my agent,
Sha-Shana Crichton, for working so hard to get me the
work! Writers are inspired by everything around them.
I'd like to acknowledge that the artists Ben Harper &
the Innocent Criminals provided great inspiration
to me in the form of their newest CD, *Lifeline*.
And the inimitable Sam Cooke also did his
part in inspiring my creativity for this book,
Seduced by Moonlight, as you will see when you read it.

Lay bare your soul for
all the world to see
Make a mere word or
gesture a sweet melody

Turn what was supposed to be just
dinner into breakfast for two
That's what a little
moonlight can do

—*The Book of Counted Joys*

Chapter 1

Harrison Payne walked through the crowd in the ballroom of the Karibu Resort in Vail, Colorado, on ski season's opening night. Every year, he got an adrenaline rush knowing that the resort was booked for the entire season, which began in mid-November. Hundreds of guests would be staying there for the next one hundred and sixty-six days.

Harry had opened the resort five years ago. In the beginning there were just fifty suites and ten hotel rooms. Today the Swiss chalet–style resort had one hundred and fourteen luxury suites and sixteen hotel rooms. And this season they were offering ten two- or three-bedroom condominiums for larger groups who wanted more privacy.

At forty-two, Harry had already enjoyed one career: he was retired from professional football. One of the few black quarterbacks, Harry was proud to have played with the Denver Broncos the last nine years of his career. Although he was a Kentucky native, Coloradans had adopted Harry as their own, and loyally frequented his resort.

He saw plenty of locals in the crowd tonight, many of whom could not let him pass them without a "Hey, Harry!" or a fond pat on the back.

He was looking for his date, Marcia Shaw. He and Marcia had been going out for three months. She was a news anchor for a Denver station. Smart, attractive and just the right age to be seriously looking to settle down, Harry thought she was perfect for him.

Harry had this "life timeline" in his brain. When he was a football star in high school, he'd said that by the time he was twenty-five he would buy his mother a house. He had met that deadline. By the time he was thirty-five, he vowed, he would be financially solvent. He was a millionaire many times over by his thirty-fifth birthday. And by the time he was forty-five he would be married with children. He'd put off getting married this long because he was of the mind that when a man married, his wife should take precedence over everything else in his life. Therefore, his business had to be in good standing before he married anyone. Plus, since his own father died when he was a small child, he wanted plenty of time to spend with his kids.

Now that he was forty-two he felt an urgent need to find that special someone and start working on fulfilling the last item on his timeline agenda.

The orchestra was playing "Clair de Lune" and the beautifully dressed guests were either dancing or standing on the sidelines conversing, with small plates filled with appetizers and glasses of wine balanced in their hands.

Harry saw Marcia across the room chatting with another woman. He made a beeline for her, but was waylaid by John Santiago, founder of a Denver ski club for minority kids. Harry knew John well because he'd donated his time and money to the club over the years. He had even hired some members of John's group to work at the resort over the weekend, giving beginning ski lessons to children of his guests.

"Harry, could I have a word with you?" John asked with a serious look on his medium-brown face. John was five-ten and stocky with powerful shoulders and great arm and leg muscles honed from skiing, no doubt.

Harry was six-two and athletically built. Every morning—Monday through Friday—he still got up and jogged, even though his knees were beginning to give him problems. He spent at least an hour in the gym seven days a week. Both men were wearing tuxedos for the black-tie event.

"Sure, John, what's up?" Harry casually inquired, his thick brows raised.

John took a DVD in its plastic cover from his inside jacket pocket and handed it to Harry. "I've never asked you to do this before, Harry, but this girl is special. She's a downhill racer. I think she has the talent to qualify for the 2010 Winter Olympics in Vancouver, but she needs a sponsor. You know what that means—she needs financial backing and the use of Karibu's facilities."

Harry started to say something, and John cut him off with "I don't want you say anything right now. Just look at this DVD, and I'll get back to you later. She's only seventeen and in her last year of high school. She lives with her mother, who's a nurse at a Denver hospital. Single mom, but she's done a great job with Danielle. That's the kid's name, Danielle Washington."

John smiled. "I'm gonna get out of your hair now." He looked around them. "Great turnout tonight, Harry."

"Yeah, thanks," Harry said, wondering what he was getting himself into.

John disappeared into the crowd and Harry continued across the room. Marcia was no longer where he'd earlier spotted her. He kept walking in that general direction anyway and saw her standing in an alcove adjacent to the white brick fireplace.

Her back was to him, so she didn't see him approaching. He could hear her distinctive voice quite well, though. "I agree, Harry's a great guy, but he's too attached to his mom. Can you believe he phones her every day? My mother would have a heart attack if I started phoning her that often." She laughed uproariously as her friend joined her.

Harry stopped in his tracks, unable to resist listening to the rest of the conversation. How could she think he was a momma's boy? Sure, he phoned his mother every day, but that was because his mother was recovering from cancer surgery and he was worried about her. He had tried to talk her in to coming out to Denver to have the surgery and recuperate so he could keep an eye on her, but Mildred had flatly refused.

She preferred to stay in her Louisville, Kentucky home where her daughter, Susanne, Harry's younger sister, could walk across the street from her house to check on her mother each day. Harry could understand so he hadn't tried to bend his mother to his will.

"I like it when a man's devoted to his mother," said Marcia's friend. "If he treats his mother well, he'll treat me well."

"That's not always true," said Marcia. "If a man wants to be with me, I need to be number one in his heart. I don't want an old lady beating my time!"

"Girl, you need to quit," chuckled the friend, obviously enjoying their conversation. "If I had a man like Harry Payne, I wouldn't be complaining about the time he spends on the phone with his mother as long as he spends time with me in the bedroom. Tell me you've seen his bedroom." She waited expectantly.

Harry held his breath. He had never been able to put up with a woman who discussed their sex life with anyone. Not her best girlfriends. Not her sister, nor her mother. That was private. He considered sex a sacred thing between a man and a woman. Unlike some of his male friends, he never talked about how a woman performed in bed with him.

"I have no complaints there," Marcia confided conspiratorially. "He's the best lover I've had in a long time. But *Marcia* needs to be the queen in his heart as well as in his bed. I will not share him with his mother. I won't have her taking away my time!"

Harry turned on his heels and walked back in the direction he'd come. He didn't want to hear any more. In fact he wished he hadn't heard as much as he had. Here he was thinking that Marcia Shaw was a sweet, unselfish woman with whom he had a lot in common, only to find out that she was jealous of the time he spent talking to his mother. In his opinion Marcia's behavior smacked of a woman who was insecure and immature.

He sighed deeply. When you were past forty, it was definitely hard to find a woman worth taking home to Mom. He supposed he could give up and marry some bimbo with hips built for breeding who was just in it for the money and the big alimony after the divorce five years down the road. But he truly wanted someone he could love. Someone who could love him for himself and not for what he could give her. Was that too much to ask for?

It's freezing out here! Cherisse Washington thought as she wrapped her arms around herself. The pashmina shawl around her shoulders wasn't doing much to keep her warm. But she couldn't stand to be inside a moment longer. Why had she let Sonia talk her into coming? She could have been at home, curled up with a good book. Instead she was in Vail at "the hot resort," as Sonia had put it. Opening night promised to be filled with plenty of unattached men looking for unattached women. Sonia had already hooked up with someone: a computer programmer from Denver who had also had the bright idea to spend his Saturday night looking for love.

If Cherisse hadn't given Sonia a ride, she would have been in her car by now on her way back to Denver. But she wasn't about to leave her best friend stranded.

So she'd come out on the balcony to fortify herself with a bit of fresh air before returning to the ballroom, and the awkward advances from men who were more out of practice than even she was when it came to talking to the opposite sex.

The moon was about the best thing she'd seen tonight. It was full and bright, the color a pale yellow. She could see the smiling face of the man in the moon. She could almost feel the warmth of the moonlight on her skin. Closing her eyes, and tilting her head back, she imagined she could feel the moonbeams dancing on her face.

"What are you, a stargazer or just a moonbeam bather?" asked a deep male voice from behind her.

Cherisse's eyes flew open, and she turned to face a tall strikingly handsome man. She had no idea he was actually the host Harrison Payne. She didn't follow football and had never been to the Karibu Resort before tonight so there was no reason that she would recognize him.

She didn't follow football because she'd had enough of the game when she'd been married to Charlie Washington, a professional football player and her ex-husband for the past ten years. She'd married him at nineteen and divorced him at twenty-seven when he hadn't been able to put his family—

Cherisse and their daughter—before his gambling habit. She sometimes missed Charlie, but she didn't miss football.

As for the Karibu Resort, she had heard it was African-American-owned, and that was all she knew about it.

The guy was tall and muscular. From what she could see of him, he had a square-jawed, clean-shaven face and short, neatly cut hair. He smelled nice, too. "The moonbeams feel good on my face. Which one are you?" she said.

"Oh, I'm a stargazer," he said, joining her at the railing and looking up at the moon. "Especially when I was a boy, I would imagine that I could fly to the moon and stars like Superman. A little moonlight can still make me believe I can fly."

"It's been known to make you do silly things," Cherisse agreed. She rubbed her arms again, thinking that she should be getting back inside. Being alone with a stranger on a balcony, looking at the moon might not be the wisest or the safest thing to do. "I think I've had enough for one night."

She went to open the door and Harry stopped her with a hand on her arm. "Wait, don't go."

She was around five-seven, had wavy dark hair that fell to the middle of her back. She was wearing a simple little black dress, and had the best pair of legs he'd seen in ages. Admittedly, the light out on the deck didn't allow him to see her face too clearly, but her voice, her presence, even the smell of her body made him want to spend more time with her.

But she obviously didn't want to get too close to anyone tonight, otherwise she would have been inside trying to hook up with someone, like the other hundred or so single women at the opening were doing.

He removed his hand from her arm. "Sorry. It's just that I rarely feel comfortable at parties like this and you're the only person I've felt comfortable with tonight. Won't you stay and talk a while?"

Cherisse didn't know why, but she liked being in his presence, too. "A few more minutes," she said.

Harry removed his jacket and placed it about her shoulders. "You looked cold."

Cherisse immediately relaxed. His jacket was warm from his body heat and smelled of Calvin Klein cologne, a very pleasant combination. "Thanks."

"What's your name?" he asked.

She cleared her throat and he took that to mean he was overstepping his bounds.

"Okay, no last names," he said with a smile.

"It's Cheri," she told him, giving him the nickname her friends called her.

"I'm Harry." He waited half a beat, expecting her to recognize him now. But she gave no indication that she had connected him to the Harry who owned Karibu Resort.

"What are you doing here tonight, Cheri?"

"A friend convinced me that this was 'the' place to meet nice men."

"And you don't agree?"

"I'm sure there are plenty of nice men here tonight. It's just that I'm not in the market for a man, nice or otherwise."

"Then you already have someone?"

"Yeah, a teenaged daughter," Cherisse said with a laugh. "I also have a job I spend way too much time on, and college loans to repay. I don't have time for a man. Or should I say the average man would not have time for me. He would soon discover that he would be relegated to a sorry fourth in my life. My daughter, my job, the loans and, lastly, him. No man would put up with that kind of ranking."

Harry laughed softly. "You would be surprised what a man would put up with to have a good woman in his life. Take me, for example. I'm dating a woman I just found out hates the fact that I dote on my sick mother. Can you believe it? I phone my mother every day. She's recovering from breast cancer surgery. Thank God they found it when they did. She's gonna be all right. But, tell me, Cheri, would you hold it against a man if he was concerned enough about his mom that he phoned her every morning just to hear her voice and assure himself that she's still breathing?"

Cherisse was a nurse in pediatrics at Mercy Hospital in Denver. She dealt with sick people every day. She believed the sick healed faster when they had people around them who cared about them.

"Have you gone to visit her, and not just phoned her?" she asked.

"She had to threaten me to get me to leave Louisville," he told her. "She lives in Louisville, Kentucky. That's my hometown."

Cherisse smiled up at him. "Every mother should have a son like you."

Harry felt like hugging this complete stranger but restrained himself. "Thank you!"

He moved farther into her personal space, but not too close. He got a good whiff of the fragrance she was wearing. He couldn't place it. It was spicy but not overly so. He liked it when women smelled good, but perfume didn't turn him on. In this instance, it had to be a combination of her skin and the fragrance she was wearing. Something about her had captured his senses and wouldn't let go. "What's your real reason for not being open to meeting a nice guy tonight?" he suddenly asked.

Cherisse turned to face him and laughed softly. "Promise not to spread this around?" she asked lightly.

"I don't know anyone you know," Harry said. "I'm pretty sure your secret will be safe with me."

"I haven't been intimate with anyone in more than six

years. If I met someone and we liked each other it would eventually come to that age-old question—your place or mine? And I'm afraid I've forgotten everything I ever knew about that aspect of a relationship. I'm not a twenty-first century girl who can sleep with anyone just for the immediate gratification. I need to like the guy, a lot! And it's been six years since I really liked a guy."

"What happened to the guy you really liked?"

"He was killed." Her voice broke.

Harry didn't know what to say. He should have kept his mouth shut. Now he could feel the pain radiating from her body, just as her lovely scent had wafted over him. "I'm sorry. I didn't mean to bring up sad memories."

"It's okay," she said, clearing her throat. "At any rate, you see my predicament, right?"

"Yeah," Harry agreed with a smile. "You would be a tough nut to crack."

Cherisse laughed again. "Exactly, and what man in his right mind would even try?"

Harry was about to say that he knew any number of men who would get in line to take her out when the balcony door opened and Cherisse's best friend, Sonia Lopez, cried, "There you are! I've been looking all over for you." She noticed Harry. "Oh, sorry, girl, I didn't know you were out here with somebody. I'm ready to leave. I have to work tomorrow. But if you want to stay a while longer I'll go wait for you in the lounge off the lobby."

Cherisse clamped onto Sonia's arm as if it were a lifeline. "I was just waiting on *you,*" she said. She gestured to Harry. "This is Harry. Harry, this is Sonia."

The two of them murmured hellos and Cherisse turned to Harry. "It was nice chatting with you, Harry. Take care."

"You take care, too," Harry said. He wanted to give her his

card, but knew it would be inappropriate. He was dating Marcia. He had to chalk this up to one of those magical nights that had no chance of going any further than it already had.

He held the door for her and watched her leave with her friend, Sonia. In the light of the ballroom he saw that she had the face of an angel. Her skin was golden-brown and she had eyes the color of a fine malt whiskey. Her face was heart-shaped and she had lips that were full and sensual, lips any man would love to kiss. He knew he was going to have dreams about her, his moonlight angel.

Still, he let her walk out the door.

A few seconds later, his ears were assaulted by the sound of Marcia's strident voice accusing him of neglecting her all night.

Harry met her in the center of the room. She had a sexy pout on her beautiful face as she walked up to him. He knew she was going to exact some kind of punishment for what she perceived as his preoccupation with business.

Tonight, though, he simply wasn't in the mood to play games.

"I'm sorry, darling," he said, taking her by the arm. "Of course, you're probably ready to go home. I'll get someone to drive you."

Marcia's light golden eyes stretched with surprise and indignation. "I didn't say anything about being ready to go home. I simply wanted to spend some time with you."

"You're right," Harry insisted. "Because I had to be sure the rest of my guests were enjoying themselves tonight, I've had to leave you on your own. I'll make it up to you. I'll call you tomorrow."

He took his cell phone from his inside jacket pocket and dialed his driver Fisher Graham's number. Fisher answered right away. "Yeah, boss?"

"Fisher, I'd like you to take Miss Shaw home. How soon can you meet us in the lobby?"

"I'll be right there!" Fisher replied. "I'm in the lounge off the lobby."

"Great," said Harry. "See you soon."

He smiled down into Marcia's frowning face. "Fisher will take you home. You can meet him in the lobby." He bent and kissed her on the cheek. "Thank you for taking time out of your busy schedule to join us tonight."

He sounded like he was talking to one of the guests. Marcia continued to stare at him. Then something horrible occurred to her. He was acting as if he were saying goodbye forever to her, not simply good-night. Was it possible he had overheard her talking to Kenya about his being tied to his mother's apron strings?

She couldn't broach the subject for fear her guess was wrong, and then he really would know how she felt about his relationship with his mother.

So she played it cool. She faked a yawn. "I am a little tired." She smiled up at him. "Maybe we can have brunch together tomorrow?"

"Sounds good," Harry said. He glanced at his watch. "It's almost time for the fireworks over Vail Mountain. See you, darling."

He walked away, and Marcia turned and went to the lobby, a feeling of dread niggling at her.

Harry went to join the other guests, who had gathered on the south side of the ballroom to watch the fireworks with Vail Mountain as a backdrop. The fireworks display was spectacular, and the guests enthusiastically applauded.

Harry smiled his pleasure. Things were getting off to a good start this season. He couldn't help thinking that meeting his moonlight angel had something to do with his positive outlook.

But he knew he had to put her out of his mind. Sure,

Marcia had given him a rude awakening tonight, but that didn't mean he wasn't going to try to make the relationship work. We all had our faults, he thought. He definitely wasn't perfect.

Chapter 2

Five Points, the neighborhood where Cherisse's family had lived for years, was bustling with activity Monday morning as she drove up Martin Luther King Boulevard. At seven-thirty, traffic was heavy, but then it usually was with all the commuters who lived in Five Points trying to drive to the metro area.

The radio in her Cherokee was tuned to a talk radio station. She listened to men grouse about their wives earning more money than they did while she watched the road. It was another sunny day in Denver. The latest tourism ads boasted that Denver enjoyed 300 days of sunshine every year. Cherisse didn't think they were exaggerating. Because of its unique geographical location—east of a major mountain range—Denver enjoyed a mild, dry, sunny climate. Temperatures dipped during the winter but there were few gray days.

Today, for instance, it was forty degrees but it would

probably warm up to fifty degrees by noon. Cherisse usually sat outside to eat her lunch.

When she got to Mercy Hospital she parked in the staff parking lot across the street. Staff who worked nights often grumbled about the long hike through the parking lot in the dark. Cherisse would be grumbling herself in three months' time because she would be changing shifts. Hospital management believed keeping the staff rotating kept their medical skills sharp. The staff would have preferred to work either during the day or at night, not both. But they didn't have a say in the matter. As head pediatric nurse, Cherisse was often told that she was in a managerial position and should side with management on the issue. But in the three years she'd held the position, she had been firmly on the side of the nurses.

This was a bone of contention between her and Dr. David Pedersen, the hospital's chief of staff. He had hired her with the intention of making sure she followed his orders. He had been sorely disappointed when she'd fought for better hours for the nursing staff. Better hours and better pay. He was chomping at the bit waiting for the day when he could fire her. However, Cherisse had an ironclad contract, which stipulated that unless her job performance fell below standard her job was safe for ten years. Then they were free to renegotiate her contract. Of course, she could resign.

Some days she felt David Pedersen was trying to make her life such a living hell that she would turn in her resignation. Today was such a day.

The minute she got to her office and put her shoulder bag and lunch away, David Pedersen tapped lightly on her door. He didn't wait for her to invite him in, and strode confidently into her office, an aggrieved expression on his tanned, sharp-boned face.

David was six feet tall, trim from jogging every day—rain, snow or shine—and wore his thick gray hair in a military-style buzz cut. Cherisse had heard he'd spent several years in the army before going to medical school. He was fifty-five now and his body was still fit and ramrod-straight.

Clearing his throat, he said, "Good morning, Cherisse."

Cherisse finished slipping into a pair of pristine sneakers and sat in her chair to tie the laces. She was wearing her usual uniform of green scrubs, which most of the staff wore. David was wearing them, too, but he wore a white lab coat over his.

"Good morning, David," Cherisse said without looking up. "What can I help you with?"

"You might channel the energies of your staff in a different direction," he said tightly. "They are wasteful with medical supplies and spend way too much time entertaining the patients instead of doing their jobs."

"The patients are children, David, children who're sick and scared. What's it to you if the staff spends a little extra time trying to cheer them up if it doesn't interfere with their duties? I have seen no evidence of anyone slacking off. As far as the medical supplies go, I'll look into it and if there is a reason for concern, I'll address it at the next staff meeting." Finished, she rose and smiled at him. Didn't he have other nurses to pester?

"Is there anything else this morning? Because if there isn't I should go post the assignments and study a few patients' charts."

David stepped aside. "There has also been more talk about Mary Thomas's love affair with the bottle. If you can't get her to go to rehab, I'll have to deal with it myself."

Cherisse sighed softly. Not again. She had spoken to Mary, a licensed practical nurse with twenty years under her belt, at least three times about going to Alcoholics Anonymous. She knew Mary's job meant everything to her.

Like any other profession, medicine had its share of drug-addicted and alcohol-addicted workers. The stress of the job could drive anyone to find a way to self-anesthetize.

The hospital's policy was to be understanding and supportive to a certain extent. Mary had had three warnings. It was time to show some tough love.

Cherisse looked straight into David Pedersen's smug blue eyes. "Please don't interfere, David. I'll handle it." She then left him standing in her office.

Taking a deep breath, she headed for the nurses' station. Mercy Hospital was one of the oldest hospitals in Denver. With 880 beds, it was also one of the smaller facilities in the metropolitan area. If the staff were not feeling the brunt of budget cuts, they were being confronted with constant rumors that the hospital was being closed down entirely. Those rumors had been circulating for years before Cherisse ever got hired. Yet Mercy was still open. She figured it was just a ploy management used to justify poor cost-of-living raises and a downsized staff.

They always had to make do with fewer nurses than were needed for the daily schedule. Today, for example, there were forty-four patients on the floor and six nurses to see to their needs. That meant each nurse was responsible for at least seven patients and two lucky nurses got to care for eight. That might not seem like a lot of patients per nurse, but considering the fact that during an eight-to-ten-hour day, vital signs had to be monitored, medications administered, IVs set up, blood drawn, baths given, beds changed and God forbid an emergency should occur that would send a code-blue team rushing to a patient's room. Every day that Cherisse went to work, she prayed for a quiet day. But her prayers were rarely answered.

At the nurses' station she greeted Sonia, her best friend and a registered nurse, and Gerald Cramer, also a registered nurse. Both were busy entering data in patients' charts. The other nurses were elsewhere on the floor working with patients.

"How is Billy today?" Cherisse asked Sonia. She peered over her shoulder. Sonia paused in her writing. She was a petite brunette with long, curly auburn hair and startlingly dark brown eyes. Billy Neale was an eight-year-old who had recently undergone a liver transplant. For the next few days the staff was praying that he didn't reject it. This was his second transplant. His body had rejected the first liver.

Sonia smiled up at her. "He's doing really well, vitals are in the normal range, and the doctor put him on limited solids today."

Cherisse liked the sound of that. She breathed a sigh of relief and turned her attention to Gerald. "And you, Gerry? How is Amy Whitehall doing?"

Gerald shook his head sadly. Amy was a twelve-year-old who had allegedly been viciously attacked by her father and left for dead. A neighbor had found her and called 911. The girl had broken ribs, a broken arm and her skull had been fractured by a blunt object. The first couple of days no one expected her to live. This was day five. Cherisse was hoping that she'd taken a turn for the better overnight.

"Still in a coma, and the infection is worse," Gerald reported. Narrowing his eyes, he added, "I'd love just five minutes alone with her father."

Gerald, thirty-two, was a huge man, six-four and well over two hundred pounds. A bodybuilder, he looked like he could bench-press a Cadillac. Part African-American, part Native-American, Gerald wore his long, black hair in a ponytail.

People sometimes joked about his being a nurse among so many women. The other nurses were happy to have him nearby because they knew that for all his physical strength, he was one of the kindest, gentlest men they'd ever known. He was wonderful with the kids.

"You wouldn't need five minutes," Cherisse said. "You could snap his neck in a second."

Gerald laughed. "Cheri, you're so violent!"

Cherisse squeezed his shoulder and left him to his work while she walked over to the large carousel atop the desk where they kept the patients' charts.

Turning the carousel, she selected a metal-encased chart and began reading the latest entry. She sat there and read every last update in every individual chart, while jotting down a note to herself as to which patients she wanted to personally check up on. Several minutes later, she had a list of thirteen patients.

While she had been checking the charts, Sonia had gone to answer a call from a patient, and Gerald had gone to get another patient ready to be taken downstairs for X rays.

Now there were two other nurses in the station: Katy McCullough, a tall redhead, and Sarah Benson, a small blonde fresh out of nursing school. Both were licensed practical nurses.

Upon entering the station, Katy had started gabbing away. "I heard you and Sonia went to Karibu Resort this weekend. Did you meet anybody interesting?"

"Just some guys more desperate than I am," Cherisse joked.

"You didn't get a chance to meet Harry, did you?" Katy asked, her light-colored brows arching over pale green eyes.

"Harry?" Cherisse asked, frowning, remembering the guy on the balcony.

"Harry Payne, the owner of the resort! He used to be the quarterback for the Broncos a few years ago. When he retired, he opened Karibu Resort. Where have you been the past ten years?"

"Right here," Cherisse said. "I just don't follow football."

She faintly recalled that the Broncos had a black quarterback with the last name Payne. So, he was the African-American who owned the resort. That couldn't be her Harry!

"Well, if you'd met Harry you would remember it," Katy said with a dreamy expression.

Cherisse laughed. "Why? Is he drop-dead gorgeous?"

"He's no pretty boy," Katy said, giving her considered opinion. "But he's definitely all man!"

Suddenly the lights connected to Amy Whitehall's life support monitors began blinking on the monitor bank. Looking up, Cherisse wondered where Gerald was. A moment later, her question was answered when Gerald's voice came over the intercom.

"I need help right now!" he yelled frantically. "Amy's seizing."

"Katy, come with me," Cherisse ordered.

They ran down the corridor to Amy's room, their sneakers squeaking on the tiles.

The girl on the bed was bucking violently, and Gerald was cradling her in his arms, trying to prevent her from hurting herself.

Cherisse immediately assessed the situation. According to Amy's chart the neighbor who'd brought her in didn't recall her being on any medications. This reaction was obviously due to her injury or perhaps due to the infection.

She was on antibiotics for the infection. The side effects of the drug did not include seizure activity.

Turning to Katy, she ordered, "Twenty milligrams of phenobarbital, stat!"

Katy didn't hesitate, she ran to get the drug.

In her absence, Cherisse joined Gerald on the bed with Amy. The girl's pale skin now glistened with perspiration. Her scalp was bandaged to protect her skull where it had been fractured. But the girl was bucking so wildly that Cherisse feared she might hit her head and reopen the wound, so she climbed into the bed and sat behind her with a pillow pressed to her bosom. Amy hit her head repeatedly against the pillow.

Katy returned with the syringe filled with the drug and Gerald held Amy down long enough for Cherisse to administer it.

It took a few minutes for the drug to work, but it was effective. Amy's body stopped jerking involuntarily, and the girl's breathing returned to normal. Cherisse gently moved away from the bed and helped Gerald place Amy in as comfortable a position as possible.

Seeing how shaken Gerald was, Cherisse told him to leave the room. She and Katy would handle everything from this point on.

When he was out of earshot, Katy said, "That seizure wasn't a sign that she's on the road to a full recovery, was it?"

Cherisse wasn't willing to give up just yet. She'd seen patients with injuries worse than Amy's pull through. "She's young and strong. And as long as she's breathing, there's hope."

Katy laughed shortly. Nurses either saw the humor in their lives or they developed ulcers or a taste for drugs or alcohol. "Okay, Mother Teresa."

Cherisse smiled at her as she took Amy's wrist between her fingers and felt her pulse.

It was still a little rapid, but was slowing down. She reached up and smoothed the crinkly black hair out of Amy's face. As pale as the child's skin was, one would expect her to have blond hair or perhaps be a redhead like Katy, but she had coal-black hair that was thick and curly. Cherisse suspected there was some African-American blood in her veins.

Denver was a diverse city with many interracial couples among its population.

"She's going to be okay," she said. It was more a prayer than a statement. Looking at Katy, she said, "Go tell Gerald he needs to contact Amy's primary and fill him or her in. He might be too upset to remember that."

Amy's primary physician was probably the doctor who had been in charge of the emergency room when she had been admitted. When parents or guardians weren't the ones to bring in a child, the child was treated like any other indigent. She got whomever was on duty.

"Amy, you've got to fight, do you hear me?" Cherisse whispered. "Fight to stay here with us."

She was still standing there holding Amy's hand when Gerald returned. "Dr. Mahoney's on the way. He says good call on the phenobarb."

Cherisse smiled. Some doctors became incensed when a nurse diagnosed and prescribed on the spot the way she had done.

Dr. Phillip Mahoney was well-liked by the nurses because of his unerring belief that good nurses were essential to the well-being of his patients.

"He's one of the good guys," she said of Dr. Mahoney. Then she left Gerald alone with his patient.

It was after one before Cherisse got a chance to grab some lunch. She sat at a table outside at the cafeteria annex on the first floor. All of the umbrella-topped tables were occupied with either hospital staff or visitors, even the occasional ambulatory patient on a normal diet who was tired of eating in his room.

It was also the only place where you could use your cell phone. They were prohibited inside the building.

She dialed the house. She and Danielle lived with her mother in a Victorian that had been in the Patterson family for over a hundred years. Her mother, Joann—called Jo by friends and family—often threatened to move to Arizona with her sister, Bettye, and leave the house to Cherisse. She never believed her because Jo was too wrapped up in the community. She thought her mother would die without her circle of friends. Besides, living in that big house without Jo around wouldn't be half as much fun.

Jo picked up on the fourth ring. Cherisse figured she'd interrupted her mom's favorite soap, *All My Children.* "Mmm, huh, hold on just a second," Jo said. "Adam Chandler's about to profess his love for his ex-wife and beg her to come back to him, again!"

"Will he ever learn?" Cherisse asked.

"I doubt it," Jo said. She laughed loudly. "Oh, my, she turned him down. That'll just make him try harder."

"Rich men," Cherisse said, "don't know how to take 'no' for an answer."

"You've got that right," Jo chortled. "That's why I like him. Okay. He's gone now. What's up, baby?"

"How did your granddaughter get to school today?" Cherisse wanted to know.

"Don't worry, she didn't take the car," Jo said. Cherisse had forbade Danielle to drive her car to school for two weeks because Danielle had let someone else drive it, violating the terms of the insurance policy on the car. The only persons listed in the policy were Danielle and Cherisse.

"I think I saw Echo's car in the driveway this morning," said Jo.

Echo was Edward James Thornton, also a senior and Danielle's best friend. Cherisse might have been leery of Danielle's spending so much time with a guy if not for the fact that Echo was obviously gay. He hadn't come out to friends or family yet, but Cherisse didn't know any straight men who could cook, sew and knew all the songs from the Broadway musical *Rent.*

Of course his being able to cook and sew could be attributed to the fact that he was the only child of a single working mother, and his mother had taught him the skills so he would be able to take care of himself in her absence. But loving musicals, in Cherisse's experience, was not a male thing. Charlie used to complain loudly and vociferously whenever she rented one. When she was growing up her father used to leave the room whenever she and her mom watched one on television.

Edward James Thornton had earned his nickname because he was always mimicking any song he heard, singing them word for word. His friends started saying he sounded like an echo, and the name stuck. His favorite singers were invariably female. Cherisse knew she shouldn't label the boy, but the signs were there.

"All right," Cherisse said of Danielle's getting a lift from Echo that morning. "I was just checking."

"She's a good girl," Jo said, defending her granddaughter.

"I know, Ma, but when she does wrong, she has to pay the price. You never let me get away with anything."

"Sure, I did," her mother disagreed. "One of them was car-related. I know you and Sonia took that little Toyota I used to own when you were in high school for a joyride one lazy summer afternoon. Your father and I had gone to Boulder to visit friends and I told you not to drive my car. I was worried you might get into an accident and your father and I would be all the way in Boulder. But the next day Bea Wilson told me she saw you and Sonia tearing out of the driveway in my car acting like a couple of prisoners let out of Alcatraz. Free at last, free at last!"

"And you never said anything!" Cherisse cried, laughing.

"Well, you didn't get hurt or cause an accident," Jo said reasonably. "And you had sense enough to put gas in the car before returning it to the garage. Besides, if I had made a big deal out of it, your father would have probably grounded you for life."

"Probably," Cherisse agreed. "Thanks, Mom."

"Just remember this the next time Danielle does something stupid," her mother said.

"Gotcha," said Cherisse. "I'd better go."

"Wait a minute," Jo said hurriedly. "John Santiago phoned this morning. He says he's found Danielle a sponsor."

Cherisse frowned. She knew she should be happy that Danielle excelled at skiing. She was undoubtedly going to be athletically gifted, with her genes: her father played professional football and Cherisse had been quite the athlete herself in high school. Even though she was only five-seven, she had been the forward on the basketball team, and what she lacked in height she made up in determination. Her team had been state champs three years in a row. These days she jogged and lifted weights.

Nevertheless, she had misgivings about Danielle's downhill skiing because it was such a dangerous sport. One spill and her baby could sustain several broken bones. She was nervous every time Danielle competed.

Recently, Danielle's coach, John Santiago, who also ran a youth program for minority kids who were interested in winter sports like skiing and snowboarding, was saying that Danielle had a good chance of qualifying for the Olympics.

Cherisse had always told Danielle she could be whatever she wanted to be. In spite of her fears for Danielle's safety she couldn't, now, start telling her to set her sights on a sport that was less dangerous.

"He's really serious about Danielle going to the Olympic trials!" Cherisse exclaimed in her mother's ear.

"It appears so," said Jo.

"Did he say who the sponsor was?"

"Harrison Payne, the ex-quarterback for the Broncos," Jo answered. Jo was a fan. She'd lived in Denver all her life and when he was alive, she and Jake, Cherisse's father, had tried to go to all of the home games.

"I keep hearing that name," Cherisse said.

"Whose name, Harrison Payne's?" asked Jo.

Cherisse reminded her mother that she'd told her about her visit to the Karibu Resort over the weekend and meeting a guy named Harry. Then she told her about her conversation with Katy about Harry Payne. "Now, John Santiago has recruited him."

"Maybe it's a sign," said her superstitious mother.

Cherisse laughed softly. "Yeah, it's a sign that I am totally clueless when it comes to football. I have a feeling he's the same Harry I had a memorable conversation with on the balcony at the resort Saturday night."

"Well, you'll find out soon enough," Jo said. "John wants you and Danielle to drive up to Vail this weekend to meet him."

"But it'll be Thanksgiving weekend," Cherisse protested. She had little time with Danielle as it was. She was looking forward to some quality time with her seventeen-year-old daughter.

"John says you've been invited to spend Saturday night at the resort. Free, of course. You can't pass that up. I hear it's pretty ritzy. Danielle will love it. If it weren't such a shameless ploy, I'd try to wangle an invitation myself."

Cherisse's beeper went off at her waist. "Mom, I'm being beeped. See you tonight."

"'Bye, baby, hope it isn't anything awful," Jo commiserated before hanging up.

Cherisse got up and quickly disposed of the rest of her bag lunch in the nearby trash receptacle. She paused long enough to glance down at the readout on the beeper's tiny screen. It had been Sonia who had summoned her. She hurried to the bank of elevators on the first floor.

As soon as she stepped off the elevator onto the fifth floor she heard a woman's voice raised in anger. It was coming from the direction of the staff lounge.

Chapter 3

Sonia was coming out of the staff lounge as Cherisse approached. Her friend looked mad enough to spit bullets. "David Pedersen just threatened to fire Mary," she reported.

"What is Mary doing here, she's not due on until eleven," Cherisse said, confused.

Sonia rolled her eyes. "Apparently she came back to get something out of her locker. Pedersen was in the lounge eating lunch and saw her."

Cherisse's stomach muscles tightened painfully at the mention of Mary coming in to work to get something she'd left in her locker. "Dear God, please tell me it wasn't liquor!"

Sonia screwed up her mocha-colored face. "You guessed it."

Cherisse strode past her, entering the lounge. Mary stopped talking as soon as she saw Cherisse, and walked over to her. "He can't fire me, can he, Cheri?" she asked loudly, pleadingly.

Cherisse went to her and grabbed her by both arms. "First of all, Mary, you've got to calm down. Remember, we've got sick children on the floor who're depending on us to provide a healing environment."

Cherisse knew that appealing to the nurse in Mary would be more effective than ordering her around. Mary, in spite of her drinking, was devoted to the patients.

Cherisse could feel the tension leave Mary's body as she held on to her. Mary looked her in the eyes. "I'm sorry, Cheri. That man brings out the worst in me."

David Pedersen was standing in front of the sink in the room that was furnished with a stove, a refrigerator and several tables and chairs for the staff's use. His arms were obstinately folded in front of him, and his eyes were cold and uncompromising. "I told you that if you didn't handle it, I would have to," he said to Cherisse.

"Handle what?" Mary asked softly, appealing to Cherisse. "I haven't done anything wrong. Have the patients complained?"

"No," said Cherisse, holding Mary's gaze with the force of her own. "No patient has complained, but several of your co-workers have smelled liquor on your breath and they—*we*—are concerned that if you can't stop drinking while on the job, things are only going to get worse. Look at yourself, Mary. What did you come down here for?"

Mary looked guilty. Her brown eyes lowered, and her bottom lip started to tremble. Cherisse knew that tears weren't far behind. But tears weren't going to make her reluctant to say what she should have said months ago.

"I'm going to have to put you on temporary leave until you get help, Mary. I have no alternative. I have the patients' well-being to think about. Plus the fact that if you're drunk on the job and there is an emergency, I don't think you'll be able to do it if you're incapacitated. Go home, Mary, and don't come back until you can show me proof that you're seeking help for your alcoholism. And when you do return, which I hope you will, if anyone reports that you're still drinking on the job, I'm going to have to let you go."

Mary collapsed into sobs. Cherisse calmly pulled her into her arms. "Now, I love you, Mary. You're one of the nurses I looked up to most when I first came here." Mary was one of the older African-American nurses, and she immediately took to Cherisse when she began working at Mercy. Already with a bachelor's degree, and working on her master's after her divorce, Cherisse had been motivated to go as far in the nursing field as she could so that she would be able to take care of Danielle and not have to rely on child support from Charlie, which never came with any regularity.

"I know you miss Trey," Cherisse continued soothingly. Trey, Mary's twenty-five-year-old son, had been killed in Iraq more than a year ago. "And that big house of yours feels so empty you probably hate to be there." Mary's husband, Clarence, died two years before Trey was killed. Now all she had in the way of relatives was a very ungrateful twenty-three-year-old daughter who had gone to Los Angeles right out of high school and became a video dancer. Not a very successful one because she was always calling her mom to hit her up for money.

"Think of Trey and Clarence," Cherisse softly said in Mary's ear. "They would want you to be happy and healthy. They loved you so much."

"I loved them," Mary said, weeping.

"Then respect their memory by living a long, happy life," Cherisse told her. "Besides," she whispered, "Eve is just waiting for you to drink yourself to death so she can come back here, sell the house and live the good life in L.A. until the money runs out. Then she'll be on the street. You can't let that happen to your little darling."

Mary actually laughed through her tears. Many nights, she and Cherisse had comforted each other about the antics of their daughters. Eve had always been a wild child and Mary had no control whatsoever over her. From the time she became a teen, Eve had been sneaking out of her bedroom window in the middle of the night to be with boys. She'd stolen money and other valuables from her mom, gotten arrested for shoplifting more than once and propositioned the cop who had booked her the last time if he would let her go.

Danielle had also been caught climbing out of her bedroom window in the middle of the night, but not to meet boys, rather to go to late-night clubs with her girlfriends. The girl loved to dance, and her mother forbade her to stay out late, so she had taken it upon herself to disobey her. Cherisse had put the fear of God in her, promising her that the next time she climbed out of her window in the middle of the night, she was going to have all the locks changed on the doors and have bars put on the windows. Plus, she was going to take her down to the local police station and ask her friend Taz Coffman, a sergeant, to put her in lockup for a few hours to see how she liked it.

Danielle had never sneaked out again.

Cherisse released Mary, and the older woman wiped her tears away with the back of her hand. Still laughing, she said, "Come on, Cheri, if you wanted me to get off the booze, all you had to do was ask. You didn't have to threaten me with the thought of Eve blowing my money when I'm dead!"

"I have to use whatever I have at my disposal," Cherisse said with a smile. "May I have what you came for today?" She held out her hand.

Mary closed her eyes momentarily and sighed. But she

went into her shoulder bag and withdrew the pint of Jim Beam wrapped in a brown paper bag and handed it to Cherisse.

"You want me to drive you home?" Cherisse asked.

"No, I took the commuter train," Mary said. Mary also lived in the Five Points area and the commuter train was convenient to that neighborhood because it ended at 30th and Downing streets, an easy walk for many Five Pointers.

"Okay," said Cherisse, looking Mary straight in the eye. "I expect you back here as soon as you get yourself together."

Mary gave her a quick hug and turned to leave the room, but not before leveling an evil glance in David Pedersen's direction.

David visibly winced.

When Mary had gone, David sighed with relief. "That woman called me everything but a child of God," he said. "I think she should see a mental health professional."

Cherisse rounded on him. "I specifically asked you not to say anything to Mary," she said menacingly, her eyes flashing angrily. Pointing a finger, she reiterated exactly what she had said to him that morning. "Please don't interfere, David. I'll handle it."

She stomped her foot. "Did you not understand me? Or was Mary's presence here too much of a temptation for you to resist saying anything? Yeah, she drinks too much. Yeah, she was caught drinking on the job and something had to be done about it. But you didn't have to scare the poor woman half to death by saying she was fired."

"I never said she was fired," David said, defending himself. He rubbed what must have been a sweaty palm down the front of his immaculate navy blue slacks. "I only said that if she couldn't control her drinking she could end up without a job. I never said she was fired."

"Coming from you," Cherisse told him, "it means the same thing. That's why nobody feels comfortable coming to you with a personal problem, David. Mary is a human being. She's a widow and her son, the apple of her eye, was killed in Iraq defending his country. Why couldn't you have shown some compassion? Or, at least, restrained yourself from causing misery to a woman who is already pretty miserable?"

"If I had known…" David began.

"If you had asked me anything about Mary's personal life, I would have told you," Cherisse said. "But, you didn't."

"I can't be expected to tiptoe around someone with personal problems," David said. "It's my job to run this hospital as efficiently as possible and to avoid as many lawsuits as I can. A drunken nurse is a lawsuit waiting to happen. It was my duty to say something to Mary Thomas. If I was lacking in tact I apologize. But I will not apologize for doing my job."

"Nobody expects you to," Cherisse said softly. And that said it all. No one on the staff would expect human kindness from David Pedersen.

Turning to leave, Cherisse said, "I've got work to do."

When she returned to the nurses' station, Sonia was waiting to get an update on the situation. Cherisse gave her a shortened version.

"I'll go check on her after I get off from work," Sonia volunteered, agreeing to look out for a co-worker and a friend.

"And I'll go the next day," Cherisse said.

Sonia snapped to when one of her patients' room numbers lit up on the monitor bank.

"That's Hilary. She probably needs to go to the bathroom again. Sweet kid, she's so happy she isn't on the colostomy bag anymore."

"Who wouldn't be?" Cherisse cracked. "Yuck!"

They both laughed.

* * *

That night, Cherisse got home after a twelve-hour shift just in time to sit down and have a late dinner with her mother and daughter.

The house sat on a quiet tree-lined street amid other older homes. Yards were kept neatly manicured and no junk cars were allowed on the front lawns, but it wasn't unusual to see a father and son—or daughter—working on their car in the driveway of their home on a Saturday morning. That's the kind of neighborhood it was—family-oriented.

While some of the original families had sold their homes to the highest bidders, most of the families on Cherisse's street were third- and fourth-generation Five Pointers.

Cherisse put her key in the lock of the front door, an oak door with a stained-glass window in its upper portion. The image in the stained glass was of an angel floating in the air, wings spread, gently nudging a lost child in the direction of home. Jo called it "the lost sheep."

Cherisse didn't get the chance to get the door fully open before Danielle swung it open and yelled, "Mom's home!"

She grabbed her mother's shoulder bag and helped her out of her coat, a normal ritual at the end of the day. Then she briefly hugged her mother and kissed her on the cheek.

"Did you hear, Ma?" she asked excitedly, her dark chocolate eyes, so much like her father's, sparkling with happiness. "Harry Payne has agreed to back me for the Olympics!" She jumped up and down with her mother's shoulder bag and coat clasped to her chest.

Cherisse couldn't help laughing. "Yes, yes, I heard. Congratulations!"

Danielle pulled herself together long enough to deposit her mother's coat on the hall tree and the shoulder bag inside the adjacent closet on the top shelf, after which she regarded her mother again. "We've got to do something about your wardrobe before we go to Vail this weekend."

Her eyes raked over her mother's body and obviously found it wanting. "And we need to tame that wild hair of yours, too."

At thirty-seven, Cherisse's hair had very little gray in it, fell halfway down her back, was thick and naturally wavy. She hadn't been to a salon in years. For one thing, she could never find the time, what with her work schedule. For another, she had no desire to waste three hours or more sitting in a salon pretending to be patient with the stylist, who had over-booked and therefore made the customers wait for hours, while she was really dreaming up ways to murder her.

"I have a perfectly functional wardrobe," Cherisse said, walking back to the kitchen where she knew her mother probably was. "And you're not touching my hair. After thirty-seven years I've finally got it the way I want it. There are no chemicals in it, and it's healthy."

Danielle, who was five-nine and weighed 155 pounds, was taller and weighed more than her mother. She had her mother's unruly hair which she tamed by having it braided within an inch of its life, and tying all of the long plaits together at the nape of her neck with colorful ribbons. With her active lifestyle, she couldn't have her hair flopping in her face every time she went flying down a mountain on skis.

She followed her mother into the kitchen where the three of them had dinner together as often as their schedules permitted. She plopped down in a chair at the table while her mother went to kiss her grandmother's cheek.

She smiled. The two women were her greatest sources of strength, and she knew it. Her mother may not have been aware of it, but she did appreciate everything she and her grandmother had done for her. Probably the greatest gift they'd given her was the knowledge that a Patterson woman—okay, she was technically a Washington because that was her dad's name but she felt more like a Patterson—could be and do anything she envisioned.

Her grandmother had been one of the first black female city council members in Denver. She had also taught school for thirty years. She was retired from teaching now but was still involved in the community. Everybody knew Miss Jo, and knew that she was the person to go to whenever you had a problem with city hall. Miss Jo knew the mayor personally and didn't mind letting him know when he was slipping in the performance of his job. She let him know that he was an elected servant of the people and hadn't been put into office to line his pockets.

The mayor good-naturedly took Jo's suggestions in the manner they were intended, out of love for the city. He had even been known to phone her and ask after her health when he hadn't heard from her in a while.

Jo called his concern *two-fold*. "On one hand," she would say, "in a strange way he probably does like me as a person. On the other, I've been a thorn in his side, and he would like advance notice if I'm about to kick the bucket and will therefore cease to be a thorn in his side!"

Danielle adored her grandmother's spirit.

She looked at her mother with a critical eye as the two women across the room started putting dinner on plates. Her mother was a beautiful woman, but she had no inkling of what she was missing by shutting herself off from the rest of the world. Or the part that males lived in.

Danielle knew Neil Kennedy's death had had something to do with it. She was eleven at the time, but she would have had to be blind not to have seen a change in her mother after Neil had gotten killed by a kid terrified of going to jail. Neil had stopped the kid for a basic traffic violation, but the kid was a small-time drug dealer and was both afraid of answering to the guy he worked for and going to prison. He had heard tales about what happened to "pretty young boys" in prison. He'd panicked and shot Neil before he even heard the reason why he'd been pulled over.

Since Neil's death her mother hadn't given another man the opportunity to get close enough to stake a claim on her heart.

Danielle was worried about her. In a few months, she was going to graduate and move on to college. Then, it would be her grandmother and her mother in this big, old house. She knew it was crazy, but she wished her mother would remarry and maybe have another child. She'd always wanted a sister or a brother.

After all of them were sitting around the table, and the blessing had been said, Danielle looked at her mother and said, "Aren't you curious about the reason I want you to look good this weekend?"

Cherisse finished chewing the delicious piece of meat loaf in her mouth before saying, "Okay, I'll bite."

Danielle smiled smugly and removed a folded piece of paper from the waistband of her jeans. Apparently, she'd been prepared for this moment. She unfolded the piece of paper and handed it to her mother. "That's why," she said. "You're going to meet him this weekend, and I'd like him to see you at your best. He's perfect for you, Ma."

Cherisse looked down at the photo that her daughter had obviously found on the Internet and printed out for her benefit. It was a photo of Harry Payne taken at the season opening of his resort on Saturday night.

She knew then, without a doubt, that Harry Payne was her Harry.

She handed the photo back to Danielle. "I've met him," she said with a smile. "He already has a girlfriend."

"No!" Danielle cried, thoroughly disappointed. "Are you sure?"

Cherisse laughed shortly. "We chatted for several minutes, sweetie. Yes, I'm sure he mentioned having a girlfriend."

"Why are the good ones always taken?" Danielle moaned.

Jo shook her head. At sixty-three, she was a petite, plump woman with big brown eyes, and salt-and-pepper hair that she wore in a short, sassy cut. Her skin was the color of coffee with only a dollop of cream in it. Smooth and brown.

Her only child had gotten her golden-brown skin from her father, Jake, but Danielle inherited her darker brown skin. She was happy to see her granddaughter taking an interest in her mother's love life. "I don't know," Jo replied to Danielle's question. "But that seems to be the case nowadays. If he's not married, he's gay. If he isn't gay, something is seriously wrong with him. Like he has twenty outside children and ten different women are the mothers to whom he's paying child support."

"Or he's been traumatized by a former marriage," Cherisse added. "And because the ex-wife was a witch, he can't trust another woman ever again."

Danielle was listening closely and agreeing wholeheartedly. "The only thing the boys I know care about is sex, sex, sex!"

Cherisse looked alarmed. "Has Echo been coming on to you?" She couldn't believe her gaydar was inaccurate. Could it be that Echo really was a blazing heterosexual?

Danielle guffawed. "You don't have to worry about Echo. He hasn't even tried to kiss me."

This attitude was new to Cherisse. Did her daughter *want* Echo to kiss her? She thought the two of them were simply buddies.

"Do you want him to think of you in that way?" she asked hesitantly.

Danielle screwed up her face. "I do think he's hot and to tell you the truth I was so happy when he started hanging round my locker and making smart aleck remarks. I thought he was interested in me. But as it turns out, he just wanted a friend who also skis. Mr. Santiago coaches both of us and he thinks we both have potential. Echo couldn't be happier."

Oh, no, Cherisse thought, *my baby's falling for a gay guy. It's gonna break her heart when she finds out!*

She couldn't believe she was saying this: "You know, sweetie, some of the happiest relationships begin as friendships." What if her suspicions about Echo's sexuality proved to be wrong? She couldn't bear to dash Danielle's hopes.

The happy expression on Danielle's face broke her heart. Her daughter truly was falling for Edward James Thornton.

Chapter 4

Marcia was in her dressing room at the station putting on her bright blue power suit. The cameras loved bright colors and her stylist said, with her coloring, she looked best in blue. It was Tuesday morning and she was about to do the seven o'clock news.

Dressed, she glanced down at her watch. The makeup artist was due any minute now. The hairdresser would follow. Marcia loved the little perks that came with her job. She could roll out of bed and come to work in sweats if she wanted to, which she didn't.

Because she was somewhat of a local celebrity, Marcia didn't go anywhere unless she was beautifully pulled together. No one was going to see her in before-and-after photos on some Web page!

There was a knock at the door. "Come in!" Marcia called and, thinking it was Jillian, the makeup artist, she went and sat in the high swivel chair in front of the big mirror where Jillian did her makeup every weekday morning.

The door opened and Marcia saw the reflection of a tall male dressed in dark clothing in the mirror. Her heart beat a staccato rhythm. Surely security hadn't been sleeping on the job and had let some nutcase sneak back here. She had had a problem with overly amorous male admirers before. A couple had gone so far as to stalk her. She'd had to get restraining orders to keep the weirdos away from her.

Quickly getting to her feet, she braced herself for a confrontation. Then, she saw who her early morning visitor was. LaShaun Gregory, star running back for the Broncos, and her ex-boyfriend. No wonder security had let him in. He used to be a frequent visitor to the station, and they loved him. They fell over themselves to get in his good graces. LaShaun often rewarded their devotion with tickets to home games.

Marcia stepped back and, with arms akimbo, asked, "What the hell are you doing here?" Their relationship had ended acrimoniously. He had left her for a woman ten years her junior. Twenty-two years old. LaShaun himself was thirty-one, a year younger than Marcia. Not a huge difference as far as they were concerned when they were in love. At his advanced age, LaShaun was considered close to retirement. Not many professional football players continued to play into their mid-thirties and beyond.

LaShaun had been besieged by sexual come-ons from women as young as eighteen. Unable to resist, he'd started sleeping with one of them. Because he and Marcia had been seeing each other for over two years and had been discussing marriage, he confessed to her that he had a love jones for a twenty-two-year-old.

Marcia had, understandably, hit the ceiling. She cussed

him out for all he was worth. Then she gave him an ultima-
tum—it was either her or the Barbie.

His manly pride hurt from being yelled at by her and told
what to do, LaShaun had chosen the twenty-two-year-old. He
regretted it almost immediately and a week later tried to phone
Marcia to see if he could come over and beg her to take him back.

By then, Marcia had had her home and cell numbers
changed. She also had the locks changed on the doors of her
house. She had even told security that if he showed up at the
station they were to escort him off the premises.

Marcia glared at LaShaun now. "Those wimps in security
are going to catch hell!"

She went to walk past him, and LaShaun grabbed her by
the upper arm. "Listen to me, Marcia. It's been six months.
Haven't you made me suffer enough? I know you've gotten
my e-mails and letters. I know you've received my gifts and
flowers. Don't you think that taking up with Harry Payne was
a bit over-the-top?"

Marcia jerked her arm free, and punched him on the upper
arm. LaShaun didn't even flinch. "No, I don't! You slept with
that bimbo for I don't know how long! I've only slept with
Harry a couple of times. I'm not finished with him yet."

LaShaun shook his head sadly. "I've apologized to you
over and over again. Unless you can let go of the revenge
scenario you've cooked up and come back to me so that we
can get on with our lives, I'm officially giving up. I haven't
slept with anyone in over five months. I kept my promise. You
need to check yourself. Two wrongs don't make a right. I love
you, and you love me. All you're doing is setting Harry Payne
up for a broken heart. He doesn't deserve that, he's a nice guy."

"I know he's a nice guy," Marcia said. "I wouldn't have
chosen him if he weren't."

"What you did was wrong, involving him the way you

have. How do you know he isn't already in love with you? You're playing a dangerous game," LaShaun said severely.

Marcia sighed and momentarily closed her eyes, wishing LaShaun and his reasonableness away. Why couldn't he have been reasonable six months ago when he chose that prepubescent over her? Yes, she was using Harry. But she truly liked him, as well. Somewhere down the line, she'd stopped thinking of him as the instrument of torture she was using to get back at LaShaun and had started thinking of him as potential marriage material if LaShaun didn't bow to her will. A girl had to have a backup plan.

Opening her eyes again she saw that LaShaun was still there, and so was her predicament. It was time for her to choose. Either Harry, or LaShaun.

LaShaun pressed his six-three, two-hundred-and-fifty-pound body against hers. Marcia's body, the traitor, immediately reacted to his closeness. Harry was hot, but she didn't love Harry. She loved LaShaun and craved him. He was right. She had to end it with Harry.

LaShaun bent his head and claimed her mouth, showing her exactly what it felt like to be kissed by a man who not only loved her, but also knew he'd been a fool and was ready to make it up to her. His kiss promised her that if she took him back, she would never regret it.

When their lips parted, Marcia stared up at him as if she were seeing him clearly for the first time. Maybe he *had* changed. "I'll break it to him gently," she said.

LaShaun hugged her tightly. "Oh, baby, you've made me so happy. We'll elope!"

Marcia pushed out of his embrace. "No way, all of Denver is going to know about it when we get married. After what you've put me through, you owe me that much."

LaShaun didn't argue, he just pulled her into his arms again and kissed the top of her head. "You can invite all of Denver if you want to."

One hundred miles west of Denver, Harry was on the last leg of his five-mile jog along a mountain road. In Vail the temperature was forty degrees. Lower than Denver's.

While Denver wasn't in the mountains, several mountains could be seen from the city. Vail, on the other hand, sat smack in the middle of the mountains. Temperatures in November would have an average high of thirty-nine degrees and a low of fifteen degrees. In the month of November they could expect almost sixty-two inches of snow, which made Vail an ideal vacation spot for skiers.

Harry's cell phone rang, and he reached into his warm-up jacket's pocket to get it while maintaining his pace.

"Hello."

"Shall I have Susanne pick you up at the airport on Thanksgiving eve?" asked his mother. Her voice was clear. The phone was getting great reception this morning.

"Nah, I'll rent a car," said Harry.

"You're out of breath," his mother said suspiciously. "Am I interrupting anything?"

Harry laughed. "Just my morning jog."

Mildred Payne laughed, too. "Oh, I thought maybe Marcia was with you."

Harry could hear the blush in his mother's tone of voice. "Marcia rarely spends the night during the week. It's an almost two-hour drive back to Denver."

"I don't think I'll ever get used to your living in the mountains. It's too cold for me," said Mildred with an exaggerated shiver. "And you really like it, baby?"

"I really like it, Mom," Harry confirmed. "So, I'll see you tomorrow night?"

"I'll be here," said Mildred. She wasn't ready to hang up yet, though. "Did you extend my invitation to Marcia like I asked you to?"

"Yeah, but she's already promised her family she's coming home," Harry said.

"Darn it, I wanted to meet her. You've been going out for about four months now, right?" Mildred said.

"More like three." Harry smiled. His mother really wanted grandchildren from him.

"Do you think she might be the one?" asked Mildred hopefully.

"I like her, Mom. Let's leave it at that," said Harry. He didn't know Marcia well enough to seriously consider marrying her even though marriage was at the top of his timeline list. He definitely had misgivings about marrying a woman who had a problem with the fact that he was devoted to his mother. What kind of life could he have with a woman who was jealous of his relationship with his mother?

He knew his mother didn't like his being so closemouthed about Marcia. Normally he told her everything about the women he dated except, of course, the intimate details.

Those he kept to himself.

"All right, I won't pry," said Mildred, sounding disappointed in spite of her good intentions. "I just want you to be happy."

For some reason, when his mother told him she wanted him to be happy, the image of his moonlight angel appeared in Harry's mind's eye. He'd been thinking about her ever since he'd met her. And all of those stray thoughts devoted to another woman made him feel as if he were cheating on Marcia. What had Jimmy Carter called it, cheating in your heart?

"I'm happy," Harry told his mother.

"Yeah, but you're not married with children," said Mildred sweetly. Harry figured she didn't want to make him feel as if he weren't on the ball. Susanne had four children and had been married for twenty-five years to a wonderful man, a dentist. He smiled to himself. The free dental work was only one of the perks his mother enjoyed as a result of her daughter being married to Dr. Kendall Welch. Four grandchildren! Harry didn't think he'd ever be able to duplicate that. He would be happy with a son or daughter, maybe a son *and* a daughter.

He laughed shortly. "Well, I've waited a little late to start having a big family."

"Nonsense," said his mother. "You're only forty-two. Men can father children for a very long time. Just marry a woman who wants a big family. Does Marcia like children?"

"She's never mentioned it," Harry admitted. Come to think of it, Marcia had never mentioned a lot of things. She had told him nothing about her previous relationships and very little about her family and her background, except her professional background. It was as if her life began and ended with her job as a news anchor.

Her choice of career didn't matter as much to Harry as what she was truly like as a person. He realized that for the past three months, she hadn't let him into her life at all. Not really. It felt as if they were just going through the motions of a dating couple. Going out when both of them were free. She had wanted to wait at least two months before they became intimate, which was fine with him. They'd made love twice.

Even then Harry had felt as if she were holding back.

On her end, Mildred waited for Harry to say something, but he was too intent on wondering why he was questioning everything about his relationship with Marcia all of a sudden.

"Harry, I'm going to let you go," she told him. "See you tomorrow night. Have a safe flight."

"Okay, Mom," said Harry. "Love you."

"I love you, too, baby," Mildred said softly.

Harry closed the phone and put it back in his pocket. Unbidden, the image of his moonlight angel appeared in his mind's eye once again. That golden-brown skin, those big brown eyes, well-shaped nose and sensual mouth. His mouth watered just thinking about her lips. And those legs!

He felt a pang of guilt again. He was being silly. It wasn't really cheating if you never saw the woman again, and he had no intention of ever looking for Cheri. Cheri. Didn't that mean "dear" or "darling" in French?

Picking up his pace, he resolved to put Cheri out of his mind and concentrate on Marcia. Marcia was accomplished and beautiful. Any man would be lucky to have her in his life.

When he got to his suite he went straight to the refrigerator to get a bottle of water. He drank it, after which he went to the bathroom and turned the shower on.

Harry spent more time here at the resort when there was construction going on as there was now. They were adding ten two-and-three bedroom, fully equipped condominiums to the resort. The condominiums would be available for leasing by people who wanted a permanent place to call their vacation home, like time-sharing. However they would also be available to those who wanted the extra privacy the condominiums would provide for a few days or a few weeks.

When Harry didn't feel the need to oversee new construction on the resort, he spent most of his time in Denver, where he owned a home on the outskirts of the city, and traveling. He was presently scouting out a location to build a second resort, this one in a warmer climate.

Peeling off his sweats, jacket and athletic shoes and socks,

Harry groaned a little. It was funny but while his body was in motion, his knees didn't bother him, but as soon as he stopped moving, they started to ache, especially the right one, the one he hadn't had surgery on yet. Football was a grueling game. He had abused his body for years and now he was paying for it. But he couldn't complain. He had known what he was getting into when he signed his first professional contract. Football players were well-compensated for the abuse they took. What other reason would a completely sane man sign up for the torture?

In the shower, he let the water sluice over his taut, muscular six-two, two-hundred-pound body. When he had been playing his weight had been around one-ninety but over the years he'd picked up ten pounds and, thankfully, not in the gut. His muscle bulk had increased due to weight lifting.

At forty-two he was more at home in his body than at any time in his life. He was no longer that cocky young man who was so confident of his invincibility. Back then, he thought he could do any physical feat put before him. Today, he was just happy that he was healthy.

After drying off, he dressed in a Hugo Boss dark gray striped suit, white silk shirt and dark gray silk tie, and put on a pair of black Italian wingtips.

He liked to present the image of a well-dressed business-man when he made his rounds at the resort. Fully dressed, he went downstairs to the main dining room for breakfast.

Breakfast at the resort was a ritual Harry had come to enjoy. At first, he wasn't at all happy with all the interruptions. But now as a provider of hospitality he took it in stride.

He was not seated at his regular table, a cup of black coffee before him, for five minutes before a couple of African-American women in their fifties sought him out.

They were dressed in athletic suits and athletic shoes, both of them no taller than five-five, and both looked as if the athletic suits weren't just for show. They were fit. One of the ladies had café-au-lait skin and wore her short red hair in a relaxed layered cut that complemented her square-shaped face. Her friend had medium brown skin and wore her graying hair in a short afro, just like his mother did.

"Mr. Payne," said the redhead, "we just wanted to drop by and let you know we're really enjoying ourselves."

"Please sit down," said Harry politely.

"Oh, no, thank you," said the one with the short afro. "Sister and I have a nine o'clock appointment to go hiking. That tall drink of water with the ponytail is going to take us into your alpine forest. I'm Adele Franklin and this is my sister, Marilyn Walker."

Harry smiled. Adele was talking about Terry Red Feather, one of their more popular guides, especially with the ladies. Terry was six-four and built. Because of his Native-American blood, he had reddish-brown skin and black hair that fell practically to his waist. Women guests got on a waiting list to have him guide them into the woods.

"Terry's a very good guide," he assured the sisters.

"Oh, he is?" asked Marilyn, sounding disappointed. "We were hoping he'd get us lost for a couple of days and we could have our way with him."

They all laughed.

"Now, ladies," Harry chided lightly. "Terry's a good kid. He's working on his master's degree in psychology at the University of Colorado. Don't scar the boy for life."

To which the sisters laughed even harder. "We'll be gentle," Adele joked. She took Marilyn by the arm. "It's eight-fifty, sister. Goodbye, Mr. Payne. Wish us luck!"

"Good luck," said Harry. He figured Terry Red Feather was the one who needed luck.

He picked up his coffee and took a sip as he watched the sisters hurry off. Nice ladies. A minute later one of the waiters arrived with his breakfast: scrambled eggs with cheddar cheese, a homemade southern biscuit and fresh fruit. He usually skipped meat in the mornings in favor of the protein in eggs. Although he wasn't close to being a vegan—he still enjoyed a juicy steak every once in a while.

A few minutes later, Harry made the twenty-minute stroll across the grounds to the site of the new condominiums. Workmen—and women—were finishing laying the floors and installing cabinetry. The condominiums would have hardwood floors, Berber carpeting, flagstone and marble tile, granite countertops in the kitchen and all the appliances, including a refrigerator, cooktops, a microwave and a conventional oven, a dishwasher and a washer and a dryer. Harry believed in sparing no cost when it came to furnishing the resort and wanted the guests to experience luxury second to none so that they would always come back.

What surprised him was that it was the little things that they raved about the most, such as the heated tiles on the bathroom floors. No stepping onto a cold floor for his guests!

The foreman of the work crew walked up to Harry as soon as he entered the first condominium. Evan Calder had worked with Harry before and knew what to expect if the work wasn't done right, and done on time. Harry knew that construction never went smoothly. He did not rant if supplies were hard to come by due to the recent building boom in the area. That was something Evan had no control over. What irked Harry was when a job wasn't done to his specifications or if the cost went way over Evan's estimate. Those were arguable offenses.

Today, Evan had nothing but good news for him. The two shook hands, their normal greeting. Evan was a short, muscular African-American with a shaved head and a thick black moustache. "Hey, Harry, we're actually ahead of schedule today. This unit is done and we should be finished in each of the units by quitting time on Friday."

The men were taking Thanksgiving off and returning on Friday morning. Harry also was taking Thursday off. He planned to be back by Friday afternoon to check on their progress.

And the ribbon-cutting ceremony, just a low-key affair with local media and his staff, would take place on Saturday, after which photographers would be allowed inside the one furnished unit. The following week, the other units would be furnished, and then guests would begin moving in. All of the units were already booked for the next six months. Therefore it was vital that the workers finish on time.

"Good, good," said Harry, pleased. "I'm just going to do a walk-through. Have a great Thanksgiving. I'll see you on Friday afternoon."

"Same to you," Evan said, referring to Harry's Thanksgiving well wishes. Then he turned and walked away, going to another one of the units while Harry stayed to painstakingly check his people's workmanship by walking on the floors, opening and closing cabinets and generally going over every inch of the finished unit.

An hour or so later, Harry left, satisfied that the work had been done to his specifications.

That left nine more units to look in on, although he wouldn't go over them as thoroughly as he'd done in the finished unit. That inspection would wait until Friday.

When he walked into his suite two hours later, he was surprised to find Marcia sitting on the couch channel-surfing.

It was only a few minutes after the noon hour. He knew she anchored the early morning news and then the five o'clock news. So for her to drive to Vail between the two shows was quite unusual. She'd never done it before.

"Marcia?"

She started as if she hadn't heard him enter the suite. Rising, she smiled wanly at him. Her lovely golden-hued eyes looked at him with an expression akin to sadness. "Harry, we need to talk."

Harry went to her and kissed her on the cheek. This didn't feel like a "kiss on the mouth" moment. He could feel the tension in the air. Marcia didn't proffer her cheek as she usually did. When his hand touched her arm as he drew near he felt her stiffen.

"What's the matter?" he asked as he turned away from her and began removing his jacket. He put the jacket on the back of an overstuffed chair and regarded her with an inquisitive expression.

Marcia fidgeted. She couldn't stand still so she paced the floor. She would look at his ruggedly handsome face then look away as if the sight of him was painful to her.

Harry tried to remain calm, but her behavior was bordering on manic. This wasn't the cool, calculating Marcia who had been plotting to become the most important person in his life. That Marcia didn't have a nervous bone in her body. This Marcia was nervous as hell.

Harry sat on the couch and looked up at her expectantly. "You wouldn't be here if you could have told me what you need to tell me over the phone," he said calmly. "So let me have it!"

His sharp tone made Marcia jump. She stopped pacing and looked him in the eyes.

"Harry, I can't see you anymore. Before you I was involved with LaShaun Gregory. We've decided to get back together."

"You never mentioned LaShaun," Harry said, trying to maintain his composure. He didn't know LaShaun well. He'd met him a few years ago. He knew he played for his old team, the Broncos, and that he was one of their highest paid and most prized players. But over the years Harry had not kept up with his old team like some of the other ex-players. In fact, he wasn't an avid fan of football. The way he looked at it, that was his old life.

Marcia went and sat beside Harry on the couch. She placed a hand on his muscular thigh and put on her most sympathetic expression. Harry swore he'd seen that same expression on her face when she was reporting on a catastrophe somewhere in the world.

He realized that her emotions were as detached from him as when she was reading a news story from the TelePrompTer. "Did you ever care anything about me?" he asked, already knowing the answer.

"I'm here to take my lumps," Marcia said bravely. "I admit, I asked you out in the beginning because you were just the type of man who would make LaShaun crazy with jealousy. But I came to like you, Harry. Truly, I did."

Harry knew he was in the company of an actor when tears appeared in her eyes as she regarded him sadly. "I know you can't forgive me right now because this is so new to you. But maybe in a few weeks you'll come to realize that this is for the best."

Harry removed her hand from his thigh and rose, looking down at her with a smile on his lips. Suddenly, he laughed.

Marcia looked personally affronted. She rose, too, and stared at him with narrowed eyes. "What is remotely funny about this situation?"

"I knew there was something missing in our relationship," Harry told her. "I just couldn't put my finger on it. The problem was you were faking it from the beginning. To believe that after I overheard you telling your friend I was a momma's boy I let that slide in favor of trying to hang on to what we had! I should have known, then, that your heart wasn't in it. How could you resent a woman you'd never met?"

He slowly circled her. "So, I was just a plaything, huh?"

Lips pressed together in irritation at being called on the carpet, Marcia didn't answer right away. A minute or so later, she sighed. "I was wrong to say what I did about your mother. I'm sure she's a lovely woman. But I can't regret what I did. LaShaun had it coming. He broke my heart. Come on, Harry. We had fun, you and I. The sex was great and now you're free to move on to the next woman. I'm sure a multimillionaire like you isn't going to lack for female companionship."

Harry wasn't paying strict attention to what she was saying. He was walking across the room to open the door and hold it for her. "You bet I won't."

Marcia walked through the door without another word.

Harry closed it and laughed again. Talk about manipulative! He actually felt sorry for LaShaun Gregory.

Chapter 5

The drive to Vail on Saturday morning was a peaceful one. Danielle had the tendency to go to sleep minutes after leaving on a road trip. So the only company Cherisse had this morning was Ben Harper and the Innocent Criminals jamming on their *Lifeline* CD.

Cherisse knew every song and sang along. The music helped to dispel the nervousness she was feeling about seeing Harry Payne again. Would he remember her? And if he didn't should she remind him of their encounter on the balcony in the moonlight? She saw no reason she should. It would probably be better if he *didn't* remember her. She had been attracted to him that night and if she wasn't mistaken, he had been attracted to her.

He had a girlfriend. She would feel very uncomfortable if he conveniently forgot that fact and started making passes at her. Worse, she would be mortified if she found herself still attracted to him in spite of it.

She had to handle the situation with kid gloves. The thing to do was not to be alone with him. John Santiago had said Harry Payne would meet them in the lobby of the resort at one o'clock. He wanted to personally show them to their suite, and then he had arranged for them to tour the facilities. Later that evening, they were supposed to have dinner together in one of the resort's award-winning restaurants. At Danielle's urging, Cherisse had bought a new dress for the occasion. She had been reluctant to do so because, contrary to her daughter's opinion, she already had perfectly good clothes in her closet, even if they didn't have designer labels.

Not many nurses could afford designer clothing.

Cherisse checked the Cherokee's clock—it was eleven-fifty and they were about twenty minutes from their destination. A few miles later, she took Exit 176 and was soon on Vail Road.

"Danielle, wake up, we're here," she said just loudly enough so as not to startle her daughter.

Danielle woke from her nap with a yawn and stretched. Blinking her eyes a couple times she looked around them. "Wow, this looks like a village in the Alps or something!"

Indeed, Karibu Resort resembled a quaint Swiss village surrounded by majestic mountains. Any minute now, Cherisse expected to hear somebody yodeling. Contrary to the Swiss image, though, she'd read that Harry Payne had named the resort Karibu because it was the Swahili word for *Welcome, join us!* He wanted his guests, he said, to feel as though Karibu was their home away from home.

When Cherisse drove up to the entrance, they were immediately set upon by an attendant, who ascertained their needs and then called for a bellhop to get their luggage and a valet to park the Cherokee in guest parking.

Cherisse had to admit to a touch of awe upon stepping onto

the golden marble floor of the lobby. *And she'd been here before.* She looked at Danielle's animated face and knew her daughter was impressed. "Oh, my God," Danielle breathed reverently. "I feel like Princess Mia." *The Princess Diaries* had been one of her favorite books when she was younger, and in it an ordinary girl learned she was royalty.

Cherisse laughed softly. Even then, she felt as if her voice echoed in the cavernous lobby. "Well, you're my princess," she said.

She stepped up to the desk. The woman behind it, a tall, attractive African-American in her late twenties, smiled at her. "Welcome to the Karibu Resort. I'm Rochelle. How can I be of service?"

"I'm Cherisse Washington and this is my daughter, Danielle. We have an appointment with Mr. Payne. Would you please let him know we're here?"

"Of course," said Rochelle. "I was told to expect you at one. Mr. Payne will be in a meeting until then, I'm afraid. He wanted to be the one to show you to your suite. Would you and your daughter like to have lunch on us while you wait? I would be happy to show you to Millie's Place. It's our cafeteria-style restaurant."

They were more than thirty minutes early. Cherisse supposed Harry Payne's schedule didn't leave room for surprises. "That would be nice of you, thank you."

Rochelle let one of her co-workers in the office directly behind the front desk know she was leaving for a few moments. Then she came around the desk and said, "It's only a short walk in this direction."

On the way to Millie's Place they passed a smart boutique and a sunny atrium that led outside to a lush garden, and encountered dozens of guests on the move between activities, no doubt. They were dressed in golfing clothes, hiking gear, ski togs and other athletic clothing, as well as casual clothing.

Cherisse had read that Karibu Resort catered to African-American skiers and was recommended by many AA ski clubs across the nation, but the guests weren't predominately black, they were from various ethnic backgrounds. She overheard at least three different languages en route to the restaurant: Spanish, German and French. French from a black couple on their way out the door with skis carried across their shoulders.

In the restaurant, Rochelle told the hostess that Cherisse and Danielle were Mr. Payne's guests. Then she said, "Enjoy your meal," and left.

Cherisse and Danielle thanked her and were told by the hostess that they could sit anywhere they liked. This was a relaxed restaurant where diners walked through the line and chose their entrees, after which they went to the register. At the register, the hostess said, Cherisse was to simply tell the cashier that they were guests of the owner.

Cherisse didn't have much of an appetite. She got a salad and a bottle of water. However Danielle appeared to be ravenous. She ordered the turkey cheeseburger with the works, thick fries and a salad, plus chocolate milk.

Danielle ate heartily. Cherisse picked at her food.

After a while, Danielle, who was sensitive to her mother's moods, remarked, "Don't tell me you're nervous about seeing Mr. Payne again."

"Well, don't you think this is a strange coincidence?" Cherisse asked reasonably. "We met as strangers and the next time I turn up I'm the mother of the skier he's sponsoring. Yes, I'm nervous."

"Don't be," said Danielle, shoving more fries into her mouth. She chewed and swallowed. She consumed her food just like her father did, quickly and with relish. Cherisse wondered if eating habits were genetic instead of learned. Danielle had spent much more time around her and her mother, both of whom were slow eaters.

"What are you most afraid of?" asked Danielle. "That he won't remember you, or he will and since that night he hasn't been able to get you out of his mind?"

Cherisse snorted. "Yeah, that'll never happen."

"It could happen," said her daughter, after which she opened her mouth wide to accommodate the huge burger and chomped down on it. She moaned softly.

Cherisse smiled. Her daughter definitely enjoyed her food. Fortunately, she was so active she had never had a weight problem. Her tall frame was exceptionally fit.

Putting down her burger, Danielle regarded her mother with a serious expression. "Let's change the subject, okay? Obviously talking about Harry Payne has ruined your appetite. Remember Dad phoned me on Thanksgiving day?"

Cherisse immediately steeled herself for dire news. Charlie was an inveterate gambler who had lost his house to foreclosure five years ago, and that was when he was a highly paid professional football player. He was retired from the game now. She imagined he was in even greater financial straits.

"Yes?" she croaked.

Danielle smiled. "It's nothing horrible. Dad told me that since he retired he's been going to Gamblers Anonymous. He has his gambling under control, and he was recently offered a recruiting job with the University of Colorado at Denver. You know, his being a hometown boy and all. He accepted. Dad's moving back to Denver!"

Cherisse couldn't help it, her eyes stretched in horror. "Denver! Charlie?! What would possess him to do that?"

Danielle laughed. "Grandma was right, you're not happy about Dad moving back home."

"You told Ma about this before you told me?" Cherisse said incredulously.

"I was trying to find the right time," Danielle explained.

"And you chose now?"

"It made you stop obsessing about Harry Payne," Danielle pointed out after which she took another bite of her burger. Chewing and talking out of the corner of her mouth, she said, "Grandma also said you wouldn't agree to Dad staying with us until he found a place."

"Staying with us?" Cherisse shouted and immediately lowered her voice. "That man has some nerve."

"He didn't suggest it, I did," said Danielle. She wiped the smile off her face and sighed. "He hasn't got anybody else in Denver, just you and me."

"You," Cherisse corrected her. "He's got you."

Danielle acknowledged her mother's comment with a nod. "Okay, he's got only me. And I wanted to spend some time with him before I started going away practically every weekend to compete in the preliminary rounds for the Olympics. I missed him a lot while I was growing up."

Cherisse couldn't help feeling a twinge of guilt at her daughter's statement. It wasn't that she had tried to keep Danielle and Charlie apart after the divorce. Charlie had his priorities: football, gambling and women. Cherisse got tired of reminding him to send Danielle a gift on her birthday, or to phone her on major holidays like Christmas and Thanksgiving if he were not able to come see her.

She looked Danielle straight in the eyes. "You and I have had this talk before. I never did anything to prevent Charlie from seeing you. Never! Now, all of a sudden, I'm supposed to bend over backwards to accommodate him because he has seen the light and wants to be in your life more? You're seventeen, practically a woman. *Now* he wants to be a father?"

"You told me when Granddaddy died four years ago that a woman will always need her father. Remember that?"

Chagrined, Cherisse had to think quickly to get out of this one. She could say that her father had been a loving, responsible parent, unlike Charlie, who visited Danielle once or twice a year and sent her checks whenever he won big at the gaming tables.

That wasn't parenting!

However, looking into her daughter's face, which held a hangdog expression, Cherisse was unable to utter those words without feeling extremely selfish. Danielle wanted to be closer to her father. How could she fault her for that?

Living with Charlie was quite another matter, though. "How long?" she asked.

Danielle immediately brightened. "Not long, a few weeks at the most. He's going to look for a place near the university."

Cherisse shook her head in astonishment. "I can't believe Ma is okay with this."

"She said you and Dad got married too young and that's why your marriage didn't work out. She said you were always more mature than Dad. But now that he's trying to get himself together and do what's right, she didn't want to stand in his way."

Cherisse had to admit that sounded just like her mother, always willing to give somebody a second chance.

"When is he supposed to move to Denver?" she asked cautiously.

"Next week," said Danielle. She visibly winced in anticipation of her mother's reaction.

Cherisse surprised her and laughed. "I'd just as well give in since it's obvious I've been outvoted, two against one. All right, your Dad can stay with us no longer than two months. Eight weeks ought to be long enough for anybody to find a place to live."

Danielle screeched with delight and, like her mother earlier, immediately lowered her voice. They'd already gotten some odd looks from their fellow diners.

Harry strode into Millie's Place two minutes after one o'clock. He wore a dark gray suit with a white shirt, a striped maroon tie and black wingtips. Gold cuff links twinkled at his wrists, but aside from his watch that was the only jewelry he wore.

Going over to the hostess, a petite brunette with brown eyes and ample hips, he said, "Hello, Alice, I'm looking for Cherisse and Danielle Washington. Rochelle told me she escorted them here."

Alice blushed. She tried her best to control the girlish reaction she got to Harry's nearness but in three years of working there she had never been able to do so. "They're the two attractive ladies over there," she said with a nod of her head.

Harry smiled at her. "Thanks."

As soon as he turned his back, Alice fanned her face. "Lord, that man is fine," she said under her breath.

Harry took his time walking across the restaurant. For one moment, his legs had gone weak under him when he saw Cherisse Washington. It was Cheri. He was sure of it. That glorious, thick, wavy black hair was a dead giveaway, to say nothing of her beautiful clear skin and warm brown eyes. He was standing less than twelve feet away from her and her daughter. Cherisse wore a classic navy blue dress whose hem fell a few inches above her shapely knees. She wore a pair of navy sling-backs with it. And as he recalled, her legs were gorgeous. A woman with legs like that—long, with slender ankles, lovely calves and exquisite knees—should never wear slacks.

She was smiling at her daughter, a cute kid in jeans, a red sweater and white athletic shoes. The kid resembled her mom a great deal except her skin tone was a few shades darker.

The daughter looked up and saw his approach. She said something to her mother and Cherisse Washington glanced up and the expression on her lovely face was priceless. He had no doubt she recognized him from last Saturday night. Now here they were a week later.

Harry silently thanked God for his good fortune. He felt like grinning but pushed away the impulse. He didn't want Cherisse to get the idea that he was especially glad to see her. He smiled his "pleased to meet you" business smile as he got closer—all lips, no teeth. "Hello, Mrs. Washington, Danielle," he greeted them.

Both mother and daughter went to get up but he gestured for them to remain seated. "Please don't get up. I'll join you." And he sat down between them. He offered Cherisse his hand. As they shook, he said, "Do you remember me from Saturday night? We chatted a while on the balcony."

Cherisse blushed. Her hand trembled a little in his grasp. She withdrew it and said with a smile, "Yes, I do. And I'm really embarrassed, now, that I didn't recognize you."

"Don't be," he said. "It's kind of nice not being recognized." He turned to Danielle, who was riveted by their conversation. They shook hands also. "Good to meet you, Danielle."

"Thanks, likewise," she told him with a huge grin. "You look even better in person than you do in photos."

"Danielle!" exclaimed her mother.

Harry thought she was probably mortified by her

daughter's candid remark. He was not in the least. He saw an opportunity to glean some information about her mother, since it was obvious the daughter was much less willing to be restrained by social etiquette.

He smiled. "At forty-two," he said, "I'm lucky to get any sort of compliment. Thank you, Danielle." He regarded Cherisse. "How was your drive up?"

Cherisse relaxed. "Very nice, the conditions were perfect for driving."

"Good," said Harry. His eyes raked over her face. She had a mole on the left corner of her full, sensual mouth. Harry thought it made her mouth all the more kissable.

He cleared his throat and sat up straighter in his chair. He couldn't let himself get turned on by Cherisse Washington while her daughter was sitting two feet away.

So he turned to Danielle. "I'm impressed by your skills on the slopes, young lady. John Santiago gave me a tape of your last race. You're amazing. How did you get interested in skiing?"

"Mr. Santiago came to our school to introduce us to his program. I was on the basketball team then. He invited anyone who was interested to go on a field trip to the Sonnenalp Resort here in Vail."

"A great resort," Harry said.

Danielle smiled her agreement. "Yeah, and I've been hooked ever since."

"Where did you get your drive, your ambition?" Harry asked. With him, he had always been a big kid and the high school coach saw his potential and asked him to try out for the team. Harry's incentive had been to become a success by any means necessary, and his talents had always been physical. Today, he was an avid reader and enjoyed learning new things. But in school he had had little interest in books and had squeaked by with a C average. Luckily, back then that was all you needed to be on the football team. In college, he had learned to apply himself more.

But he was truly fascinated by Danielle's drive at such a young age. At seventeen, he'd been happy to be on the football team and have a girlfriend. Danielle already had her sights on the Olympics.

"Mom always told me I could do anything I wanted to," Danielle told him, her eyes downcast as if she were too shy or modest to meet his gaze. She looked up at her mother and Harry could see the love she had for Cherisse reflected in her eyes.

"Mom was a fierce basketball player when she was my age," she said with a smile. "When I was growing up I always saw her doing something physical practically every day. She jogged, played tennis, even ran a few marathons. She inspired me. And my dad used to play for the Philadelphia Eagles. Charlie Washington."

Harry did grin this time. "Your father was a great defensive back. What is he doing nowadays?"

"He was just hired by the University of Colorado at Denver as a recruiter," Danielle said proudly.

Cherisse could do nothing but smile. Danielle loved her father. Even when she was little she never blamed him for not seeing her more often. She never heaped recriminations on him for not helping to support her financially over the years, either. Whenever she saw him, she was simply happy to be in his presence.

"So he's moving to Denver?" Harry asked. Here, he had to school his expression because he definitely didn't like the sound of that. Was Cherisse's ex-husband returning to reconnect with his daughter perhaps, or with Cherisse?

It wasn't an unreasonable concern, especially since he felt

more drawn to Cherisse than ever. Over the years he'd known several divorced couples who reconciled after many years apart.

Harry was happy when Cherisse spoke up. "Yes, now that he's retired, Charlie wants to spend more time with his daughter."

"That's great," Harry said. "If I had a daughter I would definitely want to be there for her."

"You're not married with children at your age?" asked Danielle incredulously.

Once again, her mother looked mortified.

Harry just chuckled. "You sound like my mother. No, I've never met the right woman, I guess." He looked Cherisse straight in the eyes when he said that.

She blushed again.

"Well, maybe you and your girlfriend will get married and have children," Danielle said, obviously fishing.

Cherisse gave Harry a look that said "I can't take her anywhere!"

Still laughing softly, Harry said, "I'm afraid we just broke up."

Danielle gave him a huge grin.

Cherisse's expression was sympathetic. "I'm so sorry, Ha— Mr. Payne."

Harry placed his hand atop hers. "Please call me Harry." He quickly withdrew his hand but not before Danielle saw the gesture and started calculating how she was going to get her mother and Harry Payne alone together.

If she let this golden opportunity pass her by she would never forgive herself.

Harry Payne was coming on to her mother!

A few minutes later, Harry was ushering them into the suite they would be spending the night in. It was a loft-style suite with exposed beams. Cherisse immediately fell in love with it.

There was a bedroom with two beds in it and a living room, all fitted with custom-made Bavarian furnishings. A gas-log fireplace was in the living room, and the bathroom had a large sunken tub, a separate walk-in shower and heated tile floors.

Cherisse and Danielle declared that everything was beautiful and thanked Harry profusely. Harry looked faintly embarrassed by their thanks and praise.

"I'm glad you like it. Danielle, this is where you'll stay whenever you come up here to use the facilities. And your mother and grandmother—John told me you and your mother live with your grandmother—are welcome to stay with you. Feel free to order anything from room service and if you need anything else we have a concierge who is very good at satisfying any whim of our guests. Make use of him when you want something that's not on the room service menu, or you awake in the middle of the night with an urge for ice cream."

"Don't tell her that," Cherisse joked. "She'll work the poor man to death."

They all laughed, after which Danielle asked, "May I go for a trial run?"

She knew her mother hated the snow. She hadn't been able to entice her to try skiing in the four years she had been a part of Mr. Santiago's youth organization. She didn't think she would be able to get her mother outside in the snow now.

With her mother left behind, maybe Harry Payne would be enticed to stay and entertain her.

"Sure you can," Harry said at once. "I'll go change into my ski gear. You and your mother do the same, and I'll meet you in the lobby in twenty minutes."

Danielle's face fell. "Mom doesn't ski," she said regretfully, her gaze resting on her mother who, if Harry wasn't mistaken, was giving her daughter a warning with her eyes.

A warning her daughter was conveniently ignoring.

"Then I'll arrange for someone to take you," Harry suggested, rolling with the punches. "And I'll give your mother a tour of the rest of the resort while you're gone."

"That sounds like a plan," Danielle said, and gleefully fled into the bedroom to change.

In her absence, Harry said to Cherisse, "She's really a handful."

"You don't know the half of it," Cherisse said with an exaggerated sigh.

Now that they were alone it was as if pretending that last Saturday night had not meant anything to them could be dispensed with.

Cherisse sat on the overstuffed couch and gestured for Harry to sit next to her. "What happened with your girlfriend, Harry? Did you argue over her insensitivity toward your mother?"

Harry remembered that he had told her about Marcia's opinion that he was tied to his mother's apron strings. "No, that wasn't it, although that has something to do with my being able to get over her as well as I am. Do you know LaShaun Gregory? He plays for the Broncos."

Even though she didn't follow football, Cherisse lived in Denver and LaShaun Gregory was the darling of the Broncos. His name was splashed across newspapers, television and radio on a daily basis, it seemed.

"I've heard of him," she said, her expression full of concern for Harry.

Harry felt warmed by her sympathy and even more warmed by her nearness. She had the kind of natural beauty that enticed him. Most of the women he knew applied makeup to walk outside to get the morning paper. And she'd come all the way to Vail to meet her daughter's sponsor with nothing on, that he could see, except red lipstick. That was utterly sexy to him. But then, looking closely, he saw that her black lashes were already full and lush, mascara wouldn't do them justice, and her skin was healthy and vibrant. What other artificial beauty enhancer did she need?

The fact that she had applied lipstick told him that she was aware that her mouth was one of her best features, she wanted to bring it out, say "look at my mouth, isn't it something?" And it was.

"Harry?" she said softly.

Harry had been lost in her mouth. He laughed softly. "Oh, yeah, we were talking about Marcia and LaShaun. Apparently they were an item before he strayed and chose the other woman over her. Angered by his infidelity, Marcia vowed to make him pay. So she set her cap for me. She used me to make him jealous and to bring him to his senses."

Cherisse shook her head. "That's so cruel."

Harry sighed. "But it worked like a dream. She says they're back together now and I should be happy I'm free to play the field."

Cherisse took his big hand in hers. "You're a good man, Harry. You'll meet someone more suited to you, someone who'll love the fact that you're so close to your mother. I don't know how Marcia could have a problem with that. I always thought a man who loved his mother had more respect for other women."

She loved the feel of his hand in hers. It made her feel safe and secure. In fact, her body was entirely too happy to be sitting this close to Harry Payne. She felt her nipples begin to strain against the fabric of her bra and was glad she was wearing a dark color that would help to conceal her arousal.

She inhaled and exhaled and realized that her heartbeat had picked up its pace. As a nurse she was trained to notice changes in a person's vital signs and she was well aware that she had no business sitting on a couch holding Harry Payne's hand.

Harry, for his part, was content to hold her hand all day long if she would let him. She intrigued him and generally threw his libido into overdrive. He wondered how he was going to get around the fact that he was her daughter's sponsor.

He knew instinctively that Cherisse would see that as a problem when he told her he wanted to date her. Date her? *Get serious, Harry,* he thought, *you want this woman in your arms, preferably naked.*

Chapter 6

Harry asked Cory Newman, one of the best ski instructors on staff, to take Danielle up the mountain and show her the trails that would challenge her. Cory, twenty-two, didn't like having to babysit some teenaged ski prodigy for the afternoon when he could have been taking paying guests up the mountain and showing off his skills to an appreciative audience.

They took the lift to Vail's world-famous Back Bowls, which was 2,966 acres of wide-open ski terrain. Cory took her to Blue Sky Basin, a spot that provided more rugged terrain and hence an exciting skiing experience.

He expected her to fall on her butt any minute now as he watched her schuss down the nicely packed light snow. Behind her, he began to admire her form and her daring, although he was a little apprehensive about the daring part. He had promised her mother he would bring her back without any broken bones.

Danielle came to a stop a few yards from the lift station and looked back at Cory through her goggles. The sun reflected brightly on the snow, so it was always advisable to shield her eyes. And the altitude was hard on the body, so Danielle made sure she was properly hydrated. She had a water bottle strapped to the back of her waist.

She took a few sips while she waited for Cory to catch up.

When he did arrive, he was laughing. "Okay, I give it to you, you're good. But you also take way too many risks. You can't go to the Olympics with a broken leg and definitely not with a broken neck."

After satisfying her thirst, Danielle was busy applying more sunscreen to her exposed skin. But she was also listening. She loved skiing and it was true that her style looked reckless because she put so much energy into it, and speed was second nature to her, but deep down she was always contemplating her twists and turns and keeping her eyes peeled for pitfalls in the terrain.

Of all her ski heroes she had never known one who did not go for broke every time they were on the powder.

"Thanks," she said with sincerity. "I'll watch it next time."

This was their second run down the mountain.

"It's safe to go one more time, then," Cory said, looking at the sky. "I think it's getting ready to snow. Visibility isn't going to be good."

They made their way to the lift, boarded and he locked them in. As the lift rose into the air, Danielle asked, "Why do you work for a resort?"

"The pay's good," Cory said, "and where else would I get the chance to ski practically every day of the season?"

"I see what you mean," Danielle said. She smiled at the short, muscular instructor.

He reminded her of a California surfer. Golden hair, blue

eyes, tanned skin. "You look more like a snowboarder to me," she told him. "Or a surfer, but isn't snowboarding derived from surfing?"

Cory looked impressed. "I see you've done your homework. Yeah, I've done some surfing in my day. And I love snowboarding. You ought to try it next time you come."

"Oh, I've already tried it," Danielle told him. "It's great, but I like the feeling of being in control I get from Alpine skiing."

Cory laughed. "You don't look like you're in control out there."

"But I am," Danielle assured him.

"Your mother probably freaks every time she watches you compete," he said astutely.

"She closes her eyes a lot," Danielle admitted.

She wondered what sort of amusement Harry Payne had found for her mom while she was enjoying the great outdoors.

"Karibu Resorts announces the grand opening of our two-to-three-bedroom condominiums. At two thousand square feet, the units boast only the finest amenities, including hardwood floors, Berber carpeting, flagstone and marble tile and granite slab countertops in the kitchens. The kitchen is a cook's dream with the latest appliances including a refrigerator, cooktops, a microwave and convection oven. And for you mermaids, there is a massaging tub in the master bedroom. As always the units will have wireless Internet access and flat-screen televisions with surround sound, plus satellite radio."

Harry and Cherisse were standing among the small crowd of staff, guests and media people gathered at the site of the new condominiums listening to Harry's general manager, Peter Wisdom, give a statement to the press.

"Shouldn't that be you up there?" Cherisse joked.

Harry smiled. "I try to stay in the background as much as possible. I derive pleasure from watching my plans for the resort come together."

"Karibu Resort is offering a lucky family of four a week's vacation in one of our new condominiums. To enter, simply go to Karibu-dot-com and sign up, or you may mail in the entry forms found in last week's local papers and trade magazines. The drawing will be held on November thirtieth. Now, the tour of the first furnished condominium is officially underway. Please join us. And thank you for coming out today." Peter finished with a flourish and people began entering the condo in an orderly fashion.

With his hand at the base of her spine, Harry asked Cherisse, "Would you like to see our new baby?"

"I wouldn't miss it," Cherisse said enthusiastically.

The condo looked like an elegantly appointed home in an upscale neighborhood.

"How many guests can stay in each unit?" Cherisse asked. It was big enough to accommodate quite a few people.

"Six in the two-bedroom units and eight in the three-bedroom units," Harry answered. "We have to comply with fire codes. There are always guests who break the rules, though, and they're hard to catch."

Cherisse laughed softly. "Yeah, I can see how that would be a problem."

Her cell phone rang. She thought of letting the message function kick in, but when she pulled it from her purse and read the name on the screen, she hurriedly answered. It belonged to Gerald, one of the nurses she worked with. Gerald had never had occasion to phone her in the past and she knew he had to have a very good reason to do so now.

"Gerry?" she answered, her voice rife with concern.

Gerald was laughing. "Oh, Cheri, I know you're somewhere in Vail this weekend but I thought you would want to know—Amy woke up!"

Tears of joy came to Cherisse's eyes and she started laughing, too. "Thank God! Has she said anything yet?"

"Yeah," Gerald reported, "she said, 'I'm so thirsty, may I have a Coke?'"

"And when you told her she could have water instead?" Cherisse prompted.

"She said, 'Aaw, man, I hate water,'" Gerald said, still laughing. He pulled himself together. "I'll let you go now. Have fun in Vail!"

"Thanks for calling, Gerry, I'm so happy for Amy. 'Bye now."

Cherisse closed the phone and put it back in her shoulder bag. Looking up at Harry, she said, "That was one of the nurses I work with. A patient, a little girl who sustained severe head injuries and was in a coma, woke up today. She wasn't expected to pull through so it feels like a miracle."

Harry was smiling because he had watched her during the entire conversation and had been highly charmed by her show of compassion. How her expression had gone from worry to sheer joy in a matter of seconds when her nurse friend had given her the good news. She genuinely cared.

"That's wonderful," Harry said.

The tour was over and they began walking toward the exit. "May I ask how she got hurt?"

Cherisse sighed sadly. "It was her father. From what I read in the paper, the girl's mother left him and didn't bother taking their only child with her. Frustrated at being the lone parent he flew into a rage and beat the child nearly to death. He then fled the scene. A neighbor found Amy and called 911."

"Did they ever find the father?" Harry asked, absorbed in the story.

"Oh, yeah, he's in jail now awaiting trial for attempted murder."

"What about Amy's mother?" Harry asked hopefully.

"She never came forward," Cherisse told him.

"So Amy goes into the system when she recovers?"

"Looks like it," Cherisse said. "But there's always the possibility of another family member claiming her."

As they left the condo, walking around others who had attended the debut, Harry suddenly heard his name being called.

He looked up and saw Marcia hurrying toward them, a cameraman in tow. Frowning, he muttered, "What the hell does she want?"

Cherisse had been unable to understand what he said, but her eyes followed his line of sight and once she saw Marcia Shaw, she realized that the Marcia he had told her about was one of Denver's most popular news anchors.

She paused in her steps, waiting for Harry to speak with Marcia in private. From the harried expression on Marcia Shaw's face, she was either late or had been forced into an assignment she did not want to do.

Harry's eyes narrowed as Marcia came up to him and said sotto voce, "The program director thought it would be more interesting to the viewers if I covered your condo opening. I haven't had the chance to tell her that you and I are no longer dating."

"Sorry," said Harry. "The general manager has already given the resort's statement to the press. The reporters from the other two TV stations and three newspapers were here on time. At the moment I'm showing an important guest around. Please excuse me. Your cameraman is free to film the condo." He gestured to the furnished condo with a nod of his head. "It's the one with all the people coming out of it."

Marcia gave him a pleading look. "Come on, Harry, be nice. It's a slow news day."

"It must be if *you're* covering a condo grand opening," Harry said dryly.

Marcia cocked a critical eye in Cherisse's direction. "Is that your important guest?"

Harry didn't reply. He turned away and began walking back to Cherisse.

"She's cute, Harry," Marcia said. "If she would do something with that wild hair she could be a stunner."

Cherisse heard that. The comment stung. She didn't know why Marcia Shaw was taking her frustration out on her. She was an innocent bystander.

She met Harry's eyes and saw by the fury in them that he wasn't going to let Marcia get away with her petty cruelty to a stranger.

But Cherisse walked up to him and took him by the hand. "Let it go, Harry. Miss Shaw is obviously having a bad day.

Harry shot Marcia such a blatantly belligerent look that she automatically took a step backward. "There's nothing here for us," she said to the confused cameraman. "Let's go."

Stiff, Harry watched Marcia quickly retreat with the cameraman lugging the heavy camera on his shoulder.

After what she'd done he was amazed that she would have the nerve to show up here asking for help with an assignment. But people like Marcia Shaw rarely worried about how they achieved their goals. The only thing that counted with them was winning. She had won LaShaun back. It didn't matter that she had strung *him* along for 90 days in order to do it!

Cherisse felt very indecisive at that moment. She didn't

know Harry well at all. Was it appropriate for her to help soothe his hurt feelings? Had he been in love with Marcia?

What he'd said earlier about his being able to get over Marcia so quickly because she had unapologetically used him to make her former boyfriend jealous didn't mean he hadn't fallen for the beautiful anchorwoman. That could have been bravado.

It might not be wise for her to stick her nose in his business.

Harry turned to her. "Cheri, may I ask you a question?"

Cherisse smiled up at him. Of course if he *asked* her to stick her nose in his business it was perfectly fine. "Ask away," she said.

"Why did you stop me from laying into that woman?"

It was an unexpected question but Cherisse rolled with it. "Because the only reason she said what she did is because she was upset that you would replace her so quickly. And with someone who is obviously unglamorous, to boot! She was livid."

"Even though she doesn't want me and has gone back to LaShaun?" Harry asked incredulously.

"She has her pride," Cherisse explained. "She saw me and the claws came out. I doubt if she even thought for a moment about what was going to come out of her mouth. It was instinctive."

"So, you forgive the comment?" asked Harry, an amused glint in his eyes.

"Of course, but if she ever insults me again I'm going to pull that weave right out of her head," Cherisse joked. "It is a weave, isn't it? Not that I've got anything against weaves, just women who wear them and then go around insulting women who don't!"

Harry laughed and took Cherisse by the elbow, directing

her away from the condo and onto the walkway that led back to the main part of the resort, about a twenty-minute walk. "That's more like it," he said. "For a minute there I thought I was in the presence of a saint."

"Saint Cherisse?" said Cherisse. "It has a nice ring to it."

"Saint Cheri, patron saint of women with beautiful, natural hair. I love your hair," Harry said, smiling down at her. Cherisse could tell that he really did like her hair, a fact that made her inordinately happy for some insane reason.

"You want to hear my theory about black women and their hair?" she asked, still in a joking mood.

"By all means," said Harry easily.

"The more we try to whip our hair into submission by chemically straightening it, the more it rebels by breaking, being lackluster and generally a pain in the butt. But when we let go and learn to love the hair we were born with, it flourishes, grows wild and abundant. It becomes boastful and prideful and that's why it stands up and says, 'Look at me, I'm the way Mother Nature made me, aren't I *gorgeous?*'" She laughed softly. "And that's why my hair is so wild and unruly. It just won't be quiet."

"I bet it keeps you up nights," Harry joked.

"All the time," Cherisse said, "usually by singing the theme song to *Hair,* the musical. It likes that song."

Harry laughed until his stomach muscles hurt. He liked this woman.

That night, as they were getting ready to go to dinner with Harry, Danielle was so excited she was bouncing off the walls. In the bedroom of the suite, both of them had laid their clothes out on the bed, showered, dressed in their underwear and done their hair. However, Danielle kept changing clothes Cherisse had left the packing to her normally sensible daughter and had no idea that Danielle had brought so many outfits with her for an overnight stay.

She had brought only the new dress she'd bought for the occasion: a beautiful royal blue wrap dress with long sleeves and a hem that fell about three inches above her knees. The soft fabric clung to her curves. She had chosen a simple black clutch and a pair of three-inch-heeled black leather Jimmy Choo sandals she'd found on sale at Shoe Emporium, her favorite place to shop for shoes.

She'd put her hair in a French twist, which made her neck look long and elegant. And the dress revealed just the right amount of cleavage. A classy look she was reasonably sure would be suitable for dinner at Solomon's, the resort's five-star restaurant.

Earlier she'd asked Harry why he had chosen the name Solomon. He told her that Solomon was his grandfather's name. And his grandfather had been a cook in a restaurant in Louisville, Kentucky, for many years. Only a cook, he had never been able to afford his own restaurant. Solomon had died when Harry was fifteen but he said he was sure that if he had lived he would have been tickled to have a restaurant named after him.

After Danielle changed clothes for the fourth time, Cherisse said sternly, "Danielle, the next items you put on stay on! What's wrong with you tonight?" She looked closely at her daughter. Danielle had fashioned her braids into an upsweep hairdo and was wearing only a black bra and bikini panties.

She met her mother's eyes, but quickly lowered her gaze again. "I met a boy on the slopes today and he said he'd see me at dinner. He's here with his family. They're from D.C., Ma. His dad works in government and his mom's a lawyer."

Danielle walked over to her purse, which she'd left

hanging by its strap on the back of the wooden slat-back chair sitting beside the closet door. Getting her cell phone, she opened it and clicked on the photo function. She showed her mother a photo of her and a tall African-American boy, both in ski gear, standing in front of the lift. He was a good-looking kid with dark brown skin, dimples and the best set of sparkling white teeth Cherisse had seen in a long time.

"His name's Dante Winters," Danielle told her mother.

"How old is he?"

"He just turned eighteen and he's a senior in high school, too."

"Wear the forest-green dress, Danielle," Cherisse said. "It looks good on you and if Dante gets up the nerve to come over to the table and say hello, stains won't show on it when you drop something in your lap."

"Aw, Ma," Danielle cried, laughing softly.

"Silly, huh?" asked her mother. "It's also silly for you to be nervous about seeing Dante tonight. You've *got* a boyfriend."

Danielle really laughed then. "You mean Echo? If it were left up to Echo asking me I would go to the senior prom alone."

"The senior prom isn't until May. A lot can happen in six months. And if Echo means nothing to you, who are you text-messaging thirty times a day?"

"He's the worst gossip in school," Danielle complained.

"Have you told him everything about your day?" Cherisse asked, curious.

"Everything except about meeting Dante," Danielle confessed.

"Why didn't you tell him about Dante?"

"Because it's none of his business," said Danielle, her tone less confident than her words were meant to be.

Cherisse shook her head. "No, you didn't tell him because you weren't sure how he would take it. How many guys have you been interested in since you and Echo have been hanging out together? How many guys have shown an interest in you?"

"None," was Danielle's reply.

"Doesn't that tell you something? You're always with Echo so the other guys at school assume you two are an item. A situation that Echo is probably enjoying if, in fact, he has designs on you."

Danielle, frowning, began texting a message to Echo. When she finished she said, "Let's see how long it takes him to answer."

"What did you say to him?"

"I told him I met a cute boy today, isn't that fabulous!" Danielle's eyes sparkled with mischief. She set the phone on the bureau top while she went to finish dressing.

Cherisse sighed and walked over to the bed to pick up her dress. She wore a beige lacy bra with matching panties and a silky slip, less because she thought the dress was see-through than for added warmth. She didn't plan on going outside tonight, but who knew? She might be tempted to step onto the balcony for a few minutes of fresh air.

She put on the dress and went to stand in front of the full-length mirror next to the closet entrance. Turning around, observing the backs of her legs, she was satisfied that she'd moisturized enough. Ashy skin was a symptom of these cold climes.

She'd slathered a light-scented lotion all over her body. Her golden-brown skin had a healthy glow to it. Smiling, she wondered if Harry were taking care with his dress this evening, as well. He appeared to be so confident that he would probably feel comfortable in anything. Although, to be honest, every time she had seen him he had been beautifully dressed. But did he agonize over what to wear? She doubted it.

A continuous beep, denoting that Danielle had a text message, resounded in the bedroom. Danielle quickly picked up the phone and began reading. "What's so fabulous about it?" Of course she was translating the shortened version of the English language that text aficionados used.

Soon, she and Echo were furiously text-messaging each other, her thumbs flying over the tiny keyboard.

Smiling, Cherisse left her daughter alone in the bedroom while she went into the living room of the suite to await Harry's arrival.

She wondered if years from now millions of teenagers would have deformed thumbs from all the wear and tear on them due to text-messaging.

Cherisse walked over to the big picture window and looked out at the lit-up resort. Even at night the resort was beautiful, an architectural dream with its turrets and other decorative flourishes reminiscent of a Swiss palace.

On her walk with Harry today she had noticed his gardeners had landscaped the resort's many gardens with plants and flowers native to this area, hardy varieties that thrived in cold weather. Cherisse was sure if her mother were here she would be able to tell her every name of every species of plant, but Cherisse was ignorant of such things. Like Danielle, her mother was going to love it here when she got the chance to visit.

A twinge of doubt suddenly wormed its way into her thoughts. She had never been happy to accept extravagant gifts from anyone. What Harry was offering to do for Danielle would cost him a lot of money. Letting her stay here and practice her skiing whenever she wanted to. Paying her travel expenses and for her ski gear: clothing and equipment. And all Danielle would have to do to repay his generosity was to wear his company's logo on the back of her jacket.

Stop it, Cherisse, she told herself. This is how the sports world works and Danielle is lucky to have somebody like Harry Payne backing her. Her logical mind told her she was right. Still, she hated being beholden to anybody.

Danielle entered, laughing. "Ma, you were right!"

Cherisse turned to face her daughter. Danielle was wearing the forest-green empire waist dress with a pair of black ankle boots. She looked as if she'd stepped off the cover of *Vibe!* The dress was modest, its bodice revealing no cleavage at all, and because of the manner in which it was designed it hung straight on her curvaceous body, but didn't display any of those curves. That was the dress's best feature as far as her mother was concerned.

It revealed her shapely legs to all and sundry, though. And because she was five-nine, her legs went on and on.

Looking her lovely daughter over, Cherisse sighed. She was already a woman. As her mother, she had to face up to that fact, but she was going to hang on to the illusion of Danielle still being her little girl for as long as she could.

"What did he say when you told him you'd met someone?"

"He wanted to know everything about him," Danielle said, smiling. "So I sent him the photo I showed you. After that, he said Dante looks older than he said he was. I should be careful. He might be one of those perverts who pose as younger guys to get close to teenaged girls. I told him I was pretty confident that Dante was eighteen like he said he was. Echo wrote back that if I couldn't be trusted to use common sense he would have to come up here and run interference. He made me promise not to be alone with Dante! Ma, Echo's not gay!"

Cherisse gave her daughter a confused look.

"You thought he was gay?"

"Well, didn't you?"

"Yeah, but I thought you never suspected."

"Come on, Ma. He cooks, sews and knows every musical that ever appeared on Broadway practically word for word. Either he was gay or very strange for a straight guy. Now I know he's just strange."

"And that comforts you?" her mother asked, amused.

"Ma, half the kids at school are strange in some way. It comes from trying to find out where we belong in the great scheme of things. There are a lot of neuroses floating around the halls of my school. I can work with strange but not gay. If Echo turned out to be gay there was no chance for us."

There came a knock at the door.

"That's Harry," Cherisse announced. She started walking to the door.

"No," cried Danielle, "let me get the door. You're supposed to make an entrance."

"You've been reading too many romance novels," her mother accused lightly.

"And you haven't been reading enough," Danielle countered, hurrying to the door. "For once, listen to me. And when you come into the room, watch Harry's eyes."

Shaking her head, Cherisse decided to let her daughter conduct her experiment. She went into the bedroom to get her purse.

When she walked back out, Harry was sitting on the couch laughing at something Danielle had said. He looked up and the laughter died in his throat.

Rising, his eyes possessively raked over Cherisse. Crossing the room to her, he suddenly found his voice again. Keeping his words low, and personal, for Cherisse's ears only, he whispered, "Damn, you're beautiful!"

Cherisse was beaming. Beautiful, he'd said, and he was

standing there looking so devastatingly handsome in his dark blue suit that he took her breath away. This wasn't working out the way she had figured. She was supposed to come here with Danielle in order for her to meet her sponsor. Not to meet a man who would leave her trembling with desire. This wasn't the right time for her and Harry Payne.

Still, she couldn't resist saying, breathlessly, "Not half as much as you are." After she'd said it she wondered where that sexy tone had come from.

Harry just smiled at her and offered her his arm. "Shall we go?"

Chapter 7

While they were leisurely strolling through the lobby on the way to Solomon's Danielle couldn't help noticing the funky beat of hip-hop in the air.

"What's that?" she turned around and asked Harry, who was walking beside her mother a couple of paces behind her.

"That's coming from the ballroom where the youth dance is held," Harry said. "What you hear is the DJ warming up. The dance starts at eight and lasts until around midnight. It's a Saturday night staple around here. It's kind of a multimedia event. The DJ plays lots of songs that also have videos, and while he's spinning the disc, the video is playing on a wide screen set on the wall. No alcoholic drinks are served."

"May I go check it out after dinner?" Danielle asked Cherisse, her tone not quite pleading, but promising full pleading mode if she got a negative reply.

"Alone?" Cherisse countered. "No. You know the rules."

Danielle started to say something, saw the warning expression in her mother's eyes and thought better of it. Earlier when she had ignored that look she had done it out of an unselfish desire to get her mother and Harry alone. This time she knew she was asking her mother to let her break a rule she had never let her get away with before: no going to dances without a suitable companion who would look out for her.

She therefore let it go and resolved to have a good time at dinner.

Once they arrived at Solomon's, Danielle noticed that several diners watched them cross the room to their table in the beautifully decorated and subtly lit restaurant. She supposed that was because of Harry. Like the captain of a ship, as the owner of the resort, many people knew him and were curious to see whom he seated at his table.

She and her mom had gone on a cruise a couple years ago and the captain had asked them to dine with him because her mother had saved another passenger from choking on a shrimp by using the Heimlich maneuver.

Harry helped her and her mother into their chairs, then he sat down between them and in less than a minute, a waiter came over with iced water and a basket of fresh baked rolls with freshly whipped butter mixed with raspberries. He then left them to peruse the menu.

Danielle was ravenous and dug right in while her mother and Harry seemed to find something to talk about in lowered voices. She didn't even try to eavesdrop since she was enjoying the delicious, flaky rolls so much.

She didn't know it, but Harry was quietly pleading her case with her mother. "I can get someone on the staff to escort her to the dance. She'd be perfectly safe," he said.

"That's nice of you, Harry, but I'd rather not allow Danielle to monopolize more of your staff's time. I'm sure they have better things to do than babysit her."

Harry had an ulterior motive: he wanted to be alone with Cheri. He had very little time left to convince her to go out with him. To state his case, he needed privacy.

Ah, well, maybe he could get her alone on the dance floor after dinner. Solomon's had a live band each Saturday night. The Delacroix Brothers, a jazz quartet from New Orleans, were playing tonight.

Harry leaned back in his chair and picked up his menu. He didn't really need to look at it. He knew what was on it like the back of his hand. "All right," he said to Cherisse's decision. Then he added "Solomon's offers a wide range of delicacies. The chef, Annette Bourne, was trained in Paris. Although she is southern born and while the menu leans toward French cuisine, it is more the French of the French Quarter in New Orleans than the French of Paris."

Cherisse was reading the menu. She loved seafood and saw an item that caught her attention. "I can't believe there's cioppino on the menu. I haven't had that in years. I'd like that with a glass of white wine."

"Then cioppino, it is," said Harry. He was fond of the fish stew himself. It was light and wouldn't leave one's breath smelling fishy. But he decided on the roast chicken.

"What looks good to you?" Cherisse asked Danielle, not looking up from the menu.

Danielle was busy smiling at Dante Winters, who had just walked in with his parents.

He had apparently asked his parents to go over to their table to meet her and her mother because they were headed straight for their table. Danielle hastily wiped her mouth and fingers on the linen napkin at her elbow, afraid that she'd gotten some raspberry butter or bread crumbs on them.

When Dante and his parents arrived, Dante said, "Hello, Danielle." Out of his ski gear he looked even more fit. He wore a pair of jeans and a black turtleneck sweater with a pair of black motorcycle boots, which Danielle thought were very cool. His father, a tall, dark-skinned gentleman in a black tuxedo, obviously enjoyed dressing up for the evening. No less than his wife, a beautifully dressed woman with café-au-lait skin and black hair that she wore in a short, sophisticated bob. Dante was at least six feet tall. His father was perhaps an inch taller, and his mother was a petite five-three, Danielle guessed.

Danielle got to her feet, as did her mother and Harry. "Hi, Dante," she said, a warm smile on her lips.

Dante graciously introduced her to his parents. "This is the young lady I was telling you about," he said to them. Then he regarded Danielle. "This is my dad, Davis Winters and my mom, Eva Stanton-Winters."

Danielle, always a charmer, said, "I'm pleased to meet you." She briefly shook both their hands. And then it was her turn to introduce her mother. "And this is my mom, Ms. Cherisse Washington. I suppose you all know our host, Mr. Payne."

"A pleasure, Ms. Washington," Eva said, shaking hands with Cherisse.

"The pleasure's all mine," Cherisse said with a welcoming smile.

Mr. Winters shook her hand, as well, and then declared, "Yes, everybody knows Harry. How are you, Harry? You know you still owe me a golf game."

"I haven't forgotten," said Harry. "How about an eight o'clock tee time tomorrow morning?"

"Sounds good," said Davis Winters. And they shook on it. "Well, we'd better get to our table. Enjoy your evening, folks."

Dante wasn't ready to go yet, though. "Danielle," he said, "would you go to the dance with me tonight? Last Saturday, our first day here, I had to walk into that room alone and I really don't want to do it again." He grinned ingratiatingly.

He's either going to be a politician or quite the lady killer when he's a few years older, Cherisse thought. *But for now, he's just a socially inept kid.*

Danielle looked to her mother for some sign of acquiescence. Cherisse smiled and said, "Maybe for a couple of hours."

Danielle beamed. "I'd love to," she said to Dante, who almost jumped for joy but was able to avoid embarrassment by controlling the impulse.

"Great!" he said. "I'll come back for you after we've all finished dinner. See you."

"See you," said Danielle.

Harry was perhaps happier than she was at the turn of events. He and Cherisse would have at least two hours alone.

Over dinner, Harry wanted to hear about Cherisse's growing up in Denver. He said he had never known anyone who was actually born there. Cherisse didn't doubt him since statistics showed that in the 1990s Denver grew by thirty percent. Approximately one thousand people moved there every week for ten years straight. Therefore Denver's population had a lot of people who were from someplace else.

"I loved the city," she told him. "I didn't know anything else so I might be biased but there was always something to do in Denver. And school was fun because the teachers, the parents, the community were all working together to keep you interested. That's why, I guess, the overall high school and college dropout rate in Denver is among America's lowest. Plus, my mom was a teacher. Teachers' kids never caught a break."

"So you graduated from high school and went straight to college," Harry guessed.

"No, I took a detour," Cherisse said with a smile and a glance in Danielle's direction.

Danielle spoke up. "What she means is she and Dad, who were high-school sweethearts, got married and had me."

Cherisse had told Danielle about the circumstances of her birth. She didn't believe in keeping things like that from Danielle because her daughter had a very inquisitive mind. Danielle would eventually find out that Cherisse was pregnant with her before she and Charlie were married. She would be upset that she had to discover it on her own instead of having been told by her parents, especially her mother.

Cherisse wondered why Danielle let Charlie slide with everything, but expressed disappointment with her if she neglected to behave like an exemplary parent. Another reason Cherisse sometimes resented Charlie.

"Charlie and I got married, he got drafted by the Philadelphia Eagles, decided to skip college and we moved to Philadelphia. I was nineteen when Danielle was born. I didn't know anything about being a wife or a mother. I just played it by ear."

"But she must have done something right," said Danielle. "I'm not crazy." She crossed her eyes. "Well, not too crazy, anyway."

They laughed.

"Charlie and I tried to make our marriage work, but we were too different," Cherisse said. "After the divorce Danielle and I moved back to Denver to live with my mother, Joann, and I went to nursing school and got my bachelor's and master's degrees."

Danielle remained silent about the reason her mom and dad's marriage didn't work. She was aware that her mom couldn't live with her dad because he was addicted to gambling. Charlie wouldn't take responsibility for his family.

Her mother had put up with it for nine years. Danielle couldn't fault her for wanting a better life for herself and her child. In fact she was glad her mother had decided to leave her dad.

Her dad had finally decided he needed help three years ago and the last time she had spoken to him he had promised her that he hadn't gambled on anything. He swore he hadn't even bought a lottery ticket in over a year.

Maybe she would eventually get the father she had always wanted.

Growing up she had accepted what little time he spent with her, not complaining because she didn't want to give him an excuse not to come see her. If he thought she was disappointed in him, or irritated with him due to his repeated lies about coming to see her or sending her a gift, he might have been too ashamed to show his face.

With her mother she could always be herself. Her mother was strong enough to take anything she dished out. That's how she wanted to be when she became a woman.

Plus, another reason Danielle figured her mom hadn't mentioned the gambling to Harry Payne was because they had just met. She might tell him the truth one day.

After dessert, Danielle was delighted to look up and see Dante coming over.

When he got to their table she rose and said her good-nights to her mom and Harry.

"Be back in the suite by midnight," Cherisse told her.

Danielle didn't try to negotiate a later curfew. "Okay, midnight."

She and Dante hurried off as if they hadn't a minute to lose.

Harry smiled at Cherisse. The Delacroix Brothers were performing "Embraceable You."

Several couples were already on the dance floor, and most of them were older couples who had undoubtedly been dancing together for years because they were quite good.

Cherisse watched them, a smile playing at the corners of her mouth and a dreamy look in her eyes.

Harry felt pretty confident that she wouldn't refuse him if he asked her to dance. He offered her his hand, which she immediately took. They rose and walked onto the dance floor and she smoothly went into his arms. From the moment her body touched his, Harry knew that they would fit well together.

Her body was firm, yet soft, and the fragrance she wore floated off her warm skin and into his olfactory senses like the fumes from a witch's brew. It was just as spellbindingly intoxicating. He was hooked.

She sighed softly, which further aroused Harry. He started talking in order to distract himself. "Emmitt Smith isn't the only ex-football player who can dance, you know."

Cherisse gave a low, throaty laugh as she looked up into his eyes. "Harry, are you nervous?"

"Kind of. Aren't you?"

"Yes."

"Why?" he asked.

"Because I'm much more attracted to you than I should be."

Harry's heartbeat accelerated at this admission. And blood rushed to a certain area below his waist. He cleared his throat. "Why did you put it that way? Is there a reason you *shouldn't* be attracted to me? Because I'm telling you now, I want to see you again. And I'm glad you feel the same way."

"I do," she said, "very much. But how would it look if it got out that you were dating the mother of the skier your company is sponsoring?"

"I don't care how it would look," Harry said calmly. "I was attracted to you last Saturday night when we met on the balcony. I didn't even know who you were then. I was tempted to look for you but you didn't give me your last name!"

"You were?" Cherisse asked with a bit of an awestruck tone to her voice.

"I was," Harry confirmed. "Now that there's nothing standing in our way, don't go inventing obstacles. Whose business is it if we date?"

"It's nobody's," Cherisse said. She wanted to believe that once the media learned Harry—who was a celebrity in Denver and Vail because not only was he a renowned ex-Bronco but he also owned one of the most successful businesses in this part of Colorado—was going out with the mother of the young woman he'd agreed to back in the 2010 Winter Olympics they would not put a salacious spin on it.

The news wasn't what it used to be. You used to be able to turn on your TV and hear serious news reported by serious journalists. Some of today's news networks thrived on rumor and innuendo. Entertainment in the form of gossip obviously helped pay the bills.

But looking up at Harry, Cherisse decided she was willing to risk it. Honestly, it could go either way: she and Harry could be left alone by the media or the media could fall on them like ravenous wolves. Either way, perhaps they would have something so good between them that they would be able to weather the storm.

"That's right," Harry said, pulling her closer against him. "It's nobody's business except ours."

For the remainder of the song, they seemed to float together on the dance floor, eyes locked, with contented smiles on their faces. Two minutes after the Delacroix Brothers finished "Embraceable You" and "It Had to Be You" and announced to their audience that they were taking a five-minute break and everyone else cleared the dance floor, Davis Winters called out, "Um, Harry, in case you hadn't noticed, the music's stopped!"

Cherisse and Harry hurried off the dance floor amid good-natured laughter from all present. "Thank you, Davis," Harry said.

"Just looking out for you," Davis said, laughing.

Cherisse blushed to her ears. "Let's get out of here."

"I was about to suggest that," Harry whispered.

They went back to their table where Cherisse collected her clutch and her wrap and they walked hand in hand from the restaurant.

Once they were clear of prying eyes, Harry wrapped his arm about her waist, pulling her close to his side. "How would you like to sit by the fire and listen to music while sipping a cup of tea?"

Cherisse smiled at him. "I'd love to."

Harry's suite was the largest space in the hotel. Like the new condominiums it had two thousand feet of living area. On the top floor, it had the appearance of a loft. Very few walls and miles of hardwood floors with expensive carpets placed strategically around the suite.

Masculine furnishings with muscle, big overstuffed couches and chairs in earth tones accented with rich woods. Once Harry ushered Cherisse into the suite he insisted that she take her shoes off and get comfortable on the couch in front of the fireplace.

He removed his jacket and went to light the fire in the fireplace. This done, he turned to smile at Cherisse and found her looking at him intently. She had taken off her shoes and was sitting on the couch with her feet tucked under her. She would have been embarrassed to admit what she'd been thinking while she had watched him bend over to light the fireplace. Harry Payne had a great butt! In fact, in his shirt-sleeves with the muscles of his arms and chest and stomach easily delineated, and the muscles of his legs and thighs working underneath his dress slacks, he was a treat to behold.

Harry didn't have to ask what she had been thinking. He could see the mischievous glint in her eyes and guessed she'd been checking out his backside. She was a healthy, red-blooded girl, after all.

"Celestial Seasonings tea," he said. "We get it by the truck-load. What kind do you like?"

"Peppermint," Cherisse told him. "It's good of you to patronize a Denver business."

"I try to use local businesses as much as possible," said Harry while strolling over to the entertainment center to select a CD. He picked up one of his favorites. "Do you like Taj Mahal?"

Cherisse looked perplexed. "I'm always open to new artists."

Harry laughed softly. "He's been around for more than thirty years. He has a kind of rock/blues/country sound. Have you ever heard of Keb' Mo'?"

"Yeah, I have most of his CDs," Cherisse said.

"Well, now you get to listen to one of the artists who inspired Kevin Moore, otherwise known as Keb' Mo'."

He put the CD on and soon the sound of a blues guitar filled the air. Taj Mahal launched into "Statesboro Blues," which had some very funky guitar riffs in it. Cherisse sat back and enjoyed while Harry went into the kitchen to put the kettle on.

A few minutes later, he returned with two piping hot cups of peppermint tea sweetened with honey and handed Cherisse one of them.

By this time Taj Mahal was singing "She Caught the Katy and Left Me a Mule to Ride" about his woman leaving on the train and his following behind trying to convince her to come back to him.

Harry sat beside Cherisse. "What do you think?"

"I like him," she said with a smile. "He sings with a lot of emotion in his voice. I believe him when he says he loves his woman, big feet and all."

Harry laughed. Setting his cup on the coffee table in front of him, he reached for her right foot and began massaging it. "You have beautiful feet."

Cherisse was glad she'd given herself a pedicure last night and had generously moisturized her feet before going to dinner tonight. Harry's strong hands felt heavenly on her feet. He even knew how to work the soles of her feet and hit that spot that sent shivers up her spine. Lord, yes, the man had talented hands.

It had been six long years since a man had… Wait a minute. She'd told Harry about her long abstinence from sex the first night they met, thinking that it was perfectly safe to spill her guts to a stranger. Someone she would never meet again.

Now here she was letting him massage her feet, a week after meeting him. Damn, he was good. Or, she was slow. At any rate, she'd come to her senses in time.

She reached down and stayed his hand. "Harry, don't do that."

He smiled that sexy smile of his. "Doesn't it feel good?"

"It feels *too* good."

"Then I'm doing it right," Harry said, still smiling sexily.

She grabbed his hand, removed it from her foot and then, still sitting, put her feet on the floor, searching for her Jimmy Choos with them.

Harry watched, confused. "What did I do?"

Shoes on, Cherisse rose and looked down at him. "Six years, Harry Payne. You know I haven't been with a man in six years. You played me like a fiddle tonight!"

Incensed, she spun around. "Look at me, standing in your love nest."

"Love nest?" Harry cried, trying his best to contain his laughter. He got it now. Because she had confided in him that she hadn't had sex in six years she thought he was putting the moves on her. Okay, he *was* putting the moves on her, but not with the intention of taking her to bed but, maybe, getting a good-night kiss. That was all. Honestly.

"I was hoping to kiss you, not make love to you," Harry told her. "I know you're not the type of woman who goes to bed with anyone on the first date, if you can call dinner and a couple of dances a date!"

Cherisse calmed down a bit and eyed him skeptically. "I guess I was letting my lust-crazed thoughts run away with me. It's hell when you meet a gorgeous male and find yourself turned on by him, knowing that you really shouldn't entertain the thought of anything other than a chaste kiss good-night when your body is saying, 'Hell, girl, you haven't had any in ages. Go for it!'"

Harry guffawed. "I'm sorry. I didn't mean to turn you on. Okay, I did mean to do it, but only enough to taste that luscious mouth of yours."

Cherisse found herself smiling in spite of herself. She walked into Harry's open arms.

"You know, we were never supposed to meet again, that's why I felt my secret would be safe with you."

"I know," he whispered, lowering his head. "It's still safe with me. *You're* safe with me."

"Oh, Harry," Cherisse breathed, and gave him her mouth.

When she said his name like that, all breathless, Harry's desire for her increased tenfold. Their mouths collided in an orgiastic dance. Harry had meant to be gentle, to make her feel comfortable in his arms until she loosened up and learned to trust him.

Cherisse had meant to test the waters, expecting to be able to maintain some semblance of control.

They were both disappointed.

One taste of her sweet mouth sent Harry on the quest for more of that addictive nectar. He devoured her. The part of his brain that wasn't lost in sensation and was still able to conjugate verbs was pleasantly surprised by Cherisse's lack of reticence.

This was not a shy, retiring celibate. She was doing things with her tongue that he hadn't even learned yet.

Cherisse knew it. The smell of Harry, his strong body and talented hands had all worked together to break down every fortress she'd built around her in the past six years. She had known he was trouble!

Now that she had tasted him, she wanted so much more.

Her feverish brain whispered, "Do it. Do it. Do it till you're satisfied!" Wasn't that from an old seventies song?

Get out of my brain! Then get your tongue out of Harry Payne's mouth and go to your own suite like a good little girl.

With some effort, she was able to tear her mouth from his, but one look into his sultry eyes, and she was kissing him again.

This time it was Harry who pulled away. "Listen, sweetness, I think I ought to walk you home before we both break our vows of celibacy."

Cherisse laughed. "You've taken a vow of celibacy?"

"Cheri." He said her name so unlike any of her other friends said it. He said it as if he really were saying "dear" or "darling." "Cheri, until you invite me into your bed, yes, I'll remain celibate. No matter how long it takes."

Chapter 8

Danielle couldn't believe it. She'd finally met a boy who could keep up with her on the dance floor! Echo enjoyed more intellectual pursuits, saying dancing was for the mentally challenged. Danielle knew he said that only because he had two left feet.

And Dante not only knew the latest moves, but his energy level also matched hers.

They had danced five straight dances before he suggested they get a drink. The DJ played some of her favorite artists: Rihanna, Beyoncé, Chris Brown, Ne-Yo and Timbaland.

The ballroom was packed. She figured kids from the surrounding area also came to the Saturday night dances. She saw kids who looked younger than she was, and quite a few who were pushing twenty-one, probably, but not that many over twenty-one. She supposed the DJ's emphasis on hip-hop attracted a younger crowd.

As they moved through the throng, trying to make it to the bar, Dante held tightly to her hand. A gentleman, he made sure the way was clear for her. When they reached the bar, he let her have the sole remaining stool on the corner and he stood next to her.

The bartender walked up to them. "What can I get you?"

"Bourbon on the rocks," Dante joked.

"Don't mess with me tonight, Dante," the bartender, a young African-American woman with spiky black hair and enormous green eyes said. She was chewing gum and popping it with alacrity.

She smiled at Danielle. "Hi, I'm Roxy."

"Hi, Roxy, I'm Danielle," Danielle said. "May I have a cranberry juice over crushed ice?"

Roxy gave Dante the evil eye. "Now that's a drink, smart boy."

"Okay," said Dante, eyes twinkling with mischief, "make mine a Singapore Sling, easy on the sling."

"I'm gonna have you slung right outta here!" Roxy warned. She glanced in the direction of one of the big, burly bouncers. There were four stationed around the ballroom, all wearing black muscle tees with the resort's logo—a skier schussing down a snow-covered mountain—emblazoned across the chest.

Dante laughed. "Fine, Roxy. Give me a Coke, regular, not diet, no ice and a slice of lime, squeeze it once into the Coke, stirred, not shaken, then put it on the rim of the glass. Make sure the glass is chilled, of course."

Roxy sighed. "Who do you think you are, James Bond? If I didn't need my job I'd tell you where you could put that slice of lime."

"Leave the lady alone," Danielle told Dante. To Roxy, she said, "He must have really irritated you last Saturday night if you remember him."

"Nah," said Roxy. "During the week, I man the bar at the pool. He has annoyed me out there, too." She started putting together their drinks, putting crushed ice in a tall glass for Danielle's drink, then bending to open the below the bar refrigerator to retrieve a can of Coke for Dante.

"She loves me," Dante said, in the way all good-looking teenage boys believe they're adored by members of the opposite sex.

Roxy presented Danielle with her cranberry juice. "You look like a nice young lady. What are you doing with him?"

"He's the only boy who would ask me," Danielle stated simply.

"Next time wait for a better offer," Roxy advised.

"Am I invisible?" Dante asked, still smiling.

"If only," said Roxy.

She put his Coke with a slice of lime on the rim in front of him. "Charge it to your room?"

"Please," said Dante.

"Done," said Roxy. She smiled at Danielle. "I was just kidding, he's a good guy."

She moved away to serve the next customer in line.

Danielle and Dante sipped their drinks. "We didn't get the chance to talk much on the slopes," Dante said casually. "Do you have a boyfriend?"

"No," said Danielle. "There's a guy I'm interested in but he hasn't given me any reason to believe he likes me."

"A guy in your class at school, somebody you see only on occasion?"

"No, I see him all the time. He's my best friend. We were texting like crazy earlier tonight."

"What's his problem?" Dante asked, looking deeply into her eyes. "You, Danielle Washington, are *hot*."

Danielle blushed. She wasn't used to compliments from

cute guys, or any guys. Frankly, even though she knew she was attractive, she was also taller than a lot of the guys in her class, an athlete of some note and on the honor roll. She intimidated guys.

She didn't try to. It just happened. Her relationship with Echo, now a year strong, was the longest relationship she'd had with a guy.

Dante set his drink on the bar and reached over to tilt her head up with a finger. Danielle had been unable to meet his eyes after he'd declared her *hot*. "You're going home tomorrow, aren't you?"

"Mmm-hmm," said Danielle shyly.

"We're staying until next Sunday," he said. "Do you think you could come back for the weekend?"

"I doubt it," she said regretfully. "There is no training session planned for next weekend. Coach Santiago gave me a schedule and my training doesn't start until after Christmas. Besides, your parents may be able to afford to stay at a ritzy place like this but my mom can't on a nurse's salary."

Dante smiled. "Is that what you think of me, that I'm some rich kid?"

Danielle smiled back. "Is that supposed to be derogatory? Being called a rich kid? I didn't mean it that way. I just thought that since you told me your dad worked in government and your mom is a lawyer, they're earning good salaries as opposed to my mom, who is in one of the worst-paid professions. They work nurses to death but don't pay them what they're worth. And she's a darn good nurse. Went to school and got two degrees. I'm sure you're proud of your parents. I'm proud of my mom, too, but she can't afford this place. I saw the rates online before we came for the weekend and my eyes bugged out!"

Dante laughed. "Yeah, so did mine when I saw them. We

kids can sometimes take the amount of money our parents spend on us for granted, can't we? You talk a lot of sense, Miss Washington. I need to appreciate my parents more."

"And stop being such a rich kid?" Danielle joked.

Dante threw his head back in laughter. "All right, I'm a rich kid. But I'm not a spoiled rich kid. I have to work hard in school and keep up my grades and by God I'm going to college on scholarship!"

"Football?" Danielle guessed.

"How'd you know?" Dante asked, truly amazed. He hadn't told her he played football.

"It's your build," Danielle told him. "I see guys who look like you every day at school. I see them when I'm working out in the gym, at lunch, at the track. Plus, my dad was a pro football player—Charlie Washington of the…"

"Philadelphia Eagles?" Dante said, beaming. "Wow, he was one of my all-time favorite players. When they went to the Super Bowl my dad took me. Were you there? It was about ten years ago but I remember it like it was yesterday. Man! I even got to meet your dad. He was so cool. He autographed my jersey and everything!"

Danielle suddenly experienced such a feeling of loss that tears threatened. She had missed that game. Oh, she had watched it on TV but she was nowhere near the stadium. That was the year her parents divorced. It was ironic really. Her dad's greatest year in football had also been the worst year of her life.

"No," she said softly. "I couldn't make it."

"Oh, you missed a great game," Dante cried, still high on the memories. Then, he suddenly realized something. "Hey, didn't you say your mother was your sole parent? Where's your dad?"

"My parents got divorced when I was seven," Danielle said,

trying to sound upbeat about it. Kids' parents got divorced all the time. She certainly was not in the minority at school. Apparently, though, where Dante came from, judging from the sorrowful expression on his face, they *were* in the minority.

"I'm so sorry," he said, and he certainly sounded sorry.

The DJ began playing a Fergie song and Danielle stood up. "Enough of this depressing conversation, we came here to dance!"

Grinning, Dante was happy to sweep her back onto the dance floor.

"I thought you were going to walk me back to my suite," Cherisse said an hour after Harry had declared his inability to keep his hands off her.

Now they were seated on the big couch in front of the fireplace, both with their shoes off, Harry sans his coat jacket, quite winded from kissing like randy teenagers for the past twenty minutes.

"And I meant to," said Harry, leaning back on the couch and drawing a deep breath. "But I kept thinking about the fact that you're leaving tomorrow and I probably won't be able to see you again until next weekend, and taking you back to your suite became less important." He smiled at the lovely picture she made, her hair mussed, her lips slightly swollen from kissing him. She was devastatingly attractive.

Cherisse leaned her head on his shoulder and Harry drew her close. "You can always write me," she said softly, her voice husky.

Harry laughed shortly. "You mean e-mail you?"

"No, write me on paper and mail it the old-fashioned way," said Cherisse, a smile lighting her eyes. "Write me, and I'll write you back. It doesn't have to be long, a line or two."

"I haven't written a personal letter the old-fashioned way

in ages," said Harry, intrigued. He liked the idea. It was hard for him to believe but he didn't have any love letters from past girlfriends. They hadn't been illiterate, they just had never thought of it, he supposed. He certainly hadn't sent any of them love letters. "I'll do it. You may not be able to understand my handwriting, but I'll do it."

The alarm on Cherisse's watch suddenly sounded. She sat up and checked it. It was five minutes till midnight. "Oh, no," she cried. "I've got to go! I don't want Danielle to get back to the suite before I do."

"Don't want her thinking you've been making out all this time," Harry joked.

Cherisse laughed. "I'd never hear the end of it. Sometimes I think she's the mother!"

She said this while she was putting on her sandals. Harry, too, quickly put his shoes back on. "What time are you leaving tomorrow? You don't have to adhere to the eleven o'clock checkout time, you know."

Cherisse thought his gesture was sweet. Smiling at him as they walked to the door, she said, "I would take you up on that if I could, but I promised a friend who is going through a tough time that I would drop by to see her tomorrow evening."

Harry held the door open for her. "When can I see you again, then?"

Cherisse paused to look him in the eyes. "Next Saturday is my first day off from work. I work twelve-hour shifts, Harry."

Harry didn't protest. "Dinner this Saturday night, then?" he asked hopefully.

"Love to," Cherisse said, and she shot through the door. Harry had to almost run to keep up with her. He smiled. She was determined to make it back to the suite before Danielle did.

They were both out of breath by the time they walked across the lobby and to Cherisse and Danielle's suite. At the door, Harry smoothed an errant hair behind Cherisse's ear. Bending close, he said softly, "Good night, beautiful."

They kissed briefly, lips only. They both knew from experience how difficult it was to pull away when the kiss deepened.

Cherisse looked starry-eyed when Harry raised his head. He smiled. "Thank you for the most enjoyable evening I've had in a long time."

Cherisse smiled back. "It was definitely my pleasure."

The provocative tone in her voice turned Harry on, a first for him. He figured he must really have it bad for her if just the sound of her voice had that effect on him.

He kissed her cheek, still reluctant to leave her side.

Cherisse had to playfully push him away. "You've got to go, Harry. If she sees you here it will have been for nothing! Help me maintain the upper hand in this mother-daughter struggle!"

"Okay, okay," Harry said, backing away.

Cherisse blew him a kiss and slipped inside the dimly lit suite.

As soon as she closed the door behind her, a voice said, "Where have you been, young lady?"

Danielle was sitting on the couch wearing her pajamas. She reached over and switched on the lamp on the end table so she could see her mother better.

Cherisse walked into the room and sat on the couch. Busted! She couldn't wipe a broad smile off her face in spite of it. "Okay, you got me. I had planned on being here when you got home, but Harry and I started talking and the time just flew!"

Danielle laughed delightedly. "Finally, I've got something

to tell Grandma about you. At long last my virgin mother has gone gaga…"

"Gaga!" Cherisse protested. "I am no such thing."

"…over Harry Payne," Danielle finished with relish. She bounced on the sofa, ending with her legs under her. "You kissed him, didn't you?" She watched her mother expectantly, her dark brown eyes sparkling. "Oh, tell me that you at least kissed him. You've known him long enough to kiss him, a whole week. It's not as if you just met him tonight!"

Cherisse was pulling off her shoes and getting comfortable on the couch. She met her daughter's eyes. "Danielle, a mother does not discuss her love life with her daughter, no matter how chummy they are. And a lady doesn't kiss and tell."

Danielle regarded her with consternation, which was hilarious to Cherisse. Laughing, she said, "Don't give me that look. The subject is closed."

Sighing loudly, Danielle rose. "I'd just as well go to bed if you're not going to tell me whether or not you and Mr. Payne kissed."

"You're not going anywhere," Cherisse told her. "Not until you tell me how your date with Dante was."

"Oh, I'm supposed to spill my guts, but you don't have to? That's not fair!"

"Life is not fair," said Cherisse with a smile. She patted the couch. "Sit."

After Danielle had sat down, Cherisse cleared her throat. "I take it Dante was a gentleman."

"He tried to kiss me good-night and I told him I never kiss on the first date," said Danielle. "So he kissed my hand instead, which I thought was sweet. We're going to stay in touch." She sat back on the couch, loosening up. "He said I was hot, Ma." She laughed shortly. "I don't know how to take that. I never thought of myself as hot. I'm an athlete. Sometimes I don't wear a dress for months at a time."

Cherisse smiled knowingly. Her daughter was beginning to recognize her sex appeal to the opposite sex. To be honest, she had thanked God for Danielle's interest in sports and her disinterest in dressing provocatively in order to attract boys. Kids these days had so much sexual content fed to them on a daily basis through TV, music videos, video games, magazines and books, that it was a minor miracle that Danielle wasn't more affected by it. Not that she naively thought Danielle wasn't aware of the bombardment. She was a smart girl. But, so far, she had chosen not to be an active participant.

"There're all kinds of 'hot,'" she told Danielle. "Dante is the type of boy who appreciates you just the way you are. You're a natural beauty who's confident enough not to buy into the video vixen brand of sexuality."

Danielle wrinkled her nose in distaste. "If I have to show my butt and my boobs to get a guy to talk to me I'll die a virgin."

Cherisse spontaneously grabbed her daughter and kissed her loudly on the cheek. "Bless you!"

Danielle grinned as she pulled away from her mother. "For what, probably dying a virgin?"

"No, for being more levelheaded than I was at your age," she said, her voice quivering a bit because she was close to tears. "I've told you that because I got pregnant with you when I was eighteen I'm sometimes harder on you than I should be. Having me as a mother can't be easy."

"Having you for a mother is a blessing," Danielle told her frankly. "I know I don't tell you often enough, but you're my greatest role model. No one in my life has influenced me more. You don't have to worry about me, Ma. I've got my head on straight."

Then she kissed her mother's cheek and told her good-night.

Cherisse sat on the couch a few minutes longer, reflecting on the night. She flushed just thinking about those passionate kisses she'd shared with Harry.

"Hold on tight," she said to herself. "This is going to be an interesting ride."

Going against her better judgment, she was looking forward to seeing where this attraction to Harry Payne, a man she would never think would be interested in her, would take her.

"Harry, you're making this too easy for me," Davis Winters said the next morning as he tapped the golf ball into the hole and finished their final round with a lower score than Harry's. "Your head simply wasn't in the game today." He laughed shortly and he walked beside Harry to the waiting golf cart. "Do I have to ask where your mind was?"

Harry was barely listening. He was consulting his watch. It was after eleven. Cherisse and Danielle would be on the road by now. God, how he had wanted to walk off the course any number of times this morning and rush back to the hotel in time to kiss Cherisse goodbye. But Davis had taken his sweet time, calculating each swing, talking through them, gossiping about mutual friends while Harry ground his teeth in frustration.

As Harry started the golf cart and Davis got in, he said, "Cherisse Washington."

"A beautiful woman," Davis said. "Danielle's a cute kid, too. Dante's smitten, but boys his age are smitten with some girl every few weeks."

The day was cold and the sky a clear Colorado blue.

Harry remained in a reflective mood as he drove. Davis, more gregarious, continued to chat in spite of his friend's silence. "You, on the other hand, are not easily smitten. You didn't look at that reporter the way you look at Ms. Washington. Why is that, Harry? Dante told me she's a nurse. An honorable profession for certain, but will she make a suitable mate for you? I think not. You're a very successful businessman, Harry. You need someone more glamorous, a woman who is well-traveled and well-educated."

Harry looked at Davis sharply. "Davis, you and I have been friends for nearly twenty years but if you say anything else negative about Cherisse Washington I'm going to pop you one right in the mouth."

Davis laughed so hard tears came to his eyes. "I knew it! Put your fist away, I was just testing you. Man, Harry. You really like Ms. Washington. Could this be the one? Dating a mother is new for you, though, isn't it? Mothers are different, Harry. Their first priority is to their children. So Ms. Washington will probably not be able to traipse all over creation with you at the drop of a hat. You're going to have to give her a break on that. And no spending the night together, either. A mother doesn't want her child, especially if it's a girl, to know she's sleeping with anyone. Touchy subject, but I'm sure when the time comes you'll handle it."

Referring to the fact that Davis held a position in the White House, Harry said, "I'm amazed they let you have security clearance. You never shut up."

Davis laughed. "I'm simply giving you the benefit of my experience."

Harry laughed this time. "What experience? You and Eva have been married since you were a senior in college. Twenty years now, right? You've never dated a single mother that I know of."

"Yes," Davis said, "but Eva has plenty of friends who're single mothers and they always bend my ear when they have 'man' problems. For some reason they look at me as if I'm one of their girlfriends."

"A fact that probably irritates you," Harry said, knowing Davis had considered himself quite a stud a few years ago.

"It's embarrassing," Davis admitted. "Now they want me to join their book club. I am not joining a book club that consists of forty-five women and a gay guy. Eva nearly busted a gut laughing when I told her. Talk about emasculating!"

Laughing, Harry said, "Davis, you lead a charmed life. You have a wonderful wife, a son who loves you and hasn't given you a lot of trouble, and now forty-five women and a gay guy want you to join their book club. Go ahead and do it, man."

Davis looked perplexed. "You think?"

"Why not," said Harry. "These days a guy's masculinity is not compromised by reading a book or two."

Davis relaxed. "I have a confession to make. Sometimes I'll read Eva's romance novels. Some of them are addictive. Good stories. The first time Eva caught me reading one she got so turned on, she jumped my bones. This from a woman who has always made me ask for it. Even beg for it. Now we'll read together in bed. I tell you, Harry, women melt when you read to them in bed."

"Oh, yeah?" asked Harry, curiosity piqued. "How do you think they respond to love letters?"

"Oh, man," said Davis, "even better than romance novels. Eva has every letter I ever wrote her." He grinned. "Hey, Harry, that reminds me. I haven't written her a love letter in years. I think it's time I composed a few for her. That ought to get me some interesting sack time."

"You're shameless, Davis. Romance novels and love letters in exchange for hot sex. What will you try next?"

Davis thought for a moment. "Don't tell anybody, but Eva loves it when I suck her toes."

"That's too much information," Harry said, laughing. "I'm not about to suck Cherisse's toes, no matter how pretty her feet are."

"She has pretty feet?" Davis asked, a bit more interested in Cherisse's feet than Harry thought he ought to be.

"You're sick, man," Harry told him, shaking his head in pity. "Eva didn't know what she was getting into when she married you."

Davis laughed. "I'm just trying to school you in the ways of women. One day you can be a happily married man who lusts after his wife, too!"

Later that day after she and Danielle got back home, Cherisse kept her promise and went to visit Mary Thomas. Since Cherisse had put her on temporary leave with pay, Mary had joined Alcoholics Anonymous and gone to meetings every day. That had been the recommendation of her counselor, who said going every day would help keep her on track. Her counselor was a short, tough black woman in her fifties who was celebrating ten years of sobriety. On her first visit to see Mary, only two days after putting her on leave, Mary had told her about Wilma, her counselor. Cherisse was glad Mary had someone like Wilma looking out for her.

Today when Cherisse arrived at Mary's house, which was no more than half a mile from her own, she found a strange car parked behind Mary's white Chevrolet.

She walked onto the porch of the single-story brick home and rang the bell. She was carrying a fruit basket that she'd picked up at the supermarket on the way over. Mary loved fresh fruit.

After a minute or so, the door was yanked open and Mary's daughter, Eve, glared at her with open hostility. "Well if it isn't the bitch who laid my mom off and told her it was for her own good. What do *you* want?"

Cherisse steeled herself for a confrontation. Eve thrived on drama. She looked as if she were itching for a fight right now. Her tall, too-thin body was fairly quivering with anticipation. Cherisse looked into her eyes. They were dilated. She was obviously on something. What, Cherisse couldn't be sure, but she would bet it was drugs she'd scored once she'd hit town. Eve had even dealt drugs at one time.

"I'm here to see Mary," Cherisse said calmly.

"She doesn't want to see you," Eve said, getting in Cherisse's face. Her lips were drawn back in a feral snarl. Her teeth were yellow and her breath smelled like an ashtray.

Cherisse tried her best not to turn up her nose. That would only make Eve more belligerent.

"You're wrong," she told Eve. "I spoke with her earlier today and she told me to come over. If I had known she had company I would have come another time. But since I'm already here, I'd just as well see her now." She hadn't really spoken with Mary today.

She pushed past Eve and went inside the dimly lit foyer. Mary usually kept a clean house but there was a foul smell in the air, a combination of stale booze, cigarettes and something else Cherisse couldn't place, probably what Eve had been smoking.

"Mary!" Cherisse called. "It's Cheri!"

She faced Eve, afraid to keep her back to her for too long out of fear that she might turn violent. "Where is she, Eve?"

Eve stood there with an angry, obstinate expression on her face. With eyes narrowed at Cherisse, she yelled, "She doesn't want to see you, bitch! What do I have to do to get you out of here, call the cops?"

"I think that's probably the last thing you want to do," Cherisse said. She walked up to Eve and shoved the fruit basket at her. "Here, why don't you go sell this and get a few bucks for your next hit."

Eve threw the basket to the floor. Apples, bananas, pears and oranges spread out on the foyer floor. "I always hated you," she said. "Mom told me how she used to go to you and talk to you whenever I got into trouble. She said you gave her a shoulder to cry on. Well, now I'm her shoulder. She doesn't need you."

Suddenly, Mary came stumbling out of the back of the house. She was wearing a ratty old white bathrobe and hadn't had the foresight to close it before she came to see who had rung the doorbell.

She wore only a pair of dingy white panties and a faded white bra underneath. Cherisse wanted to look away. She was sure if Mary were sober she wouldn't want her to see her in this state of undress.

But Mary didn't let her look away. She walked up to her and threw herself into her arms, hugging her tightly. "Cheri, thank God. You've got to make her go away. Make her go away, Cheri." Mary's words were slurred, but due to intoxication she had little control over her voice's volume, and was loud enough to be heard outside.

Eve certainly heard what her mother had said. She laughed cruelly and jerked her mother from Cherisse's embrace. Mary's frightened gaze pleaded with Cherisse to help her. Cherisse balled up her fists in frustration. What could she do to help her old friend? She had to think of something.

"Okay," Eve said to Cherisse, "you've seen her, now get the hell out of my house!"

Cherisse had no choice but to do as she was told. She turned around to glance back as she was walking down the front steps. Eve was pushing Mary toward the back rooms of the house.

Cherisse got behind the wheel of her car and immediately got on her cell phone. Maybe Taz Coffman, a police sergeant and Neil's ex-partner, could advise her.

Chapter 9

Taz wasn't optimistic. He said Mary, as the owner of the house, had to be the one to evict her daughter. Cherisse sighed as she sat in her car with the phone to her ear. "She was so drunk she couldn't walk straight, Taz. Obviously Eve has been plying her with booze in order to control her."

"How long has she been there?" Taz asked.

"I put Mary on leave last Monday, two days later I went to see her and she was sober. That was on Wednesday. I don't know when Eve got there but she must have been there a few days because the house is a mess. Mary keeps a clean house."

"I'll tell you what we can do," said Taz. "We can put the fear of God into the daughter. Maybe scare her off. You want to hear my idea?"

"Fire away," Cherisse said, feeling better about the situation. She had been thoroughly surprised when Eve had opened the door a few minutes ago. She felt horrible because on Monday she had teased Mary about Eve coming to claim her house after she had drunk herself to death. Apparently Eve was in a rush to claim the house. She seemed to be trying to hurry along her mother's death.

"How many friends of Mary's can you get together on short notice?" Taz asked.

Cherisse immediately thought of Sonia and Gerald. Her mother, who had been a friend of Mary's late mother, Rose, would also come. Plus Danielle, who would not want to be left out if her grandmother were participating.

"Four," Cherisse answered confidently.

"Good," said Taz. "Call them and tell them to meet me at Mary's house at six. It's a quarter after five now. Tell them to hang back and follow my lead. Give me the address."

Cherisse gave him Mary's address, then they hung up and she immediately started making phone calls.

Five minutes before six Gerald and his wife, Darlene, arrived in their big black SUV. Moments later Danielle drove up in her blue-and-white MINI Cooper with her grandmother riding shotgun. Shortly afterward Sonia pulled up behind the MINI Cooper in her Volvo with Ken Kesey, the guy she'd met at Karibu last Saturday. Cherisse had to smile when she saw him. He must really like Sonia to go on an as yet unknown mission with her.

Cherisse had gotten out of her car to meet Gerald and Darlene and now all seven of them were gathered around the SUV. Quick introductions were made and Cherisse told them what was happening.

"That evil little toad," said Sonia. "She's never given Mary anything but grief. Let me go in there and kick her butt!"

Cherisse smiled at her friend's moxie. "We're going to do exactly what Taz wants us to do when he gets here. He's the law. Let him handle it. He says we should follow his lead."

"Here he is now," Jo said as a huge blue SUV with its siren blasting and a flashing blue light atop its roof sped up the quiet street. Effects, Cherisse thought. He's got to make it look official. Get the neighbors out of their houses to witness the display.

When Taz stopped the SUV at the curb and climbed out of it, he immediately strode over to them. He was not a big man. He was just a trim, five-eleven Jewish guy from New York City. But after twenty years on the force he wore a mantle of authority. It was evident in his carriage and in his intelligent brown eyes.

Cherisse wanted to hug him she was so grateful he'd come. She knew a policeman going into a domestic situation could potentially be very dangerous.

Taz walked over to them. "Folks," he greeted them all with a nod of his head. Everyone there knew him except Sonia's friend and Taz's take-charge attitude told them there wasn't time for niceties. "I'm going in there and explain to Mary that if she says her daughter isn't welcome on her property that I'm there to see to it that she leaves. Cherisse, you come with me since you're the complainant. The rest of you hang back. When it's over you'll need to come in and get Mary cleaned up and sober because she can't go down to the police station to press charges smelling like a distillery. Got it?"

Everyone indicated that they understood. Taz turned on his heels and he and Cherisse went to the door of the house.

He rang the bell. No one came to the door. They stood on the porch for two minutes more, and then Taz started pounding on the door.

"Who is it!" called Eve from the other side of the door.

With a nod of his head, Taz motioned for Cherisse to speak up. "It's Cheri again, Eve. I want to talk to you about Mary.

You know she needs help. Why are you doing this to her? She's always been a good mother to you."

Eve hurriedly unlocked the door and swung it open. The odor that met Cherisse and Taz was unmistakably that of marijuana. Cherisse was surprised it wasn't something stronger like crack cocaine.

Seeing only Cherisse standing there because Taz was standing off to the side, Eve lit into her. "Back for round two, huh, bitch? You are one meddling broad. If you don't get away from here I really am going to call the cops."

"No need, I'm here," Taz said with one foot already in the doorway and his shoulder pressed against the door. Eve tried her best to shut the door but he'd anticipated her first reaction. It wasn't hard, as she was totally stoned—stoned but still ready to defend her rights. Almost losing her balance, she yelled at him, "You have to have a warrant to come in here. I don't see no warrant!"

Taz pulled a folded piece of paper from his jacket pocket and offered it to her. Eve refused to accept it, looking at it as if he were trying to hand her a writhing rattlesnake instead.

"You don't have to take it," Taz said, returning the paper to his pocket. "You can read it later." He paused for effect, standing there with his legs apart and a grim expression on his face. "Now, I want to see your mother. Go and get her."

"Momma's asleep," Eve cried pitifully. "She's sick, you can't disturb her."

"Has she passed out from drink?" Taz asked. "Have you been forcibly giving your mother alcohol to keep her incapacitated so that you can rob her blind?"

"Who told you that?" Eve yelled, looking at Cherisse.

Cherisse quietly stood behind Taz, letting him handle it as he'd suggested. She only wanted to get this over with as soon as possible. Mary had asked for her help and she would not be able to sleep tonight if she didn't do everything within her power to provide that help.

"Your neighbor, Ms. Washington, says your mother pleaded with her to get you out of her house. I would like to hear that from your mother. Please go get her," Taz said, pronouncing each word clearly so that there wouldn't be any misunderstandings. "I don't want to have to repeat myself, miss. Do it now."

Eyes red and glassy, nose running, hair sticking up on her head, Eve looked like someone who had been on a bender for days. She was breathing hard as if from exertion, but Cherisse knew it was from rage. But she huffed off and went to do as Taz asked her and a couple of minutes later she returned with Mary in the same bathrobe as Cherisse had seen her in earlier, only this time the robe was closed and properly tied at the waist.

Mary appeared to be a bit more sober, she was walking straighter and when she looked up and saw Cherisse and Taz, she gave a wan smile. Eve let go of her arm after bringing her to stand in front of Taz and she turned as if to leave the room.

"Please stay where you are," said Taz.

She stopped in her tracks and turned around to face them. Wearing only a thin white T-shirt and dirty jeans, her feet bare, she shivered as if she were cold. Eyes ringed in smeared mascara, she stood and watched as Taz asked her mother if she were all right.

"Mrs. Thomas, I'm Sergeant Taz Coffman of the Denver Police Department. Ms. Washington tells me that you wish to evict your daughter from your property. Is that correct?"

Eve said desperately, "Momma, please!"

Mary stood as straight as she possibly could but she swayed a bit. Cherisse was about to go to her and support her, but Taz motioned for her to stay where she was.

Mary looked into Taz's eyes and said, "Sergeant, she poured liquor down my throat and when I fought her she would hit me in the stomach until I let her. Please get her out of my house!"

"It would be my pleasure, Mrs. Thomas," said Taz. He nodded in Mary's direction, letting Cherisse know that she was now free to go to her.

Cherisse went and put her arms about Mary's thin waist and helped her over to the couch, whereupon Taz turned to Mary again. "Are you aware enough to answer another question for me, Mrs. Thomas?"

Mary took a few seconds to reply. "I'll try, Sergeant."

"Do you want to press charges against your daughter?"

"Momma, please!" Eve cried, more desperate than ever. "I'll go, just don't let him arrest me. I've been in jail and I can't go again. I swear I won't come back."

Tears came to Mary's eyes. "I don't believe you," she said pitifully.

That's all Taz needed to hear. He went to Eve and hand-cuffed her. Eve tried to fall to her knees in order to make his job more difficult, but Taz easily handled her slight weight. "You're just making it harder on yourself," he told her.

"I don't have any shoes on," she said, trying to postpone the inevitable.

"Don't worry, they have special shoes for you in jail," Taz assured her. He then read her her rights.

Mary sobbed on Cherisse's shoulder as she watched her daughter being taken away.

As soon as Taz removed Eve from the premises, the other six folks standing in the yard entered the house. Cherisse left them with Mary while she ran outside to catch Taz before he left.

She was surprised to see several of Mary's neighbors either standing on their porches or in their front yards watching the drama unfold.

Taz had put Eve in the back of the SUV by the time Cherisse walked up to him. The temperature this evening was in the low sixties so he had all the windows rolled up on the SUV, but still Cherisse kept her voice down, not wanting Eve to overhear, when she said, "Thank you, Taz. I love you, you're a sweetheart."

Taz smiled at her. "Love you, too, babe. You go take care of Mary. I'll call you later."

He was all business again as he got behind the wheel of the SUV, let loose with the siren once more and sped off.

Cherisse hurried back inside.

Once in the house she found everyone sitting down, chatting with Mary, who looked slightly embarrassed and happy simultaneously. Cherisse went to sit next to her on the couch, taking Danielle's spot as she did so. "Mary, Ma and I are going to take you and help you get cleaned up."

Jo, used to taking charge, took Mary by the arm and helped her up. "Come on, honey, you can show me where everything is."

In her mother's and Mary's absence, Cherisse addressed everyone else. "Thank you for coming. I know once Mary is herself again she's going to be very grateful that you did. If anyone has to leave now, I understand. But if you can stay an hour or two maybe we can put the house in order and try to sober Mary up enough so that she'll be able to go down to the station in the morning and press charges against Eve."

"Gerry and I can stay a couple of hours," Darlene volunteered.

"You know I'm down for anything," Danielle told her mother.

Sonia wasn't so sure about her new friend, but he surprised everybody by saying, "I can vacuum with the best of them!"

Sonia gave him such a beautiful smile that the poor man

almost tripped over his own feet as he went in search of said vacuum.

Cherisse smiled broadly. Mary was lucky to have such good friends.

The next day at work, Cherisse went in with the same prayer on her lips—"Lord, let today be a quiet day." And, as always, it went unanswered. Or maybe, she reasoned at around lunchtime when a buxom brunette wearing a mini-skirt, a low-cut blouse and stilettos walked up to the nurses' station and announced that she was Amy Whitehall's mother and demanded to see her, His answer was no.

There were two other nurses in the station and Cherisse let one of them handle the woman whose eyes were darting around the area as if she were afraid someone was following her. As well she should be, Cherisse thought. The police had left orders for the nursing staff to phone them if Amy White-hall's mother put in an appearance. They had been trying to locate her ever since Amy had been admitted.

"I'll take you to her," Katy said to the woman as she moved past Cherisse and gave her a furtive look on her way from behind the desk. Cherisse took that to mean Katy had also remembered that the police needed to be notified.

With her back to the woman, Cherisse mouthed to Katy, "Okay," and smiled reassuringly. All they needed today was to have to deal with an emotionally distraught parent.

After Katy disappeared down the corridor with Amy Whitehall's mother, Cherisse quickly consulted the important numbers posted on the wall next to the telephone. Getting an outside line, she dialed the number of the Denver Police Department and asked for the detective in charge of the Amy Whitehall case. In a few minutes a female's voice said, "I'm Detective Brennerman."

Cherisse told her that Amy Whitehall's mother was at that moment visiting her daughter.

"Be right there," was all Detective Brennerman said.

Cherisse figured the detective didn't have time to waste on words. They really wanted the Whitehall woman.

After Cherisse put the phone down she waited on pins and needles. She wanted to go down to Amy's room and offer moral support to Katy, who was probably making some excuse to stick around during the mother's visit because she was afraid to leave the woman alone with her patient.

But more than one nurse in the room might spook the mother, so Cherisse remained at the nurses' station, her ears pricked for any sound of a disturbance coming from Amy's room.

A few minutes later, Gerald, who had taken an early lunch, came back on the floor and checked in at the nurses' station before making his rounds. Cherisse, still waiting either for the police to show up or for Amy's mother to go ballistic, smiled nervously at him.

"Amy's mother showed up," she explained to a perplexed Gerald.

Gerald tensed. He had come to love that little girl and the thought of her being in the presence of a neglectful parent didn't sit well with him. "Who's in there with them?" he asked evenly.

"Katy," Cherisse answered. "I phoned the police about twenty minutes ago. I thought they'd be here by now."

"They should be," he said, and looked in the direction of Amy's room. "I'm going down there. I'll just introduce myself. I have been her principal nurse, after all."

"Yes," Cherisse said, "but today, Katy's the one on duty." She appealed to him with her eyes. "Be cool, Gerald. The woman wouldn't do anything stupid in a public place."

Cherisse wasn't convinced of that. In her years as a nurse she'd seen some freaky things. She didn't put anything past anybody. But she had to keep Gerald from allowing his emotions to overrule his head.

Everybody had to stay cool. The police would be there soon, and they would take the woman with them for questioning.

Now, there were two tense people in the nurses' station. Cherisse had been seated in front of the carousel going over patients' charts when the Whitehall woman had shown up. She still sat there. Gerald paced.

Suddenly, the bell over the bank of elevators sounded and when the elevator doors opened, two uniformed policemen and a woman in a gray pantsuit stepped onto the floor.

"Gotta be them," Cherisse said.

She heard Gerald give a huge sigh of relief.

The three people went straight to the nurses' station. The woman addressed Gerald with, "Doctor, I'm Detective Brennerman. Would you direct me to Amy Whitehall's room?"

Cherisse was sure Gerald wanted to let them know he was a nurse, and proud of it, and berate them for not getting there sooner, but like a good nurse he led them down the hall to Amy's room with haste.

Cherisse watched as Gerald turned around and made his way back to the nurses' station several feet away from Amy's room. And as soon as the three entered the room, Katy came walking out of there as swiftly as her skinny legs could carry her.

Shortly after that, sounds of a scuffle came from Amy's room. It sounded like chairs were being overturned. And perhaps the IV pole had been knocked over, and Amy's lunch tray had crashed to the floor.

Gerald went to leave the station, but Cherisse reached out and restrained him. "Let them do their job."

She could feel the muscles in Gerald's arm tense up.

They waited five more minutes and then the two uniformed officers emerged, each of them holding Amy's mother by an arm. She had come out of her stilettos and in her struggle she'd split her bottom lip and it was bleeding. Detective Brennerman brought up the rear, a satisfied smile on her lips.

As they approached the nurses' station, she said, once again to Gerald, "Someone should go in to Amy now. I think she's a little upset."

Gerald, now that Amy wasn't in harm's way, let the detective have it with both barrels. "I'm glad you got this dangerous criminal—" he gestured to Amy's mother, who had gone limp in the grip of the officers and didn't appear dangerous at all "—but you all took your sweet time getting here. Anything could have happened!"

Detective Brennerman, a thin, green-eyed brunette, smiled icily. "There's always room for one more in the service vehicle."

Gerald didn't hear her because he'd already turned away and was heading down the hall to Amy's room, as were Cherisse and Katy.

As far as the nurses were concerned the police officers had ceased to exist. The only person who mattered at that moment was their patient.

Amy, who in the past few days had recovered the ability to speak and move her limbs, was quiet when they entered the room. Gerald went to her and took her hand in his. "How are you, sweetheart?" he asked tenderly.

A dry-eyed Amy looked nervously at the doorway. "Is she gone?"

Cherisse came around and gently touched Amy's cheek. "You mean your mother?"

"Yes," said Amy. "Is she gone now?"

"Yes, she's gone," Cherisse said softly. "She won't be back for a while."

"Good," said Amy, and then tears spilled down her cheeks. "She hurt me. It wasn't my daddy. My daddy loves me. I remembered it when I saw her. I remembered everything."

Cherisse, Gerald and Katy looked at one another in amazement. All this time they'd been heaping recriminations on Amy's father, when it had been her mother who had beat her and left her for dead. After hearing of Amy's recovery on the news she had probably come there to either finish the job or beg Amy not to say anything.

"Did you tell the police that when they were here?" Cherisse asked.

"No, they didn't ask me anything," Amy said.

Cherisse gently squeezed Amy's hand. "Well, don't worry about that right now, sweetie. You close your eyes and try to rest."

She left Gerald and Katy with Amy and went to phone Detective Brennerman's office. The detective probably had not had time enough to make it back to the police station. She would have to leave a message.

About forty minutes later, Detective Brennerman, alone, stepped off the elevator and didn't bother stopping by the nurses' station. She went straight to Amy's room.

When Cherisse got home on Monday night, she was met at the door by Danielle, who hugged her and took her shoulder bag and coat. Her daughter's dark brown eyes danced when she regarded her. "Guess who got flowers today?" she said in a singsong voice.

Cherisse assumed they were from Dante to Danielle. Rich kid that he was, at least that's how Danielle jokingly referred to him.

So Cherisse said, "You?"

Danielle guffawed. "I wish! No, you did, mother dear, from Mr. Harry Payne."

Danielle paused long enough to put her mother's shoulder bag and coat away, then she ushered her mother into the kitchen, where her grandmother was sitting at the kitchen table reading the evening paper as she sometimes did after she'd prepared dinner.

On the kitchen counter sat a beautiful bouquet of yellow roses, at least two dozen. They smelled heavenly. Cherisse felt an impulse to float over to them and inhale their heady fragrance, but she was compelled to go and kiss her mother's satiny cheek first and murmur, "Hi, Ma, how was your day? Dinner smells divine."

Jo smiled up at her after receiving her kiss. "Hello, sweetie. Read the card already. I'm dying to know what it says, that is if the contents aren't too personal."

Jo and Danielle stood on either side of her as she got the card and silently read the note:

I was trying to think of which flower you smelled most like and this is it, the yellow rose. From this moment on I won't be able to look at one without thinking of you. Harry.

Cherisse felt warm all over. What a day she'd had. But to come home to this made it worthwhile. Smiling, she handed the card to her mother. "It's all right, you can read it," she said. "I'm going to call Harry and thank him. I'll be back in a few minutes."

They would not start dinner without her.

In her bedroom, Cherisse removed her shoes and tossed them into the closet, then she went and sat on the bed next to the nightstand. Picking up the phone, she glanced down at the personal card Harry had given her. She had entered his personal information in her address book, but had left the card next to her bedroom phone in anticipation of phoning him from that spot.

Dialing his number, her heartbeat picked up its pace. She had initially been disappointed that he hadn't been able to say goodbye to her and Danielle when they had checked out Sunday morning. Considering it a bit longer, however, she had decided that she was glad he had not. It might have been awkward. They certainly could not have kissed each other goodbye with Danielle standing there.

The phone rang four times before the machine kicked in. Cherisse hesitated. She didn't want to leave her disembodied voice on his machine. But how would it look if he checked his caller ID and saw that she had phoned and had not left a message.

She waited for the beep, but it never came because Harry picked up and blurted, "Cheri!" He sounded a bit breathless. "How are you?"

"Harry," she said, her voice husky, "I've had one of my signature Mondays where if anything could go wrong, it did, and then I came home and saw the flowers you'd sent and your gesture made me feel so much better. Thank you!"

Harry laughed softly. "I spent so much time in the florist's shop that the woman asked me if I was having a hard time choosing. 'No,' I told her, 'I know exactly what I want and I'll know it when I see it, or more accurately, smell it.' And when my nose got a good whiff of the yellow roses I knew they were the ones."

"I never thought I smelled like a yellow rose," Cherisse said. "I usually don't even wear cologne. It's not recommended at work so I rarely use it."

"But you smell so good," Harry said.

"That's soap and water and body lotion," she said, smiling. "Harry, you're making me blush, all this talk about scents is reminding me of how good you smelled Saturday night."

"Your smell, your taste, everything about you is etched in my memory," Harry said softly. "I can't wait to see you again."

Cherisse couldn't believe how turned-on a phone conversation was making her. She dug her toes into the carpet, trying to concentrate on something other than the ripening of her body due to Harry's sexy voice.

Clearing her throat, she said, "I feel the same way." Suddenly shy, she wondered how she was going to feel on Saturday night when he came to pick her up for their date. All this pent-up passion might explode and she might jump the poor guy the moment he came to the door. For that, though, she would have to make sure the house was empty. Let Danielle go out with her girlfriends or Echo, who was still pretending to be the best friend, and convincing her mother to go to the movies with the Silver Foxes, a group of ladies she had known practically all her life. That might work.

But then she thought of another obstacle. She should go ahead and tell Harry about it so he wouldn't be surprised when he came to the house. "Harry, you should know that Danielle's father is going to be staying with us for a couple of months until he finds somewhere to live. Danielle asked him to stay and as it turns out, it's okay with my mom. I've been outvoted two to one. He will be here when you pick me up Saturday night."

Harry was silent for a few seconds. "You say you were outvoted. Does that mean you have a reason why you don't want your ex to stay with you? Does he upset you in some way? Flirt with you?"

"It's not that," Cherisse told him. "Charlie and I don't have that kind of divorce. We were never the kind of divorced couple who still flirted or, God forbid, still slept together on occasion. No, there is no love left as far as I'm concerned. I'm sure he feels the same way. It's not a subject that's ever come up. It's just that I resent Charlie for not supporting Danielle more after the divorce. Not just monetarily but emotionally. And you should see her with him, she adores him. I suppose there is a bit of jealousy I have to contend with, too. I just don't think I want to come home from work and see Charlie every day for two months. I might snap at him, get everything out in the open that I've been bottling up for years. It won't be pretty. I don't want Danielle to see that side of me."

"She knows you're human," Harry said reassuringly.

"Yes, but I've kept her away from the acrimony for years. I didn't want to be seen as the villain when Charlie invariably came out smelling like a…rose!"

Harry laughed. "Okay, I've been forewarned. There won't be a reenactment of *Clash of the Titans* in your living room come Saturday night. I admire Charlie Washington as a ball player. I don't see why I can't get along with the man."

Cherisse didn't say anything but those sounded like the proverbial *famous last words*. She hoped her instincts were wrong this time.

Chapter 10

Danielle was excited. It was Thursday, the day her dad was supposed to arrive. She went through her day as if by rote, going through the motions but not really paying strict attention in any of her classes. Thank goodness there were no pop quizzes or she would have flunked them all.

Between her calculus class and her advanced chemistry class she was switching out her textbooks and notebooks at her locker in the hallway when Echo came up behind her and goosed her. Danielle elbowed him in the side.

"Ow!" Echo cried, hunching over in pain. "Girl, your skinny elbows are deadly weapons."

Echo was six feet tall to Danielle's five-nine. He wore his natural black hair in a huge afro that made him look like a throwback to the seventies. His clothing, while clean, never fit him, but hung on his trim, muscular body. But then, Danielle mused, as she eyed him, it didn't matter because Echo looked good in anything. He had flawless brown skin with red undertones, a sexy mouth and eyes the color of burnt honey.

He leaned his square-jawed, clean-shaven face closer to her as she shut the locker door. "What's the matter?" he asked softly. "Having second thoughts about your dad coming to stay with you and your mom?"

"Nothing of the sort," Danielle said. She put her chemistry book and notebook in the canvas bag she carried her school supplies in and tossed it over her shoulder. The hallway was filled with other students checking their lockers or hurrying to their next classes.

She and Echo were both in advanced chemistry so she knew when she turned and began walking in the direction of their classroom he would fall into step beside her, chatting all the while.

"You've been moody ever since you got back from Vail," he observed, his gaze on her face. "Are you missing lover boy from D.C.?"

Danielle narrowed her eyes at him. "A lady does not kiss and tell."

"He kissed you?" Echo asked, his voice squeaking.

Danielle looked straight ahead. "I didn't say."

"I get the point, Danielle," Echo said tightly. "You're not going to tell me. All right, but answer this one question for me. What does he have that I don't?"

"The nerve to try to kiss me," Danielle answered.

Echo's relief was written all over his handsome face. "You didn't kiss him!"

"No, I didn't," said Danielle angrily. "But you know what? I might just go ahead and kiss the next guy who tries."

Echo, equally upset, cried, "Well, maybe I'll be the next guy who tries!"

Nose in the air, Danielle huffed and kept walking. She

didn't even dignify his comment with a reply. Echo walked beside her, his prodigious brain calculating how he was going to wipe that smug look off her face.

"When a man loves a woman," he said quietly, "he doesn't grab her and kiss her, he picks a special moment."

This time Danielle stopped in her tracks and stared at him.

"I'm not some guy you met one night, I'm the guy who loves you, Danielle. And if it takes me a while to work up to a kiss, then so be it. I'm not just in this for the short term, but forever. You know how I was raised, my mom by herself. I saw how she struggled. And because of that I respect women. You're more to me than a quickie in the backseat of a car, or a grope in the locker room."

He opened his arms to her and Danielle walked into them. As they embraced in the hallway the other kids walked around them. "I guess it's time to take this to the next level," Echo said softly in her ear.

Charlie pulled the SUV to the curb at the Patterson home. After he turned off the engine he sat there, thinking. Why had he let Danielle talk him into staying with them until he found a place to live? He was not broke. He could afford to go to a hotel. Ever since he'd agreed to the arrangement he'd been second-guessing himself. Yes, he wanted to be close to Danielle. But he knew that Cherisse wasn't going to warm to his staying with them. No, they were not the sort of divorced couple who enjoyed insulting each other and wishing each other would suffer for eternity.

Cherisse had never forgiven him for his weakness, though. She blamed him for the divorce, as well she should. It was his gambling that put stress on their relationship. Cherisse, who had wanted to go to college and get her nursing degree while they were married, had been reduced to doing secretarial work to keep food on the table for Danielle because he owed loan sharks so much of his salary he could barely keep the roof over their heads. If he had refused to pay the loan sharks, they would have injured him so badly that he would not have been able to play football, his only money-making skill. It all became a vicious cycle. No wonder Cherisse had left him.

Today, though, he was free of the loan sharks. Not exactly free of the gambling fever. He would always be afflicted, but at least he had it somewhat under control as long as he made his Gamblers Anonymous meetings and remained vigilant at all times. No temptation whatsoever. Even a little bet between friends could trigger the fever and the next thing he knew he could be in Vegas playing craps, losing and *feeling* like crap!

It was a daily struggle, one that he gladly went through because he dearly wanted a new life.

He got out of the SUV. It was late afternoon. He knew Danielle was home from school by now, but he had neglected to ask her if her mother would be home when he arrived. Some part of him wanted to get the meeting with Cherisse over with. Another part wanted to postpone it for as long as possible.

He could take a lot of punishment, but the look of disappointment in Cherisse's eyes had always been able to do him in.

Just as well man-up, he thought as he walked onto the familiar porch. Looking around, he decided that not much had changed in the old neighborhood since his last visit. The yards were still well-kept, the streets busy with life—kids playing in them, somebody mowing his lawn, someone else washing her car, or the guy next door making minor repairs to his house or car. The neighbors were a multicultural lot: blacks, Hispanics, Asians and a few whites. It was a nice neighborhood.

He was glad Danielle had spent her formative years here.

He rang the bell and heard Danielle running to answer the door. He was ready for her when she opened the door and flew into his arms. Charlie hugged her tightly as a lump formed in his throat. She looked so much like her mother that it was spooky. The same long, thick, unruly black hair. The same nose, full-lipped mouth and short white teeth.

She was darker-skinned, like him, though, and she had his aggressiveness on the playing field. He'd been lucky enough to catch a few of her basketball games when she was younger and last year he'd seen her in a skiing competition.

In both sports she had displayed a single-minded kind of aggression on the playing field that had rivaled his.

"Dad!" she screamed. "You made it, finally!"

Charlie kissed her forehead and held her away from him so that he could look her in the eyes. "What do you mean 'finally'? I arrived just when I said I would."

Danielle wrinkled her nose and pointedly looked at the clock on the living room wall. Charlie was ten minutes later than he'd said he would be. "I hate to nitpick," she told him, "but you're late."

"That's right, you are, Charlie," Jo said, entering the room.

She stood in the doorway with her hands on her hips, looking Charlie over. At thirty-eight, only a year older than Cherisse, he was still a fine-looking man. Dark-skinned and rakish-looking, what with that moustache of his and that shaved head. She supposed he'd gotten a receding hairline like his father, God rest his soul, and had decided to go ahead and start shaving his head. It looked good on him.

Danielle let go of her dad so he could give her grandmother a hug. Jo groaned with pleasure when he did. Peering up at him, she asked, "How was your trip? Everything go all right?"

"No problems," said Charlie, moaning with pleasure. Miss

Jo, as he called his mother-in-law—ex-mother-in-law—had always given the best hugs. And even after the divorce she had not taken sides and vilified him just for the sake of showing solidarity with her daughter. She had understood that no matter what Charlie had done, he was still Danielle's father. And a little girl needed to be able to believe in her father.

"Miss Jo," he said, "you're as beautiful as ever."

Jo didn't even try to deny it. "Honey, we Patterson women hold together nicely." She let go of him and turned to Danielle. "Sweetie, help your dad get his belongings out of his car and then bring him to the kitchen for a little pick-me-up, he must be tired and hungry after all that driving."

She went back to what she had been doing in the kitchen before Charlie's arrival.

Danielle regarded her dad. "You heard her. Put me to work."

While taking a brief break in the employee lounge, Cherisse reread Harry's letter that had come in Tuesday's mail, for perhaps the fourth time that day:

I've just come from a run along a mountain road and while I was running I saw a bald eagle soaring above me. It's more and more of an unusual sight. It always makes me feel a sense of wonder. I feel the same sense of awe at your beauty, your spirit, whenever I walk into a room and see you again after a short separation. I can't wait to see you Saturday night. Harry.

"Whatcha doing?" Sonia asked as she walked into the lounge. Cherisse had been alone in the room, which was why she'd taken the letter out to read. She quickly folded it and slipped it into her smock's pocket. Harry's letters were for her eyes only.

She had told Sonia she had received a letter from him, though. "You caught me reading Harry's letter again," she confessed.

Sonia laughed shortly as she joined Cherisse at her table. "It's about time you had a little romance in your life."

"How're things with you and Ken?" Cherisse asked.

"Mmm," Sonia mused, lips pursed and eyes full of mischief. "We're taking things slowly. It's the only way. We've been to dinner a few times and when you phoned Sunday evening he was at my place helping me paint the kitchen. I've worked the poor boy hard. Painting, vacuuming Mary's house, I'm wearing him down and then when he's too weak to resist, I'll jump his bones."

"You find him attractive, then?"

"In a clean-cut, myopic-accountant kind of way," Sonia joked. "You know nerds can be very sexy."

"He's not a nerd."

"Sure he is," Sonia disagreed. "But behind those glasses are beautiful brown eyes and under those high-water pants is a pretty fit body."

Cherisse laughed shortly. "And what do you find underneath all of that?"

"A lovely soul," Sonia proclaimed. "I'm thirty-eight. I'm not looking for Prince Charming anymore. I'm looking for a HMW: Healthy Male Working."

"The best kind of male," Cherisse said wholeheartedly.

Sonia laughed again and got up. "Well, I need to go give a bath to a child who doesn't enjoy them. Pray for me."

"Done," said Cherisse.

Harry was going over business reports from his general manager in his suite's office. It was something to occupy his mind while he pondered the real question: was he going to make an offer on the resort in Montana? If he did that would mean his time would have to be divided between Colorado and Montana. But to his advantage if he went ahead with the deal it would mean he would no longer have to endlessly travel the country searching for the site of his second resort. Montana. He'd only visited the state twice and if it weren't the whitest state he'd ever been in—that honor went to Utah—it was definitely the most remote. The state was undoubtedly beautiful though, breathtakingly so.

Harry, who was in his robe after a shower following his evening workout, put down the sheet of paper he had been studying and picked up the letter from Cherisse that he'd gotten in this morning's mail.

He sighed. He could never have guessed the emotional impact of receiving a personal message from the hand of a woman he was attracted to. Her lovely cursive writing lent an air of sophistication to her words:

Dear Harry,
While your letter wasn't in the least suggestive, I none-theless found my heart racing when I read it. I'm looking forward to seeing you again, too. If only to cor-roborate certain facts I've stored up in my feverish mind about you: That your arms are strong and your mouth is sweet and your breath on my neck sends shivers down my spine. I really want to see if my memory is correct on those counts, Harry. So be prepared to demonstrate for me what my memory tells me is true. Cherisse.

Harry smiled. His first letter had been chaste because he hadn't wanted to assume she would welcome something racier. His next would be a departure from the first.

Of course, he didn't plan to write it until after their date Saturday night. By then he would most assuredly have more ammunition for his pen and would be able to fire off a missive she would never forget.

At dinner on Charlie's first night in the Patterson home, Danielle kept the conversation lively, interjecting notes on her day whenever it lagged. She seemed more than a little manic to her mother, who knew how badly she wanted her dad to feel at home.

Taking pity on her child, Cherisse was more than civil to Charlie. She even served him dessert at the end of the meal. Shortly after she put the piece of apple pie in front of him, Danielle announced that she was tired and would forego dessert tonight, an occurrence that happened about as often as there was a total eclipse of the sun, and said she was going to wash the dishes and go on up to bed. She said good-night, going to kiss both of them on their cheeks. Soon after her performance Cherisse watched as her mother, a woman who was a night owl to the core, said she, too, was feeling a bit sleepy and would turn in early tonight.

Left alone at the dining room table with Charlie, Cherisse felt certain she was the victim of a conspiracy. She smiled at Charlie. "They obviously want us to talk."

"Obviously," Charlie said and put his fork down. The pie could wait. His eyes met hers across the table. "I know you don't want me here, Cheri, and I would have said no when Danielle suggested it but I couldn't. I didn't want to disappoint her…again."

To his surprise, Cherisse's smile didn't waver. "I'm okay with your staying here, Charlie. I know Danielle dreamed it up so she could have you all to herself. She's missed you a lot. Besides, it's not as if you and I detest each other. It's been ten years. There're no bad feelings between the two of us. It's all about Danielle now."

"That's right, it's all about Danielle," Charlie assured her.

"Good," said Cherisse as she picked up her fork and daintily cut off a piece of pie with the tines. Her eyes meeting Charlie's again, she said, "I'm glad we got that out of the way."

Charlie picked up his fork and began to eat, but he could barely swallow because he was being deceitful and felt bad about it. The fact was, he was still very attracted to his ex-wife and if she gave him the slightest encouragement he would do everything in his power to win her back. There, he'd thought it even if he hadn't said it.

Earlier today, while Danielle had been helping him get his suitcases out of the SUV, she had been prattling on and on about her life and her life included her mother's life. She'd dropped an innocent enough tidbit about Cherisse dating Harry Payne and Charlie had felt his heart plummet.

Harry Payne was everything he was not—rich, successful, even richer now than he had been when he'd been a quarterback for the Broncos. Yes, they had met on the field of battle years ago and even then Harry had won. The Broncos had beaten the Eagles several times.

He bet Payne remembered that. Remembered it and was inwardly gloating now that he was dating his ex-wife. It probably gave him some sort of sick satisfaction. Cherisse was ignorant of such things. She had shown very little interest in football while they were married. According to Danielle, Cherisse hadn't even known who Payne was when they met. But it must have been quite a coup for Harry Payne to learn that she was Charlie Washington's ex.

Charlie saw no reason to pretend he was unaware she was dating Payne. The thing to do was to treat it as casually as possible.

"Danielle says you're going out with Harry Payne this weekend," he said, after which he took a bite of his pie and chewed thoughtfully.

Cherisse was at once wary of his interest. When they were married Charlie had been jealous if a man even looked her way. "Harry and I just met," she said. "I suppose Danielle also told you he's her sponsor. This will be our first date."

"Wonderful," Charlie said. "You *should* go out and enjoy yourself."

"Harry said you were one of the best defensive backs in the game," Cherisse said, trying to keep the conversation light. She gave him a sincere smile.

Charlie *had* been good in his day, a fact that escaped Cherisse. She had been too busy worrying about paying the bills. He wished he could make it up to her somehow.

Sitting there looking at her, how her mouth—he'd always loved her mouth—turned up in a smile that would melt any man's heart, and how her eyes danced with joy at the thought of Harry Payne, his stomach turned sour.

Pushing his plate away, he said, "I guess I'm full, although Miss Jo really did a fine job on that pie. She was always such a great cook."

He cleared his throat. "I think I'll turn in. Good night, Cheri."

Cherisse smiled at him. "Good night, Charlie."

He took his plate with him.

Cherisse watched him go. There was something he wasn't saying to her. She could tell when he was holding back. *But you know what,* she thought, *I don't care what's on Charlie Washington's mind anymore!*

She finished her pie and drank her coffee, then got up to go upstairs for a long soak in the tub.

About an hour later, after she'd come out of the tub, had dried off and was smoothing moisturizer all over her body, there came a knock at her door. It was by then nine-thirty and she knew Danielle was probably either finishing up homework or already sound asleep. Her daughter got up early and had never fought going to bed at night, except on weekends when she wanted to party with her friends. That left her mother.

Since her mother stayed up until one or two in the morning, she sometimes came by her room for chats after they had both bathed and were ready for bed.

Cherisse walked over to the door and opened it with the expectation of seeing her mother on the other side. Instead she found Charlie, freshly showered, wearing only a T-shirt and a pair of pajama bottoms.

"Cheri," he said, talking low and stepping into the room on bare feet, "my conscience is bothering me. I've got to come clean with you."

Charlie was six-one and weighed one-ninety-five. He hadn't been a slacker since he'd retired from the game and still made an imposing figure with tight abs, taut biceps and leg muscles. Cherisse didn't feel comfortable alone with him in her bedroom when they were both in their nightclothes.

She didn't object to his coming into the room, but she left the door open. Charlie shut it. Turning to face her, his eyes swept over her. Cherisse experienced a momentary chill when it dawned on her that Charlie was still sexually attracted to her. She supposed she would have been aware of how he felt if she had allowed herself to be alone with him for any length of time over the past ten years. But whenever he came to visit Danielle, Cherisse invariably left the room as quickly as possible, or Charlie would take Danielle elsewhere for their visits. Cherisse liked it even better when he didn't come to town at all and Danielle went to visit him in Philadelphia. That way, she didn't have to see him at all.

Well, she wasn't the inexperienced little wife who had put up with years of neglect from him. Neglect in the form of lack of support and the long lengths of time he would spend away from home on gambling binges and God knows whatever else he got into with his buddies. She suspected he'd cheated on her, too, but never saw proof of it and at the end of their marriage when she told him she was leaving him and he had begged her to stay, he had sworn that in their nine years of marriage, yes, he had gambled and put them in financial straits, but at least he had never cheated on her with the groupies who followed the team from town to town.

That wasn't enough to make her stay.

And now, this…whatever he had on his mind when he stated that he needed to come clean with her…wasn't going to sway her about him, either.

She rounded on him before he could utter another word and cried, "Charlie, if you are in this house for any reason other than to spend time with your daughter, I want you out in the morning. And *you* can explain to Danielle why you have to leave!"

Charlie looked contrite. His handsome face crinkled in a frown. Running his hand over his bald head, he sighed. "I know you don't believe me, but I have changed, Cheri. In the past three years I've gotten out of debt and I haven't gambled in years. I can tell you the exact date, but I don't think you're interested. I would never do anything to jeopardize my relationship with Danielle. But with this change that's come over me I've also been bold enough to dream of a better life, the life you and I were cheated out of because of my habit. I regret…"

"Don't say it," Cherisse hissed, trying her best to keep her voice down, but it was hard to do because she was so angry with Charlie. "Don't tell me you want to date me, Charlie

Washington, because if you do then your being here was all a ruse to get close to me and that would really hurt your daughter, who has done everything she can to finally get your sorry attention."

"But, Cheri, I know we could all be happy together. I want the chance to make it up to you. Just give me a shot."

Shaking her head in disgust, Cherisse backed away from him. "What brought this on? You haven't dropped any hints over the years. Aside from that look you just gave me I had no notion that you even thought of me, let alone in sexual terms. Why bring it up now?"

"I'm here now," Charlie said simply. "We're going to be living in the same city. And honestly, Cheri, you and I haven't been alone in the same room since we met with the lawyers that last time. What was I going to do, phone you and tell you how I felt? E-mail you? You wouldn't have spoken to me and you would have deleted any e-mails from me."

"Damn right I would've," Cherisse said vehemently. "We are divorced! There is nothing left between us. I haven't avoided you like the plague for nothing. I've moved on. I've been in love since the divorce, Charlie. His name was Neil Kennedy, he was a police officer, we were planning to get married but he was killed in the line of duty."

"I heard about that," Charlie said, to her utter amazement.

"How?" she asked, her voice sounding hoarse from disbelief.

"A friend of a friend," Charlie said. "I don't have any family left in Denver but you and I still have mutual friends here, Cheri. We have a history here. We fell in love in high school. We left here with such high hopes of a wonderful life together when I got drafted by the Eagles in college. Remember my mom wanted me to finish college instead?"

"She was right," said Cherisse.

"Yeah," Charlie admitted. "She was right. I didn't get the chance to tell her that before she died." Looking more determined than ever he strode over to her, grabbed her by the shoulders and made her look him in the eyes. "I don't want us to miss our chance. Please, tell me it's not too late for us."

Cherisse stared up at him, clearly distressed. "You're not still in love with me, Charlie. You're trying to create a happily ever after that more than likely would never have been. Aside from your gambling we had other problems. We rarely saw eye to eye on anything. Face it, our marriage was based on our being high-school sweethearts. We let our overactive hormones get the best of us. If I hadn't gotten pregnant with Danielle we might never have gotten married. That fact plus your gambling did us in, Charlie. Let it go. You've got a new job. You'll meet someone. But I'm not going to go back in time with you. This is my time and I like it. I like Harry Payne."

"He's a womanizer," said Charlie. "Why do you think he's never been married?"

"Quite a few professional athletes have had that reputation, including you," Cherisse told him, wrenching free of his hold and walking over to the vanity, where she sat down and began brushing her hair.

Charlie sighed out of frustration and sat down on the bed. "I don't see why you can't give me a chance. You're willing to give him a chance and he is twice the ladies' man I ever was!"

Cherisse met his eyes in the mirror while she braided her hair into a single plait that fell down her back. "Did something happen between you and Harry that I should know about? Why don't you like him?"

"He's trying to get my ex-wife into his bed, that's why I don't like him. That's reason enough!"

"Will you lower your voice?"

"He will use you, Cheri," Charlie insisted. "And I'm not going to sit around and let that happen, even if you don't want me."

"Stay out of my personal life!"

"Now who's shouting?"

Finished braiding her hair, Cherisse rose and began walking to the door. "It's time for you to leave."

Charlie, displaying the quick reflexes he was known for on the football field, was up in an instant. He adeptly pulled her into his arms and kissed her.

Cherisse promptly bit his lower lip.

Setting her away from him, Charlie's hand went to his injured lip. "Fine," he said. "I'll leave in the morning."

"No need for that," Cherisse told him calmly, looking away from him as though the sight of him repulsed her. "We've got everything out in the open now. You're not going to make any more advances toward me. You're going to stay out of my personal life. And Danielle never has to know you came here under false pretenses."

She looked him directly in the eye then.

Charlie got the message. Unless he ceased his campaign to win her back, she would make sure Danielle found out his secret.

"I don't like resorting to blackmail but you give me no choice," she said quietly.

Charlie smiled at her. "You don't want to hurt Danielle any more than I do. But I get you. I've stated my case. I won't harass you."

"Thank you," said Cherisse. "Good night."

"Good night." Charlie backed out of the room, smiling roguishly. His eyes slid over her one more time. "You're still a stone-cold fox, babe."

Cherisse laughed and shut the door in his face.

Chapter 11

Saturday morning dawned and Cherisse, although she sometimes fantasized about staying in bed, got up as soon as the sun filtered through her bedroom curtains.

When she got downstairs, dressed in jeans, an old purple long-sleeve cotton shirt that was baby-bottom soft due to repeated washings, and a pair of athletic shoes, she found the kitchen empty of her other housemates except for Charlie, who had put on the coffee and was leaning against the counter sipping a cup.

"Good morning," he said, smiling. His dark brown eyes possessively raked over her.

"Morning," Cherisse said, sure it wasn't going to be a good morning with him looking at her as though he wanted to rip her clothes off and have his way with her on the kitchen table.

She went and poured herself a mug of coffee. Taking a sip,

she smiled approvingly. He'd learned how to make coffee. When they were together he had not known how to turn on the coffeemaker. She peered up at him. "Didn't I make myself clear last night? I don't want you coming on to me."

Charlie took another sip of his coffee before saying, "I heard you. And I slept on it. I've decided that this is a free country and may the best man win."

Cherisse looked at him as if he'd lost his mind. Putting her mug on the counter she regarded him with steely eyes. "I am not a prize to be won. I'm the one who chooses who I want to pursue me, Charlie Washington, and you're not even in the running! You'd just as well get that through your thick skull!"

Charlie was looking deeply into her eyes and his voice was soft and intimate when he said, "Do you remember how good it was between us? When we made love something powerful happened, something magical. Did you have that with Neil Kennedy?"

Caught off guard, Cherisse found herself searching for a worthy response. Intimacy with Neil had not been the same as with Charlie. Not as intense. She had loved Neil in a different way than she had loved Charlie. Charlie was the first man she ever loved. It had been an all-consuming love that had been fed by their passion, a passion that had been extinguished by the end of their marriage.

With Neil she had gone into the relationship as a divorced woman, someone who was not looking for bells and whistles, who wanted something steady and reliable. Who was afraid of getting hurt therefore did not invest the passion into the relationship she, in retrospect, wished she had. Neil deserved that much.

But what could she say to Charlie? That smug expression on his face told her that he thought sex with him had been the highlight of her life. Passion-wise, maybe it had been. However as far as security, peace of mind and the sheer joy at having a man in her life on whom she could depend were concerned Neil had him beat by a mile!

So she gave him her stock answer. "A lady never kisses and tells."

"What a cop-out!" Charlie cried, disappointed. "You're afraid to be honest with me because you know I can compete with Harry Payne. When a woman gets to be your age she is coming into the prime of her life. She needs sexual healing, and I'm the man for that, not Payne. I'm younger than he is, and I already have a map of your body."

"Keep dreaming," Cherisse told him and walked over to the refrigerator to start taking food out in order to begin making breakfast.

"Keep dreaming about what?" Danielle asked as she strode into the kitchen still in pale blue pajamas and wiping the sleep from her eyes.

Her parents, both a little startled by her sudden appearance, each said good morning with excessive enthusiasm.

Danielle stared at them. "Did I interrupt something? You weren't arguing, were you?"

"No," Cherisse denied. "Your father claimed that he has gotten so good at chess since we were divorced that he can now beat me. I told him to keep dreaming."

"Okay, shall we test your theory after breakfast?" Charlie asked hopefully.

"Sorry, I'm going shopping after breakfast," Cherisse said with a smile. "I've got a date tonight." Her back to Danielle, she gave Charlie a triumphant smirk.

Charlie smiled at her. As far as he was concerned this war was just getting started.

As for Danielle, her curiosity had been piqued. She had felt the tension between her parents and would make it her business to find out what was really going on.

"Dad, we're still on for househunting today?"

"Yeah, right after breakfast," Charlie said, refilling his coffee cup. "Maybe I can find something in this neighborhood."

Cherisse gave him a sharp look but didn't open her mouth. She went about getting a bowl from the cabinet above the sink and then cracking eggs into it. *Let him talk,* she thought, *I'm going to have the last word because nothing he says is going to convince me that Harry Payne is bad for me.*

Charlie remained only a few feet away from her, still casually leaning against the counter, one long jeans-clad leg crossed over the other at the ankle.

"That would be so cool!" Danielle exclaimed.

Charlie waited for a reaction from Cherisse. It never came.

Danielle, who was used to helping with the cooking, went to the refrigerator to get the link sausages from the meat tray. She put several links in a skillet, put the lid on it then turned the burner on medium heat.

Seeing that her mom didn't share her enthusiasm about the prospect of her dad living in the same neighborhood, Danielle decided to inject some life into the conversation and said, "Echo told me he loves me!"

Mother and father dropped what they were doing to stare at her. Images of their own teenaged love affair flashed through their minds.

Charlie, with a rush of fear, found it hard to control instant outrage. Who was this boy to say he was in love with his daughter? She was just a baby.

Cherisse was concerned but since she knew how levelheaded Danielle was and that she had waited over a year to get some kind of emotional response out of Echo, she decided not to overreact. She hugged her.

"I'm so happy for you, sweetie!"

Charlie pulled them apart. "Happy?" He grabbed Danielle by the shoulders and looked her in the eyes. "Baby, you're only seventeen. You have years ahead of you. You have plenty of time to fall in love. After college, during college, take your pick, but don't get involved with a high school jock whose future is iffy at best!"

Cherisse suddenly had an epiphany. Charlie was talking about himself. He was that high school jock whose future had been iffy at best. Did he think he'd ruined her life by marrying her?

"Echo's not some high school jock, Daddy," Danielle said, defending her young prince. "He doesn't even play a sport. He skis and he's good at it but that's not what defines him. He has a brilliant mind. He's already won a four-year scholarship to Yale. He's going to be a scientist, a physicist. And I believe him because his life hasn't been easy. He's had to struggle. He knows what he wants and has a plan to get it."

"That's all good, sweetheart," said Charlie, holding tightly to her. "I'm happy for him. But love is not just a four-letter word. It's a serious subject, one that can't be taken lightly. I want to meet him."

Defiant, Danielle said, "No problem. He can come to dinner tonight. I'll call him and invite him after breakfast."

"Do that," said Charlie, reserving his congratulations until after he had met this paragon of virtue. He sighed wearily and looked at Cherisse. "Is this the sort of thing you've had to put up with for the past seventeen years?"

"Welcome to full-time fatherhood," said Cherisse with a smile.

Charlie let go of Danielle, who took one look at the mirth on her mother's face and burst out laughing. Charlie, relieved that his first father crisis had passed, started laughing, too, and that's how Jo found them when she entered the kitchen a couple minutes later.

"Let me in on the joke," she said. "I could use a good belly laugh this morning."

Harry didn't tell Cherisse where he was taking her on their date. He simply told her to dress as though she were going to a fine restaurant for dinner. Tonight as he got out of the Range Rover and strode up the walk to the Patterson front porch, the December air was bracing and the night sky was sprinkled with stars. He saw this as a good omen.

He couldn't remember the last time he'd shown any apprehension when he'd gone to pick up a date. But then he had never gone to pick up anyone who had her mother, her daughter and her ex-husband living with her. Harry was a big boy. None of those factors would have ever kept him away from her, but he didn't look forward to a confrontation with the ex. He knew Charlie Washington only from meeting him on the field during a game, and that one unfortunate incident that he wasn't even certain Washington recalled. He hoped not. He, for one, did not want to rehash an ugly episode from the past.

They had both been young and foolish back then.

He rang the bell.

In the house, Cherisse was upstairs stepping into a pair of three-inch-heeled black suede open-toed sling-backs. Standing in front of a full-length mirror, she looked at herself with a critical eye. She was wearing a sleeveless dark red, V-neck dress with a bodice constructed of a series of layered folds. The waist was cinched by a cloth-covered belt and the skirt fell gracefully around her shapely legs, the hem ending three inches above her knees.

She smiled at her reflection. Her hair was behaving itself

tonight. She'd parted it in the middle and it fell down her back in shimmery midnight waves. The only jewelry she wore was a pair of one-carat diamond stud earrings.

When she heard the bell, she shouted, "Danielle, would you get that? Tell Harry I'll be right down!"

However, Danielle was not in the house at the moment. She was in the detached garage with her grandmother looking for the boxes with the Christmas ornaments in them.

The only person in the house aside from Cherisse was Charlie, who was watching a game on the wide-screen TV in the family room.

He heard Cherisse and got up to answer the door.

When he got to the door, he took a deep breath and opened it.

He couldn't tell by Harry Payne's face whether or not being let into the house of his date by her ex husband startled him or not. Payne simply smiled and said, "Hello, Charlie, it's been a long time. How are you?" And then he was shaking his hand while simultaneously stepping into the house.

Charlie stepped backward. Both men were tall and broad-shouldered. Charlie was dressed in jeans and a dark blue long-sleeve cotton shirt, a white T-shirt underneath and white athletic shoes. Harry wore a tailored suit in dark gray, a black long-sleeve silk shirt with silver cufflinks at the wrists, a black silk tie and black wingtips.

Charlie felt a little out of his element, but nonetheless pressed forward with his agenda. "Harry," he said in greeting. He shut the door and turned to face him. "Cheri is upstairs. She'll be down in a few minutes. I was watching a game when you rang the bell. You want to come back to the family room and wait for her there?"

Harry was about to say no, he'd wait for Cherisse right there in the foyer, but thought, *What the heck, it's obvious*

Charlie wants to say something to me in private. Let's get this over with. So he gave an imperceptible nod and followed Charlie to the family room.

"Nice house," he commented on the way.

"Yeah," said Charlie. "It's been in Cheri's family for years."

It *was* a nice house. Harry recognized good workmanship when he saw it. The walls, hardwood floors and moldings had all been done by artisans who took pride in their work and the family had taken excellent care of it. It was furnished with well-made pieces, not ostentatious, but in good taste.

When they got to the family room, a large room with a comfortable lived-in look about it, Charlie sat down and gestured for Harry to join him on the big leather couch. Harry sat on his end and waited for the show to begin. Not the show on the television set. Charlie promptly turned that off.

"Look, Harry," Charlie said, putting the remote on the coffee table in front of him, "you seem like a nice guy. And I don't want to say anything to insult you so I would appreciate it if you would take this in the spirit it's said, that of just wanting to inform you of the situation here."

Harry was confused and looked it. He was sure Charlie was trying to be clear, but he wasn't succeeding. "Just spit it out, Charlie," he said. "What do you want me to know?"

"That I want you to stop seeing Cheri," Charlie rushed on, frowning. He stood up. Harry stood up, too.

"I want her back, okay?" Charlie said belligerently. "I screwed up. We should never have been divorced. I suppose she told you that I had a gambling problem…."

"No, she didn't," Harry said.

"Well, we're all adults here," Charlie said. "I'm going to be honest with you. She begged me to quit but I was hooked. I've since quit and now I'm trying to put my life back together. Just so you'll know, I'm not staying here because I can't afford to go someplace else, I'm staying because of Danielle. She wants me here and I couldn't say no to her."

He had not been able to look Harry in the eyes while he'd said all that, but now he did. "I'm asking you to step aside, Harry. How long have you known Cheri? It can't have been that long. I'm sure a man like you has women hitting on you all the time. She can't be that special to you. Let her go."

Harry was, frankly, tired of people telling him how to conduct his love life. First Marcia had the nerve to tell him she had done him a favor by stringing him along and then dumping him once she had brought LaShaun to heel, leaving him open to play the field. Now, Cherisse's ex-husband was telling him to be a gentleman and step aside so that *he* could have a clear shot at her.

She can't be that special to you, Charlie Washington reasoned. Well, she *was* special to him. He hadn't been this excited about a woman in years. Cherisse was everything he was hoping to find in a mate. She was smart, dedicated to those she cared about and devoted to her job, qualities he admired in anyone because they demonstrated commitment. Yes, she complained that nurses were overworked and underpaid, but he bet not once had she shirked her duties. *Plus, let's be honest, Harry,* he thought, *the woman makes you melt every time she walks into a room.*

The biggest reason he wouldn't consider doing as Charlie Washington asked was the fact that Cherisse had told him there was nothing left between her and her ex-husband and he believed her. In order for him to back off, he was going to have to be told to do so by Cherisse herself.

Therefore he said to Charlie, "Is this what Cheri wants?"

In an instant he knew it wasn't. Charlie screwed up his face, his eyes looked from side to side as he attempted to think of a quick response and none came. "Ah, no," he finally said truthfully. "She doesn't see it the same way I do."

Inwardly, Harry breathed a sigh of relief. He definitely didn't want to leave here tonight without Cheri. He'd dreamed about seeing her again all week, had even actually had a couple of dreams about her. And the truth was his heart was beating quite rapidly awaiting Charlie Washington's answer to his question. He did *not* want to lose Cheri before he'd even gotten the chance to know her!

"Then, I'm sorry, but I'm going to have to respect Cheri's wishes," Harry said, trying not to sound too happy about it. He smiled ruefully.

"Danielle, Ma, Harry? Where is everybody?"

Both Harry and Charlie heard Cherisse approaching, and both were looking toward the doorway when she entered the family room. Both of their jaws dropped when they saw her.

Harry's legs went momentarily weak. That face, that dress, that hair. That body, those legs and that beautiful smile directed at him! If he died right now he would die with a silly grin on his face.

"Hello, Harry," she said, her voice husky and inviting.

Charlie wanted to first throw something over her chest to conceal her cleavage, and then throw Harry out of the house. But he stood there, powerless, as Cherisse went to Harry, kissed him on the cheek and said, "I'm sorry to keep you waiting."

His eyes never leaving her face, Payne said, "You were worth the wait. You look beautiful."

Cherisse beamed and took his proffered arm. "Thank you, Harry. You look gorgeous, yourself." She said over her shoulder as she and Payne walked out of the room, "Good night, Charlie."

Charlie couldn't even manage a good-night. He plopped

down on the couch after they had departed and switched the set back on. Fuming, he surfed through the channels, not paying attention to anything on the screen. He saw now that he was going to have to pull out the big guns in order to win this war.

In the foyer, Cherisse paused at the closet and let Harry help her on with her overcoat. It was forty degrees out tonight. Alone with him now, she wanted to breathe him in and look closely at his face, the lines, the planes. All week, she had been recalling him from memory and she saw now that her memory wasn't close to the real Harry. He was devastatingly masculine with his clean-shaven square-jawed face, large nose, widely spaced dark brown eyes and that chin with a dimple in it. To say nothing of his mouth! She drew her gaze away from his mouth when she blushed, remembering those firm lips against hers, his clean, sweet breath mingling with hers, his tongue… *Okay now, girlfriend, quit it before you manifest the state you're in right before his eyes.*

She pulled her overcoat closed across her chest. Too late, her nipples were hardening at this moment.

Harry held the door for her and they stepped onto the porch, whereupon he closed the door and made sure it was locked before pulling her into his arms and kissing her soundly. She fell into the solid warmth of Harry. His arms went around her and drew her to his hard chest. Her breasts were crushed against him and because she was already aroused her nipples were further stimulated. She experienced a delicious sensual feeling as his tongue parted her lips. She sighed against his mouth and welcomed him inside. Her knees went weak, the soles of her feet tingled, a new erogenous zone for her.

Raising his head, Harry said hoarsely, "Hello, darling."

With her hand in his hair, her head tilted back so as to

admire him better, and a sexy smile on her lips, Cherisse murmured, "Now, that's a hello."

Harry grinned and kissed her again.

They went to Elway's on E 1st Avenue. The restaurant belonged to an old teammate of Harry's and he frequented the restaurant whenever he got the chance. Decorated in muted earth tones, the elegant steakhouse had a warm atmosphere, and Cherisse liked it upon stepping inside.

Harry had asked for a private table in the back when he'd made the reservations. He could barely tear his eyes away from Cherisse long enough to look at the menu.

Her head was bent over the menu, her wavy black hair tumbling over her slim shoulders. Harry thought he would surely make a fool of himself if he could not stop staring at her, so he asked her about work, hoping that would distract him. He was wrong. Cherisse looked up and smiled at him, her full lips curving sexily. His groin grew tight at the sight of them. And blood thundered in his ears as she opened her mouth and said, "Harry, did I tell you Amy Whitehall's father was not the one who beat her nearly to death? It was her mother. The woman had the nerve to come to the hospital to see Amy and she was arrested. Last I heard Amy's father was going to be released. I'm so glad for her. She's healing well. In fact she'll probably be released sometime next week."

"That's great news," said Harry. But what he really wanted to know was how many rooms away from Cherisse did Charlie Washington sleep, and did he sleepwalk?

No, no, Harry, he thought vehemently. *Don't go there. If you want to ask Cherisse about the current status of her relationship with her ex-husband, then do it. Don't speculate.*

He cleared his throat. Cherisse had returned to perusing the menu. She looked up.

Harry said, "You're not curious as to what Charlie said to me while you were getting ready for our date?"

She smiled. "I can imagine what Charlie said. He's under the misconception that he's going to remarry me, and he, Danielle and I are going to live happily ever after. He was probably telling you to back off."

"You know him well."

"I was married to him for nine years."

"He's persistent."

"You don't know the half of it. I told him to stop flirting with me and he told me he'd thought over my request and 'may the best man win,'" she said, laughing softly.

"So he thinks this is some kind of contest," Harry ventured.

"Yes!"

Harry narrowed his eyes. Competitive to the core, he had to rein in his first impulse: to turn on the charm and sweep Cherisse off her feet. He had money. He could take her to Paris every weekend if he wanted to. He could... *Harry, calm down. This is crazy,* he told himself. *Cheri is not the type of woman to be floored by material things.*

If you win her you've got to win her by being yourself and to do that you've got to make her a part of your everyday life.

"How would you like to go to Montana with me next weekend?" he asked. "I've got to go check out a resort I'm thinking of buying."

Cherisse was surprised he would ask her to go away with him when they'd only known one another for a short time, but she was also intrigued. She'd never been to Montana before and had heard it was a beautiful state. Besides, just because they went away together didn't mean they had to share a bed. But she had to make that clear from the get-go.

She smiled at him. "I'd love to go to Montana with you. We'd have separate rooms?"

Harry laughed briefly. "But, of course, darling girl."

Cherisse looked down at her menu once more. "Then the answer is yes, Mr. Payne."

The waiter arrived, wanting to take their orders. For starters Cherisse ordered the coconut-battered shrimp while Harry asked for the Japanese seared tuna. Then Cherisse ordered sautéed cremini mushrooms and Harry asked for the Yukon gold mashed potatoes. Cherisse wanted to try the charred red pepper soup and Harry swore by Elway's roasted corn and chicken chowder. And each of them decided upon crustaceans for their main course, Cherisse ordering the Alaskan crab legs and Harry the Australian lobster tail.

Each asked for one glass of Chardonnay since Cherisse wasn't much of a drinker and Harry was driving.

They passed on dessert.

After the waiter had gone to the kitchen, Cherisse pushed her hair behind both ears and looked Harry in the eyes. "When's your birthday, Harry?"

"October fifth," he said easily. "You already know how old I am, and you?"

"January seventeenth," Cherisse said. "I'll be thirty-eight."

"You're a lovely soon-to-be thirty-eight," Harry told her.

"May I ask you a very personal question?" Cherisse asked.

Harry steeled himself. "Go ahead."

"Don't you have that urge to be a father that men usually get after a certain age? And if so, what are you doing dating someone as old as I am?"

Harry laughed. "When you ask a question, you don't beat around the bush, do you?"

He considered her question, then gave her an honest reply. "Yes, I want children some day and I don't think that at the advanced age of thirty-seven you're incapable of giving me those children should our relationship progress in that direction. You're healthy. You've already had one beautiful child. I expect you could have more if you wanted to. *Do* you want to?"

Now he was putting her on the spot.

Cherisse rose to the occasion. "Yes, definitely. I always wanted a brother or a sister for Danielle but I certainly wasn't going to have another child without a husband. It hasn't been easy raising Danielle alone."

"Well, we got that out of the way," Harry joked. "Shall we talk about something harmless like religion or politics?"

"I'm a Christian and a Democrat," said Cherisse.

"A lapsed Christian," Harry admitted. "I haven't been to church in ages. But I'm still a card-carrying Democrat."

Cherisse looked around them. There was an eight-foot-tall Christmas tree in one corner of the dining room surrounded by wrapped gifts. It was December, after all, and many businesses already had their decorations up. "What's your take on Christmas?" she asked. "Do you look forward to it every year or do you think it's gotten too commercial?"

"A little of both," Harry said. "If I can spend it with someone I care about, I love it. If I'm alone I tend to get grumpy and become a Scrooge."

"That's understandable," Cherisse said. "We tend to celebrate it. Decorations will go up at the house in the next few days. Danielle, even though she's seventeen, will be counting down the days. On Christmas Eve we have friends and family over for a meal and, I'm embarrassed to say, we sing carols and have a bit too much Christmas cheer and sometimes have to roll a couple of friends into a cab so they won't have to drive home drunk. Yeah, Christmas is big at our house, but that's how my parents have always done it. Now that Daddy's gone, my mother has carried on the tradition. And if you don't go home to Kentucky this year, we'd love to have you join us."

Harry knew his mother would never forgive him if he didn't come home for Christmas.

But maybe just this one time, he would risk it. "I'd love to," he said. "I hope there'll be plenty of mistletoe hanging about."

"I'll make sure of it," Cherisse assured him.

By that time the waiter was returning with their appetizers and glasses of wine. After serving them, he hurried off, and Cherisse sampled her coconut shrimp, declaring that it was "delicious." She ate a forkful of the pineapple-cucumber slaw that came with it. The fresh, subtle flavors were a perfect complement to the shrimp.

Harry enjoyed his tuna, as well. What he enjoyed the most, though, was watching Cherisse eat. It was a singularly arousing experience. She licked a bit of sauce from her lips and he hardened. He had to look away.

Cherisse followed his line of sight, thinking he must have spotted someone he knew across the room. But he didn't say anything. After a while she thought she might have a bit of sauce on her chin or slaw in her teeth, something he was loath to mention.

If she had something in her teeth, she wanted to be told about it. "Harry, why are you looking everywhere except at me? Do I have something in my teeth?"

"No," Harry said hurriedly to put her mind at ease. He looked at her, but had to lower his gaze because he was somewhat embarrassed. He said, "Looking at you is doing things to my body. I have been in a constant state of semi-arousal since I picked you up this evening."

Cherisse reached across the table and clasped one of Harry's big hands in hers. "You don't know what a wonderful compliment that is, Harry. Thank you."

"It was my pleasure," Harry said, meeting her gaze. "Believe me."

Cherisse gave him a winning smile and squeezed his hand. "I'm glad to know I'm not the only one having a hard time controlling my impulses."

Chapter 12

"Montana!" cried Jo the next morning when Cherisse told her about Harry's invitation.

Cherisse was pleased to find that Charlie had slept in on Sunday morning. She and Jo had a peaceful few minutes before either Charlie or Danielle came down for breakfast.

She and her mother were sitting at the kitchen table, both in bathrobes, drinking coffee. After breakfast both would be dressing for church.

"Yes, he's going to inspect a resort he's thinking of buying."

"Why is he taking you?" Jo asked, pretending ignorance. She simply wanted her daughter's perspective on the situation. Having very little experience with men, did Cherisse actually think Harry Payne was taking her just to keep him company?

"I know how your mind works," Cherisse said, smiling at Jo. "We've already established the fact that there will be separate rooms. Why shouldn't I go? I want to be with him. I only get to see him on weekends."

"I'm not saying you shouldn't go," Jo said. "I'm saying that you should be on guard against getting too tempted. Being in Montana alone with Harry is different than being at a restaurant with him in Denver."

"So you think I'm playing with fire," Cherisse surmised.

"Yes, I do," said her mother. "God help me, I don't know if *I* would be able to resist a man that gorgeous if I were alone with him in a cabin in Montana."

Cherisse laughed softly. "Well, pray for me."

Ponderosa Pines Ranch, located in the high country of the Rocky Mountains, was not a ranch at all but a luxury resort tucked into the southwest corner of Montana.

Harry and Cherisse's plane landed at Missoula, Montana's airport, where a car was waiting to take them the seventy-five miles to the resort.

It was a beautiful clear blue afternoon, and Cherisse saw at once why Montana was called Big Sky Country—the wide open spaces made the sky appear endless. She enjoyed the drive and Harry enjoyed her enthusiasm.

The driver, Jake Hanks, a tall, dark-haired guy in his late twenties who worked for the resort, gave them a short history of the area as he drove "The resort is on the edge of the town of Darby, which looks just like it's straight out of a Western movie. We'll be driving through there in a few minutes and you'll see what I mean."

There was slush on the roads from recent snowfall but the four-wheel drive handled nicely on the wet road. "How much snow do you get every winter?" Harry wanted to know.

"Three hundred inches," Jake said. "And there are short lines at the nearby Lost Trail Powder Mountain ski area."

Harry was aware the resort wasn't designed to cater to skiers as Karibu was. The property they were going to see had several hand-hewn log cabins dotting its five hundred acres and also had a main guest lodge with sixty rooms. It was the sort of place where urban folks who wanted a genuine Western experience, but also wanted to be in the lap of luxury, vacationed.

They were coming into Darby now. As Jake had said, the town definitely had an Old West flavor. False storefronts lined Main Street. There was a tavern, a haberdashery, a general store. It really did look like the set of a Western.

Driving out of town, Cherisse noticed many log cabins. Having lived in Colorado practically all her life, she had rarely met anyone who actually lived in a log cabin. If she had had a camera she was sure she would have been doing the touristy thing and snapping photos of the homes.

A few miles more, and Jake was turning onto the road that led to the resort. As they approached, Cherisse took in the breathtaking beauty of ponderosa pines, their tips kissing the sky. Now she knew where the resort got its name. The lodge was made of hand-hewn pine, itself. The building was three stories high and blended well into the natural background of the surrounding pine forest.

She and Harry were greeted by the owners, Brian and Mitzi Raynor. Both were in their mid-fifties, Brian was tall and trim, with light brown hair and brown eyes, and Mitzi, also tall and slim, had red hair that she wore in a very short pixie cut, and hazel eyes. They spoke with marked southern accents, which delighted Cherisse, who rarely heard southern accents in her neck of the woods.

"Welcome, welcome," said Brian. He and Harry shook hands.

Harry introduced Cherisse. "This is my good friend Cherisse Washington. Cherisse, meet Brian and Mitzi Raynor."

Mitzi grinned at Cherisse and gave her a warm hug instead of shaking her hand. "Hello, Cherisse, welcome to Ponderosa Pines."

"Thank you, Mitzi. This is beautiful country. I really enjoyed the drive here."

"Isn't it?" said Mitzi, taking Cherisse by the arm and escorting her up the walk to the entrance to the lodge while the men brought up the rear. "Brian and I instantly fell in love with the ranch when we first saw it twenty years ago. We're a couple of hillbillies from Arkansas, much like Bill and Hillary Clinton, and we had never seen so many mountains and pine trees before. Wait until you see the country in the spring. The high-country meadows are just blanketed with fairy bells, lilies of the valley and violets. It's a sight to behold!"

Behind them Brian was saying to Harry, "Harry, I have to tell you I'm a fan. In my opinion, you and John Elway were the best quarterbacks the Broncos ever had."

"I'll let John know that the next time I see him," Harry joked.

Over lunch the Raynors explained why they were selling the resort "It's become too much for us to handle alone," said Brian. "We both had health scares last year—I had a minor myocardial infarction and Mitzi developed diabetes. Our doctors told us that we had to reduce the stress in our lives. And although we love this place, it is stressful sometimes. We always want to please our guests and some guests are not capable of being pleased. Am I right, Harry?"

"I've had my share of disgruntled guests," Harry agreed. He usually let their complaints roll off his back, though. When you've done everything within your power to please a guest, there is nothing else you can do except wish him a good journey back home and suggest, perhaps, another venue might be a better choice for his next vacation. Harry never encouraged disgruntled guests to try them again. Who needed

that kind of negativity? He knew he offered top-of-the-line
accommodations and excellent service. He had his standards
and they were always met by his staff or they would no longer
work for him. It was basic good business sense.

"So, we're moving back to Arkansas to be near our
children," said Mitzi. "We have a son and a daughter and six
grandchildren between them."

"Mitzi, you don't look old enough to have six grandkids,"
said Cherisse, smiling at her hostess.

"Don't I know it," said Mitzi, grinning back. "But I'm
thrilled to be a grandma. They range in ages from fourteen
to two. We had all of them here for Thanksgiving, and boy,
oh, boy, did they wear me out!"

"And she's looking forward to seeing them every day,"
Brian joked.

After lunch, it was agreed that a trail ride would give
Harry and Cherisse a good overview of the property, so they
all retired to their rooms, Harry and Cherisse to a cabin a few
yards from the main guest lodge and Brian and Mitzi to their
suite in the lodge, to change into riding gear.

The cabin had a living room, kitchen and two bedrooms
with their own baths. Cherisse put on jeans, a flannel shirt,
leather boots and her down coat. It was colder in Montana
than it had been in Denver. And from the lowering of the sky
it appeared as if snow was imminent.

She met up with Harry in the living room. He was simi-
larly dressed in jeans, boots, a long-sleeve denim shirt and a
fur-lined jacket. He was also wearing a brown Stetson.

He stood with his right hand behind his back, admiring
her. "You make a very cute cowgirl, Ms. Washington.
There's just one thing missing." And he presented her with
a Stetson just like his.

Grinning, Cherisse took it and put it on her curly mane.

She'd put her hair into a ponytail and now the hat fit snugly over her thick hair. "How does it look?" she asked Harry, eyes sparkling.

Harry stepped forward and adjusted the hat at a jaunty angle. Then he bent and kissed her, slowly and with passionate intensity. It was the first time they'd been alone since getting on the plane in Denver. Harry vowed not to miss an opportunity to kiss her whenever they were alone.

"Mmm, that's better," he said, raising his head and smiling at her.

"The trouble with you, Harry, is one kiss is just never enough," she said, and kissed him back.

When she let go of him, Harry had to struggle to control the tightness in the groin area of his already tight jeans.

Cherisse, as if oblivious of the state she'd left him in, flounced to the door and turned back to smile at him. "Coming, Harry?"

She's going to be the death of me, Harry thought, and followed her out the door, hoping that once he hit the cold December air his problem would subside.

The Raynors took them into the pine forest to a ridge that allowed them to look down on Ponderosa Pines Ranch. As the four of them sat on their horses and gazed down, Brian said, "It's one of the last best places on earth."

Harry had to concur with that. The ranch was so beautiful and peaceful that those attributes alone should draw guests from far and wide. However, as a businessman he knew that guests liked creature comforts. Beauty, yes, but comfort, ultimately. The ranch provided both. He was seriously thinking of making the Raynors an offer. But he would sleep on it. Tomorrow he would know for sure.

It started to snow on their descent.

At one point they had to go down a hill in a single line. And since it had begun to snow, the horses now had to step gingerly on the terrain. Brian went first, followed by Mitzi then Cherisse on a gentle pinto pony that Mitzi said was called Slowpoke for a reason, followed by Harry on a more spirited mount.

Slowpoke was almost at the bottom of the hill when a sound like a buzz saw split the air. All of the horses were startled, but the three more experienced riders instantly knew how to control them. A horse that is properly halter broken would not pull against pressure on his halter even when startled. Harry, Brian and Mitzi applied sufficient pressure to keep their horses from panicking. However Cherisse wasn't aware of this trick and did not. Slowpoke henceforth took off at a pace that belied his name.

Cherisse held on for dear life.

Harry took off after her, and Brian and Mitzi followed Harry.

The culprit behind the earsplitting nose, a teenaged boy riding a dirt bike, kept going, unaware of the chaos he'd caused. Slowpoke made a beeline for the pine forest and Harry yelled, "Cheri, duck!"

Cherisse did duck, but apparently not low enough because a low-hanging branch effectively unseated her and she wound up on her back on the pine-needle-covered forest floor looking up at the tips of the pines, in a world of pain. The air had been knocked out of her, but she soon began breathing again and knew that a lung hadn't been punctured by a sharp twig as she had at first imagined. She had managed to hang on to her hat, which she suspected helped her escape a concussion. Her head didn't hurt and her thinking wasn't fuzzy.

Harry reached her and quickly dismounted. Running to her side, he knelt beside her. By this time, Cherisse was trying to get up.

Putting a firm hand on her stomach, he said, "Don't move, darling."

"Nothing's broken," Cherisse said a bit breathlessly, up on her elbows.

Brian and Mitzi arrived and assessed the situation. "I'm going back to the lodge to phone 911. Cell phones don't work up here," Brian said. He galloped off on his horse.

Mitzi dismounted and knelt beside Cherisse. "Where does it hurt, Cherisse?"

"At the moment, my back and my ankle," Cherisse said. "But I don't think anything's broken. I can feel all of my extremities. My ankle might be sprained, but otherwise I'm okay."

Mitzi smiled at her and then smiled at Harry. "She's not talking out of her head, is she? How can she be sure nothing's broken? That was quite a fall."

"She's a nurse," Harry answered, concern written all over his face. He met Cherisse's eyes. "But in this instance, she's not going to diagnose herself. She's going to the hospital."

That's how Cherisse wound up in the emergency room of the Marcus Daly Memorial Hospital in the nearby town of Hamilton, Montana.

In all her years as a nurse she'd never ridden in an ambulance. It was a sobering experience, one she didn't want to repeat anytime soon. For one thing, looking up at someone from that awkward angle, seeing his nose hairs and other things lurking within was no fun.

Harry wanted to ride with her in the ambulance but was told it was against the rules. He took one of the ranch's vehicles and followed the ambulance to Hamilton and by the time he found a place to park, Cherisse had already been carted inside the emergency room and been put in a curtained-off examination room, where a nurse had come and taken her blood pressure and jotted down her various complaints. Now she lay on her back looking at the ceiling.

When Harry drew the curtain aside and strode in and she

saw his deeply furrowed brow she gave a short laugh. "Stop worrying about me, Harry. I'm fine. This isn't exactly my idea of a romantic weekend, though. And I hope Slowpoke didn't come to any harm, poor baby. He must have really been spooked to take off like that!"

Harry grabbed a tall stool that was sitting in the corner of the room and set it next to Cherisse's exam table. After sitting, he grasped her hand in his. "I'm sure Slowpoke knows the way home. How're you feeling?"

"I'll be sore in the morning, but I'm doing okay right now. My back and my ankle are a little sore but otherwise I feel fine."

"No one has examined you yet?" asked Harry, turning to glance at the entrance to the cubicle. "Maybe I ought to go light a fire under somebody."

Cherisse held on tightly to him. "See that?" she said, indicating her ability to hold on to him with such strength. "That means I don't have any nerve damage, which speaks well to my not having any damage to my spine. A nurse has been in. I'm waiting on the doctor. Stay with me, Harry, and tell me how gorgeous I am."

Harry laughed softly. Her hair was damp from melted snow but, resilient hair that it was, it hadn't lost its waves. But somewhere between the ranch and here she'd lost the black tie she'd used to put it in a ponytail. It was a loose halo about her head on the pillow now. He gently ran a finger along her jawline. "You're breathtaking."

"She's definitely a sight for sore eyes," said a male voice from the open curtain.

A dark-skinned man in his early thirties with black hair and brown eyes came into the exam room and shoved his hand into Harry's. "Dr. Mehta," he said in a British accented voice. "When they told me there was a black woman in exam room three I didn't believe them. I've been here for two years and I've never seen anyone who looks like me. I'm from India." He smiled, showing perfect white teeth in his brown face. "Hello, Ms. Washington."

Cherisse didn't know what to think about this gleeful human being's delight at seeing her and Harry. Shouldn't he be examining her? "Dr. Mehta," she acknowledged.

After his introduction he immediately dropped Harry's hand and turned his attention to Cherisse. "Fell off a horse, did you?" He examined her eyes with a penlight. "Looks good. How does your head feel?"

"No pain. I think my new Stetson protected it when I fell."

"Love those Stetsons," said Dr. Mehta cheerfully. "Although I recommend a helmet the next time you go riding."

"There won't be a next time," Harry said.

"Now, now, one must get back on the horse," admonished the good doctor. "Isn't that the old saying?" He put on his stethoscope. "Deep breaths, please, Ms. Washington."

Cherisse breathed deeply while he listened to her lungs and then her heart. She knew to remain silent while he was listening but as soon as he finished, she said, "Is it true, I'm the only black patient you've seen since you've been here?"

"Oh, yes, the population of black and brown people is practically zero in this area."

"Well, what kind of reception have you gotten?" Harry asked.

"Mostly the people are perfectly nice," said Dr. Mehta. "Although there was the incident of someone writing the 'N' word on my car with spray paint. And I haven't been able to get a date since I've been here."

Cherisse didn't know why that should be. He was a good-looking guy. Kind of reminded her of a Bollywood actor.

"I suppose Montana is still very remote," Cherisse said.

"It shouldn't be surprising that this area is predominately white, but I thought that at least ten percent of the people would be of other races."

Dr. Mehta laughed. "Yes, that's what I thought before coming here. America as a melting pot, you know? Then I got here and learned I was the only black bean in the pot."

"Gave you a shock, huh?" said Harry, warming up to the guy even though he was spending an inordinate amount of time holding Cherisse's hand when he wasn't even taking her pulse.

"I'm still in shock. I sometimes fly to New York City on weekends, where I have friends and relatives, just to get my perspective back." He once again gave all of his attention to his patient. "You complained about your right ankle hurting, as well?"

"Yes," said Cherisse.

Dr. Mehta went to the end of the examination table and gingerly removed Cherisse's boot and sock and then ran his hand all over her foot, gently twisting it this way and that way, making sure her ankle had normal range of motion. "Nothing's broken," he said after a few minutes of this. "But I do believe you have a minor sprain. I'll wrap in for you and prescribe a mild painkiller, unless you've got extra-strength Tylenol at home."

"I always carry a bottle in my purse," Cherisse said.

"Then you can use that," said Dr. Mehta. "When you get home, take a long hot bath, really soak. It may ward off some of the soreness you're going to have tomorrow, it may not. But it won't hurt. If you suddenly start having double vision, nausea, or a headache that won't go away, come back and see me. Your injuries may be more serious than I'm judging they are right now. But I truly don't believe you have anything to worry about."

The doctor was still holding Cherisse's foot in his hand as he delivered his diagnosis.

Harry cleared his throat. "You said something about wrapping her ankle."

"Ah, yes," said Dr. Mehta, smiling foolishly at Cherisse and gently putting her foot down on the exam table. Humming, he went to the supply cabinet located next to the sink in the nine-by-nine-foot room.

After he had all the supplies—Ace bandages, scissors and the metal clamps that would hold the Ace bandage together once he had it wrapped around Cherisse's ankle—he returned and began applying the bandage.

Harry stood aside with his arms akimbo, not cracking a smile. Cherisse turned her head to smile at him while Dr. Mehta was humming and wrapping her ankle.

Harry smiled back and his heart thudded in his chest. He blamed himself. He should never have let her get on that horse. Sure, she had insisted, saying that even though it had been years since she'd been on a horse, she wasn't a novice and was looking forward to the trail ride. Still, he should have shown more circumspection. It was okay to risk his own neck on a strange animal, but not hers!

When Dr. Mehta finished wrapping Cherisse's ankle he asked her to get off the table. He wanted to know if her ankle hurt when she put weight on it.

She did, and it did.

Harry saw her wince in pain, and yet, heard her say, "It's not so bad," as she hobbled around the exam room.

Dr. Mehta had obviously not been convinced, either, because he said, "What are you, a martyr? Sit down. And you're not walking out of here. You will get into a wheelchair. So don't give the nurse any problems when she comes for you. Stay off that ankle for at least twenty-four hours. Let your husband carry you. He's a big guy." With this he smiled nervously at Harry.

Harry picked Cherisse up and put her back on the exam table. "You heard the doctor." Then he offered Dr. Mehta his hand. "Thanks, Doctor."

Dr. Mehta heartily shook Harry's hand. Then he smiled at Cherisse. "It was a pleasure meeting you, Ms. Washington."

"And you, as well, Doctor," said Cherisse with a warm smile.

Dr. Mehta blushed and beat a hasty retreat.

In his absence, Harry said, "Now that you're done flirting with the doctor I want to say how sorry I am that I let you get on that horse."

Cherisse was in the process of trying to put her sock back on, but stopped to stare at Harry. Harry stepped forward and took over putting the sock on while she found the appropriate words with which to lash out at him, he was sure. Her lovely eyes were narrowed to slits, and she was breathing erratically, all signs she was irritated with him.

After Harry had put the sock on he gestured to her foot with the boot. "The sock was hard enough to get back on, forget the boot," she said. Then, she grabbed him and kissed him with all the passion she could muster. Harry thoroughly enjoyed that kiss.

That is until Cherisse pushed him away and said, "Harry Payne, you didn't *let* me get on Slowpoke, it was my choice! I've been taking responsibility for my own actions for quite some time now."

Harry started to say something and Cherisse cut him off with, "I don't want to hear anything else on the subject. My accident was my fault, not yours. I'm sure if I'd remembered what I'd been taught about controlling a spooked horse this never would have happened, but I panicked, Slowpoke panicked and here I am." She laughed. "I think they ought to rename him. Call him Speedy Gonzales or something more appropriate."

Shaking his head at her resilience, Harry laughed. He thought *she* ought to be renamed, something like Mrs. Harry Payne. He could get used to that. Of course, it was much too early to declare his love for her. Although love her, he did. He knew it with a clarity and a certainly that blew his mind. He was a man who did not believe in love at first sight, or second sight, or third, but he had known this woman would bring something special into his life the night he'd met her. At first he'd chalked it up to the moonlight and the fact that upon meeting Cheri he had been disappointed in Marcia.

A man would always grasp at the kindness of the next woman who came along when the present woman in his life mistreated him or proved herself inconsistent with his image of her. He thought that was why he considered Cheri his moonlight angel.

However when he had seen her again a week later, he had had to throw that theory out. She was in reality more wonderful than the imaginary moonlight angel because, really, he had had to attribute imagined personality traits to his angel. The real woman came with her own set of personality traits. Traits he had found extremely enticing.

Now, after learning more about her he knew he could spend the rest of his life getting to know her and would never learn enough. Isn't that what a marriage was, continually discovering your mate, day by day, year by year?

How long did it take to choose a mate? Harry was a pragmatist. He made business decisions based on possibilities. It was always a gamble. He might have crashed when he'd invested in Karibu nearly six years ago. But he'd taken the risk and the resort was a resounding success. So much so that he was able to consider buying another property.

Not that loving Cherisse had anything to do with business. The woman, most of all, made him itch in a profoundly sexual way. Okay, so he had known many women who turned him on, just not to this extent. It was as if the two of them were meant to be, that's how strong the attraction was. He could no more ignore it than he could ignore the fact that his hands were attached to his wrists. It just *was*.

Was he excited by this revelation? Yes! Would he let Cherisse in on it? Not anytime soon. She was a woman who took things by degrees. She was swept off her feet by Charlie Washington when she was eighteen. Would she ever let herself be swept off her feet again by any man, no matter how charming? Not hardly.

Harry had to bide his time.

He laughed when Cherisse suddenly shook him and cried, "Harry, why are you staring at me like that?"

"I just think you're the cutest invalid I've ever seen," Harry told her, and kissed her forehead.

A nurse, a petite brunette in her late forties, interrupted whatever response Cherisse had on her tongue. She bustled into the exam room pushing a wheelchair and talking rapidly. "Your chariot awaits, my dear. Dr. Mehta told me to take good care of you."

"Allow me," Harry said and effortlessly lifted Cherisse and put her into the wheelchair.

"My, he's handy to have around, isn't he?" said the nurse with a flirtatious wink at Harry. Cherisse smiled up at her. "He's good to look at, too."

Harry walked behind them, Cherisse's boot grasped in his hand, a smile on his lips and a bounce in his step. Now he knew what his happily married buddies knew. You can love one woman forever. Love her, and revel in it.

"What's your opinion of the property so far?" Cherisse asked Harry on the drive back to Ponderosa Pines Ranch. She was wondering if he were thinking the same thing she was—that no matter how wonderful the resort was it wouldn't matter if blacks felt unwelcome in the area.

Harry briefly smiled at her before returning his attention to the road. "I like it. But I don't know if I want a resort that's this remote. The guests I've come to know like to explore the surrounding area. I don't know if I want to integrate this area. I'm a businessman, not a civil rights leader. I know that may sound selfish but that's how I feel."

"It doesn't sound selfish, Harry. It sounds reasonable. This is 2008 for goodness' sake. I'm also tired of fighting battles with ignorant people. There are other properties around the world where the racial climate is friendlier. On the other hand, you can't base your opinion on one man's comments."

Harry smiled. "Did you see any other black folks in the hospital?"

"No."

"Did you notice any on the streets of Hamilton before we got out of town?"

"No."

"I'll speak plainly with Brian and Mitzi when we get back," Harry said. "If they confirm what Dr. Mehta said then I'll have to pass. But that conversation can wait until the morning. The rest of the evening will be devoted to taking care of you."

Remembering Dr. Mehta's suggestion that she soak in a tub to ward off future soreness, Cherisse glanced over at Harry. "You're not giving me a bath!"

"Doctor's orders," Harry said with a lascivious grin in her direction.

Cherisse laughed. "I don't care if they were God's orders."

About an hour later, however, she had to eat those words. She had gotten into the tub with very little trouble, hobbling about the bathroom, trying to keep her weight off her right foot.

When she tried to get out of the deep tub, she wasn't so successful. Every time she reached for the handle and pulled herself forward, she wasn't able to get traction because she was right-handed, and the handle was on the left side. After several awkward attempts she wound up calling Harry.

Harry came to the bathroom door. "Yes, darling girl?"

Did he sound smug, or was that her imagination?

"I can't get out of the tub. You're going to have to help me," she said too softly.

"What was that, sweetheart?"

"I've fallen and I can't get up!" Cherisse yelled.

Harry was through the door in an instant.

Cherisse covered her breasts with her hands as best she could. The suds provided cover for her lower half. "Okay, I didn't really fall. But I do need your help getting out of this death trap."

Her breath caught in her throat when she saw the expression in Harry's eyes. She knew she was in good shape but she also knew she was no ravishing beauty. Maybe ten years ago she could have competed with some of the women Harry Payne was used to seeing naked, but not now.

So, why was he standing there like an idiot when she needed help getting out of this tub! "Harry, please, the water's getting cold."

Harry grabbed the smallest towel on the shelf. "Will this do?"

Now she knew he was not as clueless as she had assumed. He was *messing* with her!

Cherisse pursed her lips. There wasn't a Patterson woman on earth who couldn't outsmart the male animal.

"Forget the towel for now," she said. "Just pick me up and put me on my feet, I'll do the rest."

Harry contemplated her request. In order to fulfill it, he

would have to touch her naked body. She would have to put her arms around his neck and he would have the full-length of her in his arms. It was all to his advantage. Pretty much like winning the lottery, intimacy-wise. Short of making love to her, that is.

"All right," he said, sounding unsure of himself.

"And keep your eyes closed the whole time," Cherisse added.

Harry didn't like that clause but didn't protest. He was going to hold her in his arms naked. A man couldn't afford to be greedy with a woman like Cheri.

Harry complied. Eyes shut, he bent down and had to rely on Cherisse to position him so that she could put her arms around his neck. He then slipped his left arm about her waist and his right underneath her thighs and lifted her from the tub.

She smelled wonderful and her wet body was warm and firm, but soft, in his grasp.

Cherisse's face was pressed against his, and he inhaled her sweet breath. He stood quite still with her in his arms. Then he gently set her feet on the warm tiles of the bathroom floor. Cherisse sensually slid down his body. His hands were now supporting her bottom as she got her footing.

Harry grew hard instantly and Cherisse could feel him through his jeans. He was not the only one who'd become aroused. Her nipples were distended and she was quite moist between her legs and it wasn't from the bathwater.

Harry kept his word and kept his eyes closed. Cherisse, however, could look at him as much as she pleased, and the sight was hugely satisfying. She loved the way his lips curved, the way his lashes curled, that dimple in his chin. She wanted to kiss his face all over. She wanted to taste him, and spend the night discovering every inch of him.

"May I kiss you, Harry?" she asked softly.

"If you do, I'll embarrass myself by coming," Harry groaned.

She knew by the solid feel of him on her thigh, he wasn't lying. "Okay, I won't," she breathed against his mouth. "Just release me and leave."

Oh, what the hell, Harry thought, *I'm already wet anyway.* And he turned his mouth a fraction of an inch. Cherisse sighed helplessly against his mouth and gave herself to him.

Lips were tasted and parted, and tongues eagerly danced against one another and delved into the sweet nectar that was their mouths. No matter how many times Harry kissed her he always found something new to enjoy about her sweet mouth. This time it was the fact that she could suck his tongue in such a sensual manner that it made him feel as though she were actually tonguing him elsewhere. He grew so hard his erection was becoming painful.

He really was about to climax, standing there kissing her on the bathroom floor.

Somehow, he found the strength to break off the kiss, and set her away from him.

However, in the confusion, he forgot to keep his eyes closed and he saw her in all her glorious nakedness. Full, gorgeous breasts, tips pointing north and as hard as he was at that moment, a slim, tapered waist and flat stomach with a lovely belly button, shapely hips, arms, muscular legs and thighs, dark curly hair between her legs and an ass that he wanted to bite.

He could not stop devouring her with his eyes.

Suddenly, though, it finally dawned on his sex-crazed brain that they had agreed on separate rooms and even if she did change her mind, it was a woman's prerogative, he had not brought any condoms with him on the trip so that he would not be tempted.

"I'm sorry, I got carried away," he said, looking into her eyes. "I'll leave now."

Cherisse smiled and said, "We're both adults. We're not going to let a little thing like nudity spoil our chaste weekend, are we?"

Harry didn't know whether she was serious or not, but he knew he had to get out of there or he was going to literally explode in his pants.

"I'll be taking a cold shower if you need me," he said hoarsely and stumbled out of the bathroom.

Cherisse reached for a towel and began drying herself off with it.

A few minutes later both she and Harry were dressed in their pajamas and robes and sitting down to the meal they had ordered from room service. Harry had insisted on their staying in tonight even though Cherisse had declared that she felt up to going to the lodge's four-star restaurant for dinner.

They had ordered simple meals of baked chicken for her and fried trout, a local favorite, for Harry. They enjoyed garden salads and freshly baked dinner rolls with it. Cherisse passed on the wine because she had taken several Tylenols since her return from the hospital. Harry had a glass of white wine, thinking it would help him sleep with Cherisse only a few feet away from him.

After dinner, they curled up on the white leather couch in the living room and watched an old movie. Cherisse fell asleep in Harry's arms and he carried her to her bed, where she woke up long enough to put her arms around his neck and murmur, "Lie down with me, Harry."

He did, and they fell asleep in each other's arms.

At around 2:00 a.m. Harry awoke and found Cherisse pressed firmly against his body as if she had been sleeping with him for years.

He found the sensation it gave him an entirely pleasant one and he bent to place a chaste kiss on her lips. Cherisse moaned softly and opened her mouth to let him in and soon they were kissing just as urgently as they had earlier.

"Cheri, darling, we can't do this."

"Why not, we're both single and way over the age of consent?"

"Unless you want to get pregnant with my child in the next few minutes, you'll let me get the hell out of here. I don't have any condoms. I didn't bring any because we agreed on separate rooms, remember?"

"Yeah, but I was open to being seduced."

Harry laughed softly. "Then you might have shared that bit of information with *me*."

Cherisse sighed and opened her eyes all the way, sleep now gone from their depths.

"Am I a loose woman because I want to make love to you? It's harder for a woman to make that decision, especially a woman with a child. I have to set an example."

"I think you've set a fine example," Harry told her. "Six years of celibacy."

"Yes, but I wasn't tempted by anyone during those six years. I'm tempted now and I'm failing miserably. I want you so much, Harry. You can't imagine how much."

Harry put her hand on him. "Can't I?"

Cherisse pushed out of his arms. "All right, go to your room, Harry. And tomorrow we'll go back home, both of us unsatisfied. And I'll keep my status as Mother Teresa. Did I tell you some of the other nurses call me that?"

Harry kissed her on the forehead. "You're breaking my heart." He got out of bed.

Looking down at her, he warned, "Next time, it's on!"

Cherisse covered her face with her pillow. "I can't watch you leave."

Chapter 13

"I was wondering when you were going to ask about that," Brian said over breakfast the next morning. Harry had asked him if Ponderosa Pines Ranch's clientele consisted mostly of whites or if other races figured in the numbers and had told him and Mitzi about his and Cherisse's encounter with Dr. Mehta.

"I want to be certain that all of our guests will feel comfortable visiting this part of the country," Harry said.

Brian, who was sitting beside Mitzi, nodded calmly. "Yes, and it's an understandable concern. To be perfectly honest, Mitzi and I would never think of excluding anyone based on the color of their skin but the fact is we have never had guests of any other race here." He laughed nervously. "Whether this area is predominately white because the folks around here are unfriendly toward people who don't look like them, we don't know. Mitzi and I never questioned it because, well, I guess because we're white. I'm sure Dr. Mehta had a different perspective on the situation."

"This poses a problem," said Harry. "We all know that a resort can't exist in a bubble. Guests like to explore the surrounding area when they come to a resort, to go shopping at local stores, or eat away from the resort in local restaurants or take in a movie. Would blacks be welcome? From what you've just said, I don't think so. I like Ponderosa Pines Ranch. I think you two have done a wonderful job on it but I'm sorry, Brian, Mitzi, I'm going to have to pass on your offer."

"We're sorry, too, Harry," Brian said honestly. "Mitzi and I like you and Cherisse. We were hoping the ranch would go to a couple like you, someone we felt would look after it the way we want it to be looked after. But I understand your point of view."

He and Harry stood and shook hands. "You won't want for buyers for long, Brian. This place is too great. In fact, Ernest Hallowell is looking for a small outfit in the west, something he can turn into a couples-only resort. You might want to make your pitch to him."

Brian brightened. "I had no idea he was in the market for something small," he said. "He owns resorts all over the world."

"Yes, but he's never satisfied," Harry said. "The Montana wilderness may be just what he's looking for. Good luck."

"Thank you, Harry."

Cherisse and Mitzi also rose and hugged briefly. "Wonderful to have met you, Mitzi," Cherisse said with warmth.

"Same here, Cherisse," Mitzi said with a grin. "Now, remember, next time a horse goes nuts on you…"

"Put pressure on his halter," Cherisse finished, to which everyone laughed good-naturedly.

Half an hour later, she and Harry were en route to the Missoula airport with Jake Hanks at the wheel of the SUV they were passengers in.

A few hours after that they touched down in Denver, Harry drove her home, carried her luggage inside and deposited it in the foyer where Jo, Danielle and Charlie were waiting to welcome her home.

Harry got a strange feeling watching Cherisse's little family hugging her hello as if she had been gone a month instead of overnight. Being hundreds of miles from his family in Kentucky, he didn't enjoy that kind of closeness.

This was the first time he'd met her mother, Joann, and he saw the resemblance to Cheri in a second—same cheekbones, overall beauty, undoubtedly the same strength of character if he could judge by the unwavering manner in which she was regarding him.

"So you're Harry Payne," she said. "You know in the fourth quarter of your last Super Bowl game, you should have passed to Kenji Burns. You missed that call."

It wasn't the first time Harry had heard that complaint from a fan. He was surprised he was hearing it from Cherisse's mother though. He smiled. "I've regretted it ever since."

Jo threw her head back in laughter and took him by the arm. "You're staying for dinner!" And she started giving orders. "Danielle, take your mother's luggage to her room. Cheri, I'll need help in the kitchen. You men can make yourselves scarce for a few minutes while we get the meal on the table."

Charlie was glad for the opportunity to get Harry alone.

While the women went off to various tasks, he put his arm about Harry's shoulders and said, "Come on, old buddy, I'd like to hear all about your trip to Montana, mainly about the sleeping arrangements."

"Charlie, behave yourself," Cherisse called from the hallway.

In the family room, Charlie muted the TV and turned to Harry, who had taken a seat on an overstuffed chair next to the door. "Well?" he asked expectantly.

"Well, what?" asked Harry.

"Did you, or didn't you?"

"Did I what?"

"Oh, is that how you're going to play it?" asked Charlie, smiling pleasantly. "Did she *sleep* with you? Because if she did I know she's gone on you and I don't have a chance but if she didn't, I'm still in the running."

"As I understand it you were never in the running," Harry stated.

"She's just saying that to get under my skin," Charlie blustered.

"Is it working?" asked Harry.

"You look smug now," said Charlie. "But I have an advantage you don't—I'm the father of her child."

Harry wanted to say "And I'm the father of her future children." He managed to restrain himself. Instead he said, "She's a great kid."

Charlie softened. "Yeah, thanks. And thanks for sponsoring her, by the way. I don't think I'd thanked you."

"No need for thanks," said Harry. After a short lull in the conversation, he asked, "Having any luck finding a place to stay?"

Charlie shook his head in the negative. "What are you afraid of—that I'm beating your time with Cheri when you're not around?"

"No, I just don't like seeing my woman irritated on a daily basis, and you're the main source of her irritation. She gets enough stress on her job. Why don't you go stay at the resort until you find a permanent place? It would be quite a commute but if you got up early enough it might work."

Charlie laughed shortly. "I must be making you nervous."

"Oh, yeah, I forgot," said Harry, "your reason for staying here is to spend more time with Danielle. Staying at the resort would defeat that purpose."

"Sarcasm won't get you anywhere," said Charlie.

Both men laughed.

"You know," said Harry, "you're an okay guy, someone I wouldn't mind being friends with if only for one thing."

"I'm trying to steal your woman?" Charlie said with a smile.

"It puts a damper on the whole friendship thing," Harry admitted.

Charlie's expression suddenly darkened. "I've got to ask you something and I would appreciate it if you would be honest and straightforward with me. I haven't beaten around the bush with you, I've told you I want Cheri back so I'm not going behind your back or anything. I'm asking you to respect me in the same way. Are you going to tell her about that night in Philly?"

Harry was afraid this subject would rear its ugly head before long. "I have no intention of mentioning it, no."

"Are you for real? Not even if I'm beating your ass when it comes to winning Cheri back? You won't use it as a trump card?"

"Neither of us should have been at a party where there were hookers," Harry said. "I would be embarrassed to tell Cheri I was there, let alone that her husband had been. Plus, I left, remember? I have no idea what you got up to after that."

"Nothing, man, I never cheated on Cheri. I was there for the gambling, that's all."

"Whatever you say," Harry joked. "But the last time I saw you a leggy blonde had her tongue in your ear."

Charlie shuddered, remembering that night. Too bad he

wasn't a drunk as well as a gambler back then. At least that memory would have dissolved in an alcoholic haze.

He remembered everything.

"One of the worst experiences I've ever had," he said.

"Coming in," Cherisse announced as she strode into the room carrying a tray of raw vegetables and dip. "Stop talking about me."

She set the tray on the coffee table in front of Harry then she bent and kissed him on the cheek. "In case you want an appetizer," she said solicitously. After which she turned to leave the room.

"Where's *my* kiss?" Charlie called to her retreating back.

"Get your own girl, Charlie Washington," she replied.

"She loves me, she just doesn't know it," Charlie said to Harry.

"Here's to her never finding out," Harry said as he picked up a carrot stick, dipped it into the sour cream concoction on the tray and ate it. "Delicious."

That day was the first of many such days that Harry was welcomed into Cherisse's family, which included her ex. As December raced to a close, Harry wanted more and more for his family to meet Cherisse. His love for her grew with each passing day and with it the desire to ask her to marry him. He resisted that impulse, though, because he still wasn't certain Cherisse would take him seriously.

Seeing her with Charlie convinced him that she didn't take relationships lightly. He realized that she was still fond of Charlie and probably always would be. But Charlie had let her and Danielle down and she couldn't totally forgive him for that.

When Harry asked her to marry him he didn't want her to be able to raise any objections. So no proposal for a while yet, but that didn't mean he couldn't set up a meeting between her and his family.

On a Sunday morning in mid-December, he placed a call to his mother in Louisville, Kentucky. It was after eleven and he knew she should be home from church by now. She went to the eight o'clock service.

Sure enough, Mildred answered on the third ring. "Hello?"

"Good morning," said Harry.

His mother screamed in his ear. "Harry! I was just thinking about you. Maris Stephens tried to get me to sell her my wedlock quilt today and I told her I was saving that quilt for you and your wife. The woman actually laughed in my face, Harry. She said you were never going to get married. I'd just as well sell her the quilt. I tell you, after today, she'll get that quilt over my dead body! Even if you never get married! How is Cherisse?"

"She's beautiful," said Harry, wondering if his mother had taken a breath yet.

"Oh, Harry, the sound of your voice when you talk about her, you're really in love this time!" said his mother excitedly.

"Yes, I'm really in love," Harry told her. "And I want you to meet her. I want all of you to meet her. Come here for Christmas, I'll pay for everything. My house in Denver will finally have a family in it."

"I'd love to," Mildred immediately accepted. "Let me get with Susanne and I'll get back to you. Traveling over the holidays can be a hassle. We'd better make arrangements as soon as possible, so I should get on the horn with Suse right now. Call you back, Harry."

"Oh, Mom?" said Harry.

"Yeah, baby?" intoned Mildred.

"Bring that quilt with you. Or ship it to me ahead of time. I want to give it to Cherisse as a Christmas gift."

"I would be honored," said Mildred, sounding close to tears.

"Thank you, Mom. I love you."

"I love you, too, baby," Mildred said. *Yes,* Harry thought, before he hung up, *she's crying.* Harry smiled and got up from his desk in the study of his suite at Karibu.

Last night he'd taken Cherisse and Danielle to dinner and then to a performance of *The Nutcracker* at the Denver Performing Arts Center. He had enjoyed himself. Danielle had shown him a great deal of attention, which made Harry envious of Charlie. One day he wanted a daughter as wonderful as she was.

He and Cherisse now regretted not consummating their relationship while they had been alone in Montana since in the past week they had not been able to steal any alone time.

He missed her so much when they were apart that he had her photograph as a screensaver on his PC. Plus a photo of her on his nightstand so that her face would be the last one he saw before falling asleep.

They tried to keep their daily phone calls down to two a day, whenever the desire to hear the other's voice became too overpowering to ignore, which to him came much more often than twice a day but he was Harry Payne and he had a reputation to uphold!

Luckily, he was not going to have to wait until Saturday night to see her again. He was taking her to the red-and-white ball, a fund-raiser held by the Denver Business Association to raise money for disadvantaged children in the city of Denver, this Friday, December 19. White tie and tails for the men and either a red or a white evening gown for the women. He couldn't wait to see Cherisse in her gown.

He had reserved a suite for them at Hotel Teatro, one of Denver's most intimate and luxurious boutique hotels. It was across the street from the Denver Performing Arts Center where the ball was to be held. In fact, if memory served, that was how the hotel had gotten its name. Back in the day it had been the hub of the Denver theater crowd.

Cherisse was happy that her workweek had been so busy that she hadn't had time to fret about the red-and-white ball. The only affair she'd ever been to at which she had worn a gown had been her wedding to Charlie. And then the gown had been borrowed. It had belonged to her mother. For the red-and-white ball she and Sonia had combed Denver looking for just the right dress. She had spent way too much money on it and Sonia had advised her to save the price tag because she knew how to reattach that sucker so they could return the dress on Monday morning.

Cherisse had looked down at the price tag and had been sorely tempted.

What if Harry took one look at her and realized what a poseur she was? She wasn't the type of woman you took to posh balls. She was the type of woman you took to a rodeo, or to the company Christmas party. They were more her speed. What was she going to say to the mayor? Her mother, now, her mother could chat with the mayor and tell him when he got gravy on his tie and advise him to chew with his mouth closed. Her mother was no respecter of persons. She didn't care who you were, she felt perfectly comfortable in your presence. Cherisse wished some of her mother's nerve had rubbed off on her.

Then, suddenly she remembered that she'd done fine in Montana. Of course Brian and Mitzi Raynor had been down-to-earth people who made her feel at ease.

"Cheri, you go clean up, I'll finish here," Gerald told her. "Chill out, girl, things are looking up. Although Pedersen might think it's a bad thing, patient numbers are at an all-time low in pediatrics. That's good news."

"Thanks, Gerry," Cherisse said and went into the adjacent bathroom to remove her shoes and place them in a white trash bag. Her ruined shoes in the bag, she left the patient's room and went to the lounge.

In the lounge Cherisse dropped the shoes into the trash receptacle designated for noncontagious refuse and then went and changed.

She was about to leave the lounge after putting on her spare Nikes when David Pedersen strode into the room. She hadn't seen him since Monday. He had other nurses on other floors to harass, after all.

"David," she said, "what brings you here? The coffee in your office isn't as good as ours?" She nodded in the direction of the coffeemaker. She was leaving in about twenty minutes in order to race across town to start getting ready for the ball. All of a sudden she felt like Cinderella. And here was her mean old stepmother, David Pedersen, about to spoil her day.

"It's about Mary Thomas," he said. "What's going on with her? We can't afford to continue paying her salary if she's on a drinking binge we're footing the bill for."

Cherisse got great satisfaction in saying, "I hate to disappoint you, David, but Mary is doing great! She's going to AA every day. She hasn't touched liquor in weeks. She will be returning to work on Monday."

David sniffed derisively and turned on his heels. "Probably won't last," he said in parting.

Cherisse saw red. She went and grabbed him by the arm, forcing him to look at her. "Why can't you be happy for Mary? That she's trying to pull herself together? Do you get some kind of sick satisfaction in watching people fail? What is it with you, David?"

With a pinched expression on his face, and his wiry gray hair practically standing on end, Pedersen fairly vibrated with pent-up tension. "Nobody ever gave me a break, and I made it. I don't truck with coddling people. I heard what you did, getting the police to go to her house and rescue her from her druggie daughter. You had no right to interfere in her life. She works for you, she isn't your friend!"

"She works for me, *and* she's my friend," Cherisse corrected him. "The two aren't mutually exclusive except in your case. I work for you but I'm definitely not your friend."

David Pedersen walked off in a huff.

Cherisse sighed and rolled her eyes. He was never going to change so she would do well not to waste any brain cells thinking about him. She went to her office to finish up a little paperwork before she left for the day.

Arriving at the ball felt like a night at the Oscars. The red carpet had been rolled out and the moment Harry pulled the car to a stop, someone was there to take his car keys, and someone else to open the door for Cherisse and hand her out.

As they made their way up the carpet, Cherisse in a red strapless ankle-length gown and Harry in a white tuxedo, newspaper photographers and cameramen from the local TV stations took pictures and filmed them. Harry flashed his signature smile.

It was obvious to Cherisse that the media adored him. She smiled lovingly up at him, realizing that in his presence she wasn't as nervous as she thought she would be.

"Hey, Harry, who's the doll on your arm?" called a reporter.

"This is Cherisse Washington," Harry called back. "Two *S*'s in Cherisse, get her name right, Ben."

The reporter named Ben laughed. "Okay, Harry, you

don't have to remind me that I spelled your last name wrong a few times."

They walked on amid flashing lights until they reached the entrance, where a uniformed doorman ushered them inside and said, "Good evening, Mr. Payne, miss, welcome to the red-and-white ball."

"Thank you," said Harry and allowed Cherisse to precede him.

Upon entering the ballroom, Cherisse unconsciously held her breath. The huge crystal chandelier dominated the high-ceilinged room. The marble floor gleamed, making the expensively dressed revelers look as if they were walking, or dancing in some cases, on water. She and Harry stood at the top of the stairs. They would have to descend a long flight of stairs to get to the dance floor.

"May I present, Mr. Harrison Payne and Ms. Cherisse Washington," announced an elderly gentleman in white tie and tails, his booming voice resounding against the walls of the cavernous space.

She and Harry slowly descended the stairs and were at once set upon by a couple of Harry's old teammates with their wives. Cherisse was introduced all around, and then Harry said, "Good to see you, guys, but I came here to hold Cherisse in my arms, not to talk about the good old days." He said it in such a way that it elicited chuckles from his old friends. "After all," Harry added, "you two have been happily married for years. I'm still trying to achieve that blissful state."

"Poor Harry," said one of his ex-teammates, smiling. "Cherisse, put him out of his misery and marry him."

"Yes!" exclaimed one of the wives. "And don't forget to invite us to the wedding because *this* we've got to see!"

Harry pulled Cherisse close to his side. "Don't rush her.

I'm sure she'll propose when the time's right." And he smiled into her upturned face.

Cherisse laughed softly and directed her comment to the woman who'd asked for an invitation to the wedding. "Yes. Maybe tonight if he's a good boy."

With that she and Harry melted into the crowd.

The orchestra was playing "You Send Me," and the singer, a young attractive African-American guy with short, neat dreadlocks was doing a pretty good imitation of the soul legend Sam Cooke.

After checking their coats, Harry pulled Cherisse onto the dance floor and took her into his arms. Harry sighed with satisfaction. "Thank you for this."

Cherisse smiled up into his eyes. "For what?" she asked softly.

"You're my fantasy come to life in that dress. I just want to take you somewhere and take it off you and make love to you all night long."

"I'm glad you like it," she said. "But let's dance a while first and then go rip each other's clothes off. We did get dressed up."

The orchestra launched into another Sam Cooke song, "Bring It On Home To Me."

"Are they doing a tribute to Sam Cooke or something?" Cherisse said. "That's the second song of his they've done since we've been here."

"What do you know about Sam Cooke?" asked Harry with a teasing smile. "You're too young to know his music."

"Get real," said Cherisse. "I have several Cooke CDs. I know lots of his songs."

She began singing in Harry's ear. Harry couldn't believe it. She had a deep, sexy tone to her voice that had an immediate effect on his…well, he was getting turned on standing there with her voice in his ear.

She sang the entire song and at the end, Harry was ready to sweep her into his arms and carry her out of the ballroom with the entire assemblage watching, knowing exactly where he was going with her and why.

Cherisse innocently smiled up at him at the song's conclusion and said, "Not bad, huh?"

Harry pressed her lower body a little closer to his. She gasped. "Oh, Harry, I'm sorry, I had no idea!"

Harry laughed softly. "Just don't sing anymore and I'll be okay."

Cherisse batted her eyes at him. "Okay, no more singing until I get you alone."

Harry was looking up at the entrance. "What the hell?"

Cherisse followed his line of sight. Marcia Shaw had arrived with a short white guy on her arm. Cherisse could guess why Harry had reacted with surprise. Marcia had made a big deal about her and LaShaun Gregory getting back together and she hadn't arrived at the social event of the year with him on her arm. That could mean only one thing—they had broken up again.

"I guess it didn't work out between her and LaShaun," Cherisse commented without rancor. She had no reason to dislike Marcia Shaw. In fact, she owed her a debt of gratitude: she'd broken up with Harry.

"That guy she's with is the station manager," Harry said. "Nice guy, but definitely not her type."

"We're just speculating," Cherisse said. "Maybe LaShaun was sick tonight and that's why he's not here with her."

That theory was blown out of the water when, fifteen minutes later, LaShaun strode into the ballroom with a curvaceous sister on his arm in a dress so tight it looked like her breasts were going to break free at any minute.

Cherisse suddenly felt sorry for Marcia Shaw. She bet

practically everybody who read the gossip columns knew that she and LaShaun *were* a couple. Now, to have been reduced to attending the ball with her station manager while LaShaun had walked in with someone who looked like a Playboy bunny!

"Okay," Cherisse said when LaShaun and his date were descending the stairs to the dance floor. "You were right. He isn't at home nursing a cold."

Harry bent and rubbed his face against hers. "Forget about them. This is our night."

And Cherisse did just that, dancing with Harry for a good forty minutes to song after song from Sam Cooke's catalog of hits. Harry was a great dancer, he could move smoothly from a fox-trot to a waltz to the jive with ease. They matched each other in ability and stamina. What's more there was such joie de vivre in their dancing that it gave pleasure to those who watched them, as evidenced by the applause from their fellow ball-goers when they got down and dirty to "Twistin' the Night Away."

They danced the jive to that one, Harry tossing Cherisse over his back as she landed on her feet and came back up twisting sexily and then Harry twirling her around the dance floor on the balls of her sling-backs. It was heavenly, and so smooth, it felt dreamlike in its perfection. She was sure she would never forget this night.

After "Twistin' the Night Away" they agreed that they were in need of liquid refreshment so Harry went off to order them drinks at the bar and await her return from the ladies room.

As always at functions this large there was a line in front of the ladies' room. Cherisse got in line behind several other women in either red or white gowns. She had been standing there a couple of minutes when someone tapped her on the shoulder.

She turned to find Marcia Shaw smiling at her. Marcia wore a white Grecian-style gown and her hair was done up in a French twist. "We meet again," she said, smiling at Cherisse. "Or to put it more correctly, we meet for the first time. I'm Marcia Shaw."

She offered Cherisse her hand. Cherisse took it. "Cherisse Washington. I've watched your newscast, you're very good."

Marcia's smile got broader. "Thank you." She wiped the smile off her face. "I wanted to apologize for that catty remark of a few weeks ago. I'm sorry. Your hair is lovely, really. I was just in a rotten mood. When your life is in turmoil you tend to lash out at those you think are having a better time of it. I guess Harry told you about me and LaShaun."

"He expressed concern that you aren't together tonight," Cherisse admitted.

"It's sad," Marcia said with a sigh. "You know how you can put so much faith in something that it blinds you to the truth? That's how I was with LaShaun. I bent over backward to be with him. I dealt dirty with Harry because I wanted him back so badly. Then two weeks after we got together again I caught him in bed with the woman he brought to the ball tonight. I feel like a fool. But, you know what? I learned a valuable lesson. You have to always deal with people in a fair and honest way or else it comes back to bite you in the ass." She laughed shortly. "I can't believe I'm spilling my guts to Harry's new girlfriend. You must think I'm nuts."

Cherisse laughed, too. "No, I think you're very human. And I like you, Marcia Shaw."

Marcia smiled warmly. "I like you, too."

Soon, they were in the restroom and went into separate

stalls. When they came out they stood side by side at the sinks, washing up and checking their makeup.

"Tell Harry I'm okay," Marcia said as she reapplied her lipstick. "I know he's wondering. That's just the kind of guy he is, one of the good ones." Their eyes met in the mirror. "Tell him I'm happy he met you."

With that she left the restroom.

Cherisse went to join Harry at the bar and found him surrounded by several male football fans, who were recounting some of the stories from his career in the game.

Harry solicitously helped her onto the stool beside him. "I ordered you a chilled white wine, is that okay?"

"Yes, thank you," she said shyly. She took a sip of her wine.

Harry turned to the football fans. "Gentlemen, if you don't mind, my date is back and I much prefer looking at her beautiful face than your mugs."

The men laughed and good-naturedly patted Harry on the back and returned to their end of the bar.

Cherisse smiled at him. He certainly had a way with people.

Harry bent close and kissed her fragrant cheek. "Are you enjoying yourself?"

Cherisse turned to meet his gaze. His eyes held an amused glint in them, which promised future mischief, no doubt. She wondered what kind of mischief they could be getting into in that suite he'd reserved at Hotel Teatro.

"Immensely," she told him. "I just had a chat with Marcia in the line for the ladies' room. She told me to tell you she's doing okay after her breakup with LaShaun and she's glad you met me."

Harry looked fleetingly surprised. Then he smiled. "I'm glad I met you, too. In fact, I've never been happier." He looked deeply in her eyes. "I wish I'd met you ten years ago. I wish I'd known you when you were a girl. I bet you were cute."

"My hair was even more unruly than it is now and I was fat," Cherisse said. "I didn't lose my baby fat until I was thirteen and I joined the track team, played baseball for a couple of seasons and finally settled on basketball. Discovering sports saved me."

Harry laughed softly. "I don't care if you were fat, you were probably adorable." And he bent to kiss her mouth. She tasted of the wine she had just sipped. He tasted of the Rémy Martin he'd had in her absence. But they both tasted unbearably sweet to each other.

"I think I'm falling for you, Harry," Cherisse told him in all earnestness when they parted. "With a very small push I could fall all the way."

Harry's heart thudded. Excitement suffused him and he got off his stool and lifted her off hers. Setting her on her feet, he said, "Well, then, darlin', let's blow this joint and I will give you all the pushing you need."

Cherisse grinned. She liked the sound of that. They didn't waste time going to collect their coats and rushing out into the cold night. The only holdup was the seven minutes they spent out front waiting for Harry's car to be brought around.

Once on the road, Harry had only to drive across the street to 1100 Fourteenth Street.

They were at their destination in only a few minutes. Once again the valet service took charge of the car but this time Harry hurried around to help Cherisse out. He got the pleasure of looking at her long legs unfolding from the confines of the luxury car.

The doorman bowed. "Welcome to the Hotel Teatro, sir, madam. I hope you'll enjoy your stay."

Harry said a hasty thank-you and soon he and Cherisse

were standing at the desk while a very friendly woman quickly checked his reservations and announced, "Yes, Mr. Payne, your suite is ready and our concierge service has supplied everything you asked for and it is all waiting in your suite." She handed him two key cards. "Enjoy your evening."

Harry snatched the key cards. "Thank you!"

On the walk across the lobby to the bank of elevators, he handed Cherisse one of the key cards. She slipped it into her clutch. Harry pulled her close to his side as they waited for the elevator to arrive. "Do I appear eager?" He smiled down at her.

Cherisse was excited herself. "No more than I do, no doubt. I'm nervous, Harry."

Harry embraced her, and that's how they were standing when the elevator doors opened and perhaps five people exited the conveyance. She and Harry stepped inside, the only people getting on at that moment.

Harry pulled her into his arms as the doors closed. "Why should you be nervous? I'm the one. You haven't seen me naked yet. I've seen you in all your glory, remember?"

Cherisse blushed. "Oh, yes, how could I forget it?"

Harry grinned. "I definitely haven't. I've had some very nice dreams about you since then."

"Oh, no, *dreams*. How will I ever compare to your dreams?" Cherisse playfully lamented.

"Shut up and kiss me, woman," Harry said.

Chapter 14

They stepped onto an Indonesian flagstone foyer as they went into the suite. Harry secured the door behind them and immediately began to help Cherisse out of her coat.

He bent to kiss the side of her neck as he did so, and Cherisse turned out of the coat, leaving him holding it in his hands. "A little trick I learned when I was in high school and the boys tried to steal a kiss while helping me off with my coat," she said with a mischievous glint in her eyes.

Harry hung her coat on the convenient hall tree next to the door and she walked up to him and placed both hands on his chest, slid them outward and around, helping him off with his coat. She took it and hung it on the hall tree.

Then she tiptoed and kissed him, taking her sweet time and relishing him. She ended by taking his lower lip between her lips and gently sucking on it. "You taste good."

Reaching up to remove his bow tie, she said, "Since you've

already seen me naked, I think it's only fair that your clothes should come off first. I'll do the honors."

Harry smiled. "Wear yourself out."

Being a nurse, Cherisse knew a little about anatomy. Being a woman, she was incapable of removing Harry's clothing without being aroused by the sight of his well-defined musculature, evidence of a life devoted to sports. All of those crunches, running up and down stadium steps and hours in the weight room had wrought a body that was strong and beautifully constructed.

Not a woman given to swooning, she felt quite close to doing just that. Heart beating rapidly, hands trembling slightly, she peeled off his jacket, the cummerbund and his shirt, grimacing when she came to the heavy onyx-and-gold cuff links because they stubbornly resisted her efforts at first. She had to grasp the clasps in a certain way to make them loosen their grip on his cuffs. Damned cuff links, she thought irritably.

All the while Harry was standing there as still as a statue, smiling.

"Do you find this amusing?" she asked.

"I thought you might cuss when those cuff links wouldn't come off fast enough."

Cherisse sighed as she caressed his naked chest, and what a chest. He was indeed hairy. Not too hairy, but curly dark brown hair covered his pectorals, wasn't as thick on his washboard stomach, thickening lower and disappearing inside his waistband.

She kissed his chest. She heard him moan with pleasure. Running her hands over his nipples she gave a little moan herself. And found that she couldn't prolong the ecstasy sure to come any longer.

"Harry, I'm sure you can undress yourself much quicker

than I can. I'll meet you in the bedroom," she said breath-lessly, looking at him with smoldering eyes.

She gave him a quick kiss and ran into the bedroom.

Harry grinned. Now, it was on. He kicked off his loafers and shucked his slacks in a matter of seconds. Then the socks had to go. Whoever thought leaving your socks on while making love was sexy was a fool!

When he got to the bedroom, Cherisse was struggling with the zipper on that clinging red dress. Her breasts were heaving enticingly with the exertion and she was breathing erratically.

Harry went and pulled the zipper down. The dress fell to the floor in a soft clump.

Cherisse went into his arms dressed only in a very reveal-ing natural-colored strapless bra, bikini panties and—he got an erection just looking at her in them—stockings with a garter belt.

"Let me help you out of those," he said, dropping to his knees at her feet.

He kissed her bare stomach, licking her skin. Her skin was warm and soft and tasted wonderful to him.

He felt Cherisse tremble, and he didn't think he could wait one minute longer before tasting her sweet nectar. She was standing with the backs of her legs against the bed. Harry rose and gently pushed her backward onto the bed and coaxed her up farther on the mattress.

"Is this a bra designed to drive men crazy trying to get it off?" he asked tightly. "Because if it is, I suggest you take it off. I feel about bras the way you feel about cuff links."

Cherisse reached behind her and unhooked the clasps. Harry pulled the bra off and tossed it onto the bed. Heaven! Her breasts fit nicely in his big hands. He bent and licked them, up, down, underneath. Her skin smelled of the melon skin lotion she liked.

Harry took a nipple into his mouth. It was delectable on his tongue. He gently sucked, enjoying her reaction. She sighed delightedly, licked her lips and raised her hips off the bed as though she were ready for more than the sensation of his mouth on her breasts. But Harry had waited too long to rush toward the denouement. No way was he going to sleep tonight without exploring every inch of her body.

He raised his head and grasped the waistband of the garter belt. It slipped easily over her hips. He enjoyed removing each stocking. The panties, silken and tiny, were a little more difficult to get off, but he persevered and was rewarded at last when he rolled them off her and she opened her legs to him. He removed his Jockeys.

Harry's mouth watered when he saw the beautiful lines of her sex, and her clitoris peeking from between the lips of her vagina seemingly beckoning him. He didn't have to be asked twice. He plunged right in and feasted on her with slow deliberation.

"Oh, God," Cherisse moaned loudly. She felt like a virgin experiencing her first orgasm, deeply astonished that it felt so damn good! "Harry, I'm coming!"

"Then come on, sweetness," Harry paused long enough to say, then redoubled his efforts. He grasped her by the backs of her legs and pulled her closer.

Cherisse continued to moan loudly until she exploded and quietly sighed on her way down from the peak of pleasure.

Harry knew the moment she came. He felt her throb with release. Kissing the insides of her thighs, he waited until she had stopped trembling before getting up to get a condom from the bedside table.

His eyes devoured Cherisse, her golden brown body glistening, her breath coming in short intervals causing her breasts to rise and fall enticingly with each inhalation.

Her legs were spread, revealing the wet promise of her sex. He could hardly get the condom onto his penis fast enough.

Cherisse raised up on her elbows to look at him on his return to the bed. He was huge, as she suspected, but she had to see with her own eyes. She wanted to remember every detail of this night. And seeing Harry in all his magnificence was now etched in her mind.

Harry didn't enter her immediately. He straddled her and bent to kiss her mouth, her throat, to tease her breasts, lick her nipples. Cherisse moaned with pleasure expressing extreme satisfaction for his efforts. Six years of pent-up sexual energy was being unleashed tonight!

Harry finally placed the tip of his penis at the opening of her vagina and gently pushed. Cherisse pushed back and he entered her by degrees. She was tight around him, tight and deliciously warm and wet. He closed his eyes, fully appreciating the moment. Yes, he realized, making love to a woman you cherish *is* different!

He wanted to please her. He wanted to hear her little moans of delight, feel her sweet breath on his skin as she panted, cared that she got her pleasure before he got his.

He opened his eyes and found that Cherisse had been watching him. Their eyes met and held. He saw in her depths the love she had for him, and it was that revelation that pushed him over the edge. He came with a shout and thrust into her with rapidity.

It was sheer sweet torture!

Holding himself up with his powerful arms, he continued pushing until he had come down from his high. Cherisse's hips were raised off the bed, fully meeting his thrusts with her own.

He pulled her to him and rolled over, bringing her to rest on top of him. Sighing, he lay back with his hands behind his head and admired the view, Cherisse sitting on top of him, her beautiful breasts full and enticing, their nipples erect and pointing upward. He smiled at her. "Marry me."

"Huh?" said Cherisse, totally taken by surprise.

"I don't mean fly to Vegas tonight," Harry said with a gentle smile. "How about New Year's Day? We could go to Zurich for our honeymoon. There's a ski resort there that I want you to see. It's what I'm aiming for in a resort. As my wife, I want you to learn every aspect of the business. You'll be a part of it, after all, a wonderful asset. I saw a sneak-peek of how good you're going to be when we went to Montana. You're naturally good with people, and they like you right away."

Cherisse's mind was racing. Had Harry said anything about being in love with her before he'd started talking about what a great asset she would be to his business? No, she didn't think she'd heard him say he loved her.

"Is that what this is, Harry?" she asked, climbing off him. "An interview for the position as your wife whom you see as a business asset?"

Harry grasped her wrist. "No, no, I love you, Cheri." He rose and pulled her into his arms. "I'm such a fool. I was so excited about the fact that I love you that I rushed right to the proposal." He kissed her chin, her neck. "I love you, baby, I love you so much that I can think of little else!"

Cherisse teared up. "Are you sure? Because I love you, too! I think I fell in love with you in Montana."

"Montana?" Harry said, trying to keep the excitement out of his voice, but failing. "I fell in love with *you* in Montana!"

Tears rolled down Cherisse's cheeks. "Why didn't you say anything then?"

"Because I figured you wouldn't believe me. You're such a sensible woman, Cheri. Look how you've raised Danielle on your own. It seems like everything you've done since you got up the nerve to leave Charlie has been methodically thought out. You came back to Denver because you knew your mother would welcome you and would be a built-in babysitter for Danielle. You put yourself through college with your eye on the head nurse position. You're a formidable woman, baby. I figured you would not believe me if I said I loved you after knowing you for only three weeks! So I gave it a few more weeks, hoping that by then my proposal would be more believable to you."

Cherisse sniffed. "Yeah, I've been sensible. I had to be sensible. I'd married my childhood sweetheart without knowing him well enough and toughed it out for nine years. I figured I'd better be sensible about the rest of my life's decisions. Danielle deserved at least one dependable parent. But when I met you, Harry, I realized that my sensible way of life could sometimes be put on the shelf in favor of red-hot passion!

"That's what you made me feel again, Harry, the passion that had been missing in my life! I love you like crazy and I look forward to spending the rest of my life loving you."

Harry, big tough Harry, sniffed back tears. He pulled her into his arms and they lay in bed holding one another. "So, New Year's Day?" he asked softly.

"That's less than two weeks away," said the sensible Cherisse.

"The resort's available," said Harry.

"We're going to shock everybody we know by getting married so quickly," Cherisse warned.

Harry grinned. "Believe me, we're not going to shock anybody, least of all our mothers. Your mother can tell how I feel about you, and my mom knows because I told her I loved you. And Danielle has been trying to hook us up from the beginning. The only person who'll be shocked is Charlie."

Cherisse laughed. "I forgot about Charlie."

"How can you forget about a man who wants you back?"

Cherisse snuggled closer to him and looked him in the eyes. "You don't really believe Charlie was serious about a second chance, do you?"

Harry frowned. "Didn't you believe him?"

"If I can make myself clear," Cherisse began, "I believe *he* thought he was serious, but deep down I think it was just a cry for forgiveness. I never forgave him for choosing gambling over me and Danielle. I believe in some screwy way Charlie thought that if we were a family again all of his sins would be forgiven."

"Makes sense," Harry agreed. He kissed her forehead. "How about a shower and then I have a couple of things I want to share with you."

Cherisse readily agreed. "A shower sounds good. And just for future reference, I'd like the chance to freshen up a bit before, you know…"

"You mean before I kiss you down there?" Harry asked, looking amused. His fiancée wasn't as wanton as she'd seemed a few minutes ago.

Cherisse looked embarrassed. "Yes, down there."

"You bathed before dressing," Harry said. "A woman's natural scent is not offensive to me, darling. I find your smell, your taste totally pleasing. I enjoyed you tonight."

Cherisse grimaced. "You must think I'm a prude."

"No, I think I'm going to have a good time teaching you to enjoy your body more, because I'm definitely going to enjoy it."

He pulled her up from the bed and playfully spanked her bottom. "Come on, I want to see just how turned on you can get in the shower."

The luxurious bathroom was huge with a deep tub and a

walk-in shower. The floor was heated and, best of all, the towels were thick and plush and there were two comfortable-looking terry-cloth bathrobes with the hotel's logo in gold lettering on the breast pockets hanging on double hooks behind the door.

Cherisse pinned her hair up and stepped into the shower stall, followed by Harry, who turned on the water. "Hot, warm, lukewarm?" he asked.

"Warm," said Cherisse.

Harry adjusted the temperature and grabbed a thick wash-cloth and squeezed some of the milk-and-almond body wash onto it. "You first," said Harry and moved aside so that Cherisse could step under the spray. He gently rubbed the washcloth over her back, her shoulders, her chest, slowing down when he got to the intersection of her thighs. Cherisse closed her eyes and stood with her back to him and her hands pressed to the tiled shower wall, legs slightly spread.

"Your skin is flawless," Harry murmured. "How did you escape getting scars being so active in sports?"

"Oh, I have scars," Cherisse told him. She turned around to face him and pointed out an inch-long scar on the inside of her right arm. "I got that from another player's cleat when I was sliding into home and his shoe connected with my arm. I played on the boys' baseball team."

"Why the boys' baseball team?" asked Harry. "The girls didn't have a softball team?"

"Yes, but I wanted to play baseball, not softball, and my mom was feisty enough to go up against the school board to make sure I got the chance to do it. I played for two seasons. Then I moved on to girls' basketball."

Harry kissed her scar. "My tough little Cheri," he said softly as he dropped the washcloth, backed her against the wall and kissed her breath away.

Sinewy muscles rubbed against soft, fragrant skin. Her

breasts were crushed against his hard chest and Cherisse spiraled into a state of arousal to rival any she'd ever experienced. Making out in the shower was something new to her and she wondered why her other two lovers had not thought of it. Why *she* had never thought of it.

Harry raised his head. "Now you're loosening up." Looking deeply into her eyes, he said, "Tell me your fantasies, sweetness. I want to hear what you dream of doing with the man you love."

Cherisse's female center throbbed at the sound of blatant sensuality in his voice.

The possibilities were endless. She was a woman who had not had a man make love to her in more than six years. She had a lot of desires to satisfy. "I want to make love to you in unusual places," she breathed, her heart pounding with excitement. "Not someplace we might get caught, I'm not that freaky, but in your office with the door locked. On the deck of a boat under moonlight…"

"Outdoor sex," said Harry contemplatively. "I've never done that before, too afraid of photographers with telephoto lenses."

Cherisse laughed. "Yeah, that would be embarrassing."

"The beach?" asked Harry.

"Sand getting in my hair? No thanks."

"Ever did it in a hammock?"

"No, but it's worth a try."

Harry laughed. "So basically you are a missionary-style woman, sex in the bedroom with the man on top."

"Harry, what good does it do talking about sex when you could be demonstrating it?" Cherisse said suddenly, bending to pick up the washcloth Harry had earlier dropped and rinsing it out under the spray.

"I want to know what you're used to so I won't shock you,"

said Harry. "It's obvious I've had more experience than you've had."

"You're an ex-football star, Harry. Of course you've had more experience than I have. You've undoubtedly had more experience than the average man, let alone a woman who has had only two lovers in her entire life!"

"That's all?" Harry asked, brows arched in surprise. "Darling, you're thirty-seven."

"Don't even tell me how many lovers you've had, Harry Payne. I don't want to hear it. And, yes, only two for me because I married the first guy I ever made love to and the next man I loved got killed. That didn't exactly make me want to go out and have sex with a lot of other men!" Cherisse stated emphatically.

"Okay," said Harry mildly, a smile on his lips. "I'm not complaining about your lack of experience, I'm just surprised by it. You're almost a virgin."

"You know," Cherisse said, "'almost a virgin' would make a good book title but it doesn't describe me. I like sex. I just don't go around having it with every Tom, Dick and Harry! Now, turn around and let me wash your back."

"Yes, dear," said Harry and turned his muscular back to her.

Cherisse's righteous anger faded as soon as she saw his butt. She could bounce a quarter off that baby! She didn't pick up a washcloth with which to rub his body down, she used her hands. Harry just smiled.

Harry had planned ahead. He'd ordered a repast for them that included cold spicy crab legs, fresh garden salad, crusty rolls and fresh fruit—Cherisse's favorites—and for dessert, rich double chocolate cake. Champagne had been left chilling in an ice bucket by the hotel's staff.

Harry had lit the candle in the center of the table and

poured the champagne by the time Cherisse came into the room, wrapped in one of the bathrobes. Harry was wearing the other one.

He held her chair for her. "We didn't have dinner before the ball," he said. "I figured you must be famished by now."

Cherisse's stomach had been growling off and on since ten o'clock. It was now nearly eleven. "I am. Thank you."

"I ordered the spicy steamed crab legs you like," Harry said. "Eat up."

Cherisse did. The spices weren't nearly as hot as she liked. She expected her eyes to water when she ate crab legs, but these had a nice delicate flavor and had fresh, succulent meat on them.

Harry had fun watching her lick those plump lips of hers.

Cherisse knew he was watching her and licked her index finger indolently, drawing it from between her lips with slow deliberation.

Harry's groin grew tight. He looked down at his own untouched plate and picked up a cracked crab leg and began to methodically peel the shell away from the meat. "What do you think of announcing our engagement at the Christmas party?" he asked.

Cherisse gave it some thought. "All right, that would cover all of my friends and family but you would have to phone your folks."

"Oh, didn't I tell you?" said Harry. "My family will be coming here for Christmas. I invited them a few days ago and they'll be here on the twenty-third. They'll be staying until the first week of January."

Cherisse swallowed hard and had to take a sip of her champagne to get the crabmeat to go down. All of sudden, her head was spinning. Harry Payne didn't play around when he made a decision, did he? The next thing he would be telling her would probably be that he had already planned the wedding and all she had to do on the fateful day was show up!

"Today is the nineteenth, Harry. In four days your family will be arriving and you're just telling me?"

"I wanted it to be a surprise, like the rest of tonight," Harry told her, smiling as he tossed the crab leg onto his plate and rose. He went into the bedroom and came back out carrying what looked to Cherisse like a folded quilt. When he got closer, she saw that it was a quilt.

She loved quilts. Carefully wiping her hands on the cloth napkin, she rose as Harry placed the beautiful work of art in her arms. She carried it over to the couch, not wanting it anywhere near the food where something could get spilled on it, and sat down with it on her lap. She looked at Harry, her eyes questioning. "Where did you get this? It's the most beautiful quilt I've ever seen." She ran her hand over the delicate stitching. "See that design? Those are supposed to represent interlocking wedding rings." Her eyes stretched. "This is a wedlock quilt, Harry!"

Harry smiled his satisfaction, walked over to her and sat down beside her. "You know your quilts. My mom will be pleased. She made it for me and my wife."

Cherisse burst into tears. That was the sweetest, most dear thing she'd ever heard. His mother had made him a special quilt for when he got married. No wonder he doted on the woman.

Laughing softly, Harry put his arms around her. "I can tell Mom it's a hit with you, huh?"

Too choked up to speak, Cherisse nodded. Harry kissed her cheek. "I love you."

He rose again. "But the quilt's not the only gift I have for you tonight, darling girl."

He didn't leave the room this time. He simply reached

inside the pocket of the robe, withdrew a ring box and knelt on one knee in front of her. He opened the ring box and presented her with a five-carat white diamond solitaire in a platinum setting. "Asking you to marry me while we were having sex didn't seem the proper way to go about such a solemn occasion." He smiled up at her. "Will you be my wife? Will you let me love you and care for you until the day I draw my last breath?"

"Only if you'll let me love you and care for you for just as long," Cherisse said through her tears.

"Agreed," said Harry happily.

"Then, yes, I *will* marry you," Cherisse said and held out a trembling hand for Harry to place the ring on her finger.

Harry held her hand firmly in his while he slipped the ring onto her finger. Then he leaned forward and kissed her tenderly. Parting, he said, "You've made me a very happy man."

Cherisse laughed and jumped into his arms, catapulting both of them to the floor, where she kissed him soundly. Once he could disentangle himself, Harry reached up to pull the thick, heavy quilt onto the floor and pushed Cherisse back onto its plush softness. "Let's christen this baby."

Kneeling over Cherisse, he loosened his robe's belt and pulled it off, tossing it somewhere behind him, then he removed the sash around Cherisse's waist and ripped open her robe, revealing her luscious naked golden-brown body underneath.

His semi-erect penis achieved hardness as soon as he laid eyes on her. She was a visual delight, long limbs and womanly curves, hair splayed out around her beautiful face, that beauty mark next to her sensually curved mouth winking at him. He bent and kissed her mouth, his tongue parting her lips. Cherisse kissed him back hungrily, rising from the quilt.

Harry pulled her to him, their bodies warm and naked, hot and bothered, alive with sexual need.

Harry was about to impale her right there on the floor when he remembered the condom in his robe's pocket.

He kissed her belly. "One minute, baby, I forgot the latex."

Once the condom was in his hand Cherisse took it from him and placed it on his hard, throbbing penis. Then she pulled him down for a deep kiss as she opened her legs, welcomed him inside of her, and wrapped herself around him.

No words were needed as they achieved the right rhythm, hands caressing, and their mouths drank the nectar each freely offered, gently at first and then more urgently.

Bodies entwined, they somewhat resembled the yin-and-yang symbol, Cherisse's body being a lighter brown than Harry's, but both bodies together meeting in perfect synchronicity.

Harry had never felt this kind of exultation before and thought his heart might explode inside his chest, he felt such joy. How could he have known that a stranger he met on the balcony on a moonlit night would come to mean so much to him?

Cherisse ended up on top and Harry had to close his eyes against her intense beauty, afraid he would not be able to hold back the powerful climax he felt building within him.

Cherisse closed her eyes, as well, and threw her head back, riding him, feeling his penis rubbing against the sensitive walls of her vagina and worrying her clit until she thought she might scream.

She bent and whispered in his ear, "So this is what a little moonlight can do."

Harry came in an instant because he knew exactly what she was referring to. The very thing he had been thinking only moments ago. How fate had brought them together that night on the balcony at Karibu.

At that moment, his love for her knew no bounds.

Cherisse came with a loud moan, and Harry pulled her down to hold her in his arms while her body went through its spasms of release.

Chapter 15

On Monday Cherisse tracked down David Pedersen to tender her resignation. She was required by the terms of her contract to give six weeks' notice. She admitted to some misgivings about quitting nursing. She had gotten her master's degree when she was thirty, but she had worked as a registered nurse for a year prior to that. Would she miss the daily grind of the past eight years? No. However she would certainly miss the patients and the easy camaraderie she shared with her colleagues.

She finally caught up with David at lunchtime. She paged him, he called her and they agreed to meet in the cafeteria.

Cherisse got there before David and sat down at a table in the back, a salad and a tall glass of iced tea in front of her. She didn't wait for David, but began eating. If he decided not to show up, she still had to get back to work on time.

He arrived about ten minutes into her salad, carrying a tray to the table and sitting down with a tired sigh. Cherisse thought the bags under his eyes were fuller than usual.

And his carriage wasn't as erect as it normally was.

"Hello, Cherisse," he said softly, looking at her with red-rimmed eyes.

Cherisse dearly wanted to ask him if he'd stayed up all night, but wouldn't give him the satisfaction of knowing she was in the least concerned about him. For three years he'd given her a hard time. Was she now going to try to end their association with tenderness and compassion? No. David wouldn't accept it, anyway.

"Hello, David," she said. She put her fork down and regarded him. "I'll make this short. I'm quitting."

David's eyes stretched, but he didn't say anything. He placed his stethoscope on the tabletop. The weight of it in his lab-coat pocket bothered him when he was sitting. Then he met Cherisse's eyes. "Don't be ridiculous, Cherisse. Where are you going? Has some other hospital made you an offer? Is that it? You'll be swallowed up by bureaucracy in one of those places. Sure they seem nice at first, better pay, better benefits, but would you find satisfaction with them? The kind of satisfaction you get from challenging me at every turn?"

Cherisse smiled at him. Could it be that David Pedersen had found their adversarial relationship stimulating and would miss her when she was gone? If it were true he would never admit it. "No, I haven't been recruited by another hospital," she told him. "I'm getting married."

"Lots of nurses get married and continue working. I'll tell you what I'll do. I'll give you a month's leave. How is that?" His smile was warm, even solicitous.

"That won't be acceptable. I'm going to be working with my husband in his business. So I won't have the time to continue working here."

David frowned. "It's true then? I heard rumors that you were seeing Harry Payne. I figured they were lies. Well, this is a fine mess, Cherisse! It's going to take a hell of a person to take your place. You're leaving me high and dry. How can you do this to me?"

Cherisse laughed. "I'm giving you six weeks' notice, David. That's not leaving you high and dry. What's more, if you're going to be hiring within, I suggest Sonia Lopez for the job. She has more than ten years' experience…"

"She doesn't have a master's degree," David pointed out.

"She's working on it," said Cherisse. "She's been going to night school for two years. She graduates in June. I don't see why you can't consider her for the job! You know it would be more cost effective instead of having to bring someone in from the outside. Of all the nurses in pediatrics, she's the one the others look up to. They would accept her as their leader."

"You think you've got it all figured out, don't you?" said David peevishly. He bit into his ham-and-cheese sandwich almost viciously, chewed, swallowed and took a swig of apple juice. "If I had known you were going to marry a millionaire and leave me three years from the date I hired you, I wouldn't have hired you!"

Cherisse was shocked by his reaction. "I thought you would be happy to see me go!"

David sighed. "I rode you so hard because I knew you had potential, Cherisse. I will not be happy to see you go. You have yet to achieve your full potential."

"You mean I haven't yet bowed to management," Cherisse said. "I'm not sorry to disappoint you, David. This is one nurse who is going out unbowed and with her dignity intact."

"Let me leave the position open for six months," David suggested. "Sonia can do the job for that long. You may change your mind. Rich men often change their minds about the women they marry. What if he kicked you out? You would have nothing to fall back on."

"I'm touched by your concern," Cherisse said sarcastically. "But the answer is no."

"Then my answer to the Sonia Lopez question is no," David stubbornly told her.

"Go ahead, David, bite off your nose to spite your face. But you're going to lose many more good people unless you start showing some compassion, a shred of interest in your staff as human beings and not just as bodies to perform tasks around this hospital."

She rose and collected her tray. "My written resignation will be on your desk by the end of the day."

David threw his head back in laughter.

Cherisse looked down at him. "Have you gone crazy from lack of sleep or something? You came in here looking like death warmed over and now you're acting peculiar."

David gestured to her empty chair. "Sit, sit." His eyes danced with amusement.

Cherisse sat back down and glared at him.

"Didn't it feel good to have one last knock-down-drag-out, Cherisse?" he asked smugly. "Of course I accept your resignation. Yes, I'll be sorry to see you go, but I'm happy for you. You deserve happiness, and if Harry Payne makes you happy, then, wonderful!"

Cherisse looked around them suspiciously. "Are we on some kind of hidden camera TV show? Am I being punked?"

Still laughing softly, David explained, "Nothing of the sort. I'm just tired of being a tight-ass, Cherisse. I spent most of my life, both as a civilian and in the military, being the one who never let his standards fall below excellent. My wife left me three weeks ago. She said she and I had nothing left. I was my job, and she didn't want to be married to a job. I haven't been able to sleep well without her beside me. I didn't realize how much I depended on hearing her reassuring soft snores next to me in order to get a good night's rest. Not that her snoring is the only thing I miss about her. It's just an example of one of the things I never appreciated about her."

"Oh, my God, David, you've just shared something personal with a colleague. Will you now keel over and die?"

David laughed anew. "You're not going to give me a break?"

"Why should I give you a break? It's obvious you drove the poor woman away. I would have left you much sooner. How long have you been married?"

"Twenty-five years."

"She's a saint! I would've killed you in your sleep two years into the marriage."

David had tears in his eyes, he was laughing so hard. And Cherisse knew why. He was finally releasing some of the pent-up stress he'd been carrying around since his wife had left him.

"I would tell you that you have a good chance of winning her back if you cleaned up your act, but I have too much sympathy for the poor woman. She's suffered enough."

David wiped his eyes with a paper napkin and regarded Cherisse. "Thanks, I needed that."

Cherisse smiled. "You needed me to insult you?"

"I needed somebody to be brutally honest." He sighed. "I'll seriously consider Sonia Lopez for the job. I can't promise to stop being a tight-ass. It's too ingrained in me. But I will definitely try to get my wife to come back to me. I love her and I believe she loves me. I can leave the job here from now on, and actually start to have a life outside of work."

"Just my luck," Cherisse quipped. "You're turning into a human being just as I'm leaving this place."

"You could stay."

"Not on your life," said Cherisse. "And another thing, I'm going to need ten days off starting on January first."

"You're busting my balls!" David cried.

"A girl has to have a honeymoon, David," Cherisse said, rising. She picked up her tray. "And if you have got your wife talking to you again by January first, I'd like you to bring her to my wedding in Vail."

"You're inviting me to your wedding?" David asked, genuinely moved.

"I'm inviting all of my friends, David."

Charlie liked his job. He went to area high schools and community colleges to recruit students into the sports medicine program at the University of Colorado at Denver. He had so much fun talking to the students that he often felt let down when it was time to go home after work. But then he figured the reason he didn't want to return to the Patterson home at the end of the day was because he felt guilty. He had found a nice house not too far from campus but he hadn't told anyone about it yet. He wanted to be around the Patterson home for a while longer.

His big plan to win Cherisse back, to get Danielle on his side and therefore work on Cherisse's sympathies as a mother, had failed miserably because Danielle saw through his ruse in about a minute and called him on it. Cherisse had raised a very astute young lady. Basically, Charlie was now out of ammunition when it came to the big guns he was supposed to have brought to bear in the war to win Cherisse back.

Harry Payne was winning big-time. Charlie suspected that Cherisse had slept with Payne even though he hadn't overheard her talking about it with her mother or anything. Cherisse was notoriously closemouthed about that sort of thing.

Still, she looked exceptionally happy to him. She glowed. He hoped she wasn't pregnant!

What's more, lately, she was being very polite to him. She no longer avoided him and when she looked at him he saw a softening in her gaze as if she could finally stand the sight of him without rolling her eyes or cursing under her breath. He didn't know if that was a good sign or a bad sign. It could be a bad sign if she were so gone on Harry Payne that his presence was no longer a blip on the radar. It could be a good sign if she were genuinely beginning to consider Charlie as a rival for Payne.

Charlie wasn't going to hold his breath.

It was two days before Christmas and Charlie had gone shopping on his lunch break and gotten Danielle that new cell phone she had been dropping hints about, Cherisse a gold bracelet and Miss Jo a pair of pearl earrings. He'd had the bracelet engraved with the words *I'll Always Love You.*

When he got home in the afternoon, Miss Jo and Danielle were in the kitchen cooking. They had started cooking two days ago for the Christmas Eve bash. The freezer on the back porch was full of goodies that only had to be thawed and reheated.

Charlie had even been put into service last night when they had baked cakes and pies for the party. His right arm was sore from whipping cake batter. He didn't mind, though. This was the first time in years he was going to spend Christmas with people he loved.

Danielle looked up from chopping celery and went to him and kissed him on the cheek. "Hey, Dad, how was your day?"

"It was fine, baby, how was yours?"

"Hectic, as usual," said Danielle. "Grandma's trying to work me to death."

Charlie went and kissed Miss Jo on the cheek. "Miss Jo," he acknowledged with a smile.

Joann smiled back. "Hello, Charlie. Refresh yourself then

wash up and join in the fun. There are still potatoes to be peeled for the potato salad."

"I'm a pro at peeling potatoes," Charlie said gamely.

Joann winked at Danielle. "Isn't that something? If he stays here long enough we'll have him cooking entire meals."

Charlie suddenly decided it was time to come clean. "I'm afraid I'm going to have to disappoint you, Miss Jo," he said regretfully. "But I've found a house. I'll be moving at the first of the year. I found an owner who's agreed to rent it to me before I decide to buy."

"Well, that's nice," said Joann. She was wearing an apron over a smart gray A-line dress that nicely fit her plump body and a pair of black flats as she stood at the counter cutting carrots into three-inch-long sticks for appetizers. "I'm going to miss you around here."

"I will, too," said Danielle. She wore jeans and a red sweater with a pair of white sneakers. Her thick hair was braided and held back by a brown leather tie.

She smiled at her father. "But all good things come to an end. Things stay in flux. I learned that in physics. Even though we're not aware of it, the earth, everything is continually changing. Change can be good."

Charlie looked into her eyes. Was she trying to tell him something? Perhaps prepare him for some shocking news.

Danielle seemingly spoke to his fears when she said, "Dad, I got a letter from Yale today. I've been accepted. I start the fall semester of next year. And since Mom put me in that young achievers program when I was eight, my tuition will be paid for the first four years."

Charlie couldn't believe his ears. Yale. His little girl had gotten into Yale. On a scholarship!

He went and picked Danielle up and spun her around in the middle of the kitchen.

Danielle squealed like a little girl. "Daddy, let me down!"

Charlie put her feet back on the floor and squeezed her tightly. "I'm so proud of you, baby girl, so proud! And your mother, she must have grinned from ear to ear when you told her."

"I haven't told her yet," Danielle said. "I'm waiting until she gets home so I can see her face when I tell her."

"I've got to have my camera ready," said Charlie. He glanced up at the kitchen clock.

Cherisse wouldn't be home for two and a half hours. He had plenty of time to get the digital camera prepared.

Then something troubling occurred to him. He frowned at Danielle. "Wait a minute. Didn't you tell me Echo was going to Yale?"

Danielle smiled widely. "I wondered when you'd remember that."

"You mean you and he are going to be alone hundreds of miles from here?"

"Daddy, I'm nearly eighteen. Don't you trust me to do the right thing?"

"I trust you, but I don't trust him!" Charlie almost yelled.

Joann was laughing softly. Danielle was just like her mother. She hadn't been able to talk Cherisse out of marrying Charlie twenty years ago, either. Well, the chickens had come home to roost now. Charlie and Cherisse would get a taste of how frustrating it was being the parent of an obstinate child. Or should she say, in Danielle's case, a child who knows her own mind. Joann had complete faith in Danielle's ability to attend Yale without difficulty and to handle any advances from Echo.

Joann also believed that Echo was a fine boy. A little flaky, but then geniuses were often flaky. He and Danielle made a good couple. Danielle was so grounded she would be able to pull Echo back down to earth when he began to float into the stratosphere.

"Now, now, Charlie," Joann said in placating tones. "You said you liked the boy when he came for dinner."

"I do like the boy," Charlie said. "I'm just against his and Danielle's going to the same college." He regarded Danielle. "Haven't you applied to other colleges?"

"Yes," Danielle said. "But Yale is my first choice. I'm not giving up my first choice, Daddy."

Charlie went to the refrigerator to pour himself a glass of water. He suddenly felt warm. After drinking half the glass, he said, "All right, go to Yale. Go to Yale with Echo. I guess I was overreacting because I've just got you back in my life and now you're talking about leaving. But I have to get used to the notion of letting you go sometime. All fathers have to face that at one time or another, right?"

"I'm not leaving for months, Daddy," Danielle said.

Charlie cheered up somewhat. A lot could happen between now and next fall. Echo could decide that the love he felt for Danielle was only infatuation. Danielle could decide that she liked the kid from D.C. better. What was his name? Dante, Dante Winters.

And Cherisse could break up with Harry Payne and when it came time to drive Danielle to college, she and Charlie would do it as a couple. Just a couple making sure their darling daughter was settled in at school. The way their lives were supposed to have turned out.

Charlie set his glass of water on the counter and went to start whittling down the pile of potatoes Miss Jo had earlier suggested he might enjoy peeling.

Things might work out his way.

On Christmas Eve cars lined the street where the Patterson house stood. Joann had gotten permission from her neighbors for the cars to park in their driveway and in front of their houses. They were amenable to the request because most of them would be attending the party, as well.

The early birds started arriving at seven. Jo knew how to handle people who came an hour too soon—she put them to work.

She, Danielle, Echo, Cherisse and Charlie were all dressed by seven and downstairs putting food on the tables. Dinner would be served buffet style and consisted of all the traditional Christmas fare that the African-American community in Five Points had come to expect from the Patterson Christmas Eve party—glazed ham, roasted turkey, roast beef, with various sides like collard greens, fresh acre peas, fried okra, butter beans, potato salad, macaroni and cheese, candied yams, corn bread, dinner rolls, fresh garden salad and, for dessert, ice-cream pound cake made with frozen vanilla ice cream instead of milk in the batter, sweet potato pies, egg custard pies and pecan pies. The potables were provided by guests who knew it was a "bring your own brown paper bag" affair. They generously provided cases of beer, liters of vodka, gin, brandy and whiskey. No one left with a clear head unless they were teetotalers. And Cherisse made sure that there were designated drivers aplenty. What's more, she had the local cab company on speed-dial.

The party was in full-swing when Harry arrived with his mother, Mildred, his sister, Susanne, her husband, Kendall and their four children: Kendall, Jr., sixteen; Kara, fourteen; Sandrene, thirteen; and Sage, ten.

Cherisse had already met them, having had dinner with them the night before. She met them at the door and invited them in, receiving hugs from Mildred and Susanne as they entered. The large foyer was as always elegant, but the rails on the stairs were now strung with holly vines and poinsettias lined the entrance. The hardwood floors gleamed and the air was redolent with good food smells. Christmas carols sung by soul singers like Otis Redding, Aretha Franklin, Lou Rawls, Marvin Gaye and other Motown artists were on the CD player, which could be heard throughout the house thanks to the sound system Echo had hooked up.

When Harry and his family walked through the door, Otis Redding's rendition of "White Christmas" was playing. Tonight Cherisse was wearing a sleeveless, scoop-neck royal blue dress with a hem that fell two inches above her knees. She looked sophisticated with her hair in an upswept style that framed her heart-shaped face nicely and made her neck look long and graceful.

Mildred thought she looked like a young Dorothy Dandridge. Mildred was fond of old movies, especially those with Dorothy Dandridge and Sidney Poitier in them. She pictured Cherisse as Dorothy tonight in her pretty frock and Harry as Sidney Poitier in his dark blue suit.

Mildred herself was in a tailored black pantsuit. Susanne also wore basic black, but hers was a simple black dress that had a square neckline and a low-cut back, but not too low. Her husband Kendall wore a blue suit similar to Harry's. The boys were in dress shirts and slacks and the girls wore dresses, although Cherisse noticed that the youngest girl, Sage, looked very uncomfortable in her frilly dress. She guessed she was like Danielle had been at that age, a tomboy.

Cherisse made the introductions in the foyer. Jo, Danielle, Echo and Charlie were introduced in turn: Joann wearing a beautiful bronze-colored dress with bronze accessories that accentuated her gray hair. Danielle in a multicolored, diamond-design short shift trimmed in black with a pair of chunky-heeled black leather sandals. She looked both young and trendy. At her side, Echo was wearing his usual geeky dress-up ensemble of a white long-sleeve shirt, black dress slacks and black Adidas. But from the adoring expression in fourteen-year-old Kara's eyes, he was quite handsome. Danielle smiled when she saw the way the girl was looking at Echo. She didn't blame her one bit.

Kendall and Kendall, Jr. were duly impressed when Cherisse introduced Charlie. They were football fans and considered Charlie to be one of the best defensive backs in the history of the game.

Cherisse was gratified to see the three of them, along with Harry, launch into an enthusiastic conversation about football as soon as the introductions were over.

Danielle and Echo took it upon themselves to show Sandrene and Sage around and make sure they were supplied with food and ample entertainment. Joann and Mildred took one look at one another and saw kindred spirits. Joann took Mildred by the arm and took her across the room to introduce her to a couple of eligible bachelors of a certain age. One was a retired English professor and the other was Joann's minister, Reverend Alastair McLeod who bore a striking likeness to actor Billy Dee Williams.

Cherisse was happy to have some alone time with Susanne.

"You have a lovely home," Susanne said as Cherisse directed her to the buffet tables laden with food in the corner of the large room. "I'm really fond of old houses. How old is it?"

Cherisse smiled up at the taller woman. Susanne was five-nine, wore her black hair in a pageboy cut that was shoulder-length, and had beautiful medium-brown skin and golden-brown eyes. She didn't look anything like her older brother, Harry. Cherisse had been told they had different fathers. Harry's father had died when he was a small boy, and Mildred had married Susanne's father.

"Thanks," Cherisse said, smiling. "It belonged to my

mom's parents. Granddaddy Patterson was a Pullman porter with the railroad back in the twenties. He built this house for his much younger wife, I'm told she was twenty years his junior, in 1927. It's been renovated since then of course. More rooms have been added, modern plumbing, thank goodness!"

Susanne laughed. "Hey, I'm from Kentucky, I've heard of outhouses." She was putting food on her plate as she talked. Around them, guests chatted, ate with gusto and some who had imbibed were dancing to and singing along with the music on the stereo.

"I have to tell you, Cherisse, I never thought my brother would actually settle down. For years I've been trying to talk him into finding someone special but he always put work first. I'm glad he's found you. Now, maybe, my kids will finally get some first cousins. I hope you two want a big family."

Cherisse didn't know what to say. She and Harry were supposed to keep their engagement a secret until tonight. Had he confided in his sister? Or was Susanne fishing for information?

Cherisse wasn't even wearing her engagement ring so as not to tip anyone off about the announcement to come later in the evening.

"Well, I love kids and Harry loves kids," she said hesitantly.

Susanne laughed softly. "I'm sorry," she said. "I'm jumping the gun with all this talk about you and Harry having kids. You must not know Harry's history when it comes to women. He never introduces them to his family. That's why I assume that he's very serious about you. I mean, he invited us to Denver expressly to meet you. That says a lot."

Cherisse breathed a silent sigh of relief. "No, I had no idea Harry kept his former girlfriends away from his family." She smiled. "But I'm happy to have been the first one to meet you." She felt a little deceitful talking to Harry's sister when in a few minutes Susanne would know they were soon to be sisters-in-law. But she was sure she would be forgiven.

Susanne speared a piece of ham with her fork and doused it in candied yam drippings then put it in her mouth. She chewed and swallowed. "Delicious. Good caterer."

"Oh, we didn't hire anybody," Cherisse said off-handedly. "Mom, Danielle and I did the cooking. I'm glad you like it."

Susanne eyed the buffet tables. "You must have been cooking for days!"

"Three days," said Cherisse. "But we had fun doing it. You know how it is when three women get in a kitchen, magic happens and before you know it, you're laughing and talking and it doesn't seem like work at all."

Susanne was smiling and shaking her head in agreement, remembering the times she and her mother had been lost in the shared give-and-take of creating culinary delights in the kitchen. "Yeah, good times," she said.

She suddenly grabbed Cherisse by the arm. "Oh, you've got to make Harry bring you to Kentucky in the summer. We have a family reunion every summer and this year I'm doing a cookbook of all the family recipes. You know, just a self-published softcover book with photographs of the finished recipes and the recipes along with homespun stories about the origins of the recipes."

"That's a fabulous idea," Cherisse said and meant it. "I don't know why I never thought of it. My mom has a box filled with hand-scribbled recipes from her mother, her grand-mother and various aunts. That's something that should be preserved for future generations. Our daughters should know these things even though they're all going to have careers and won't be housewives."

"Exactly," said Susanne. "My girls are already turning their noses up at kitchen duties but I make them help me cook for their own good. One day they'll thank me."

Cherisse thought of Danielle, who had always been underfoot whenever she was in the kitchen, and adored helping her grandmother cook. She supposed that was unusual for a teenage girl nowadays.

Speaking of their daughters, all three of them suddenly emerged from the crowd and Danielle said to her mother, "Ma, is it all right if Sandrene and Sage and I go upstairs for a while? They say they've never been skiing before and I wanted to show them my competition videos. We'll be back in a few minutes."

"If it's all right with Susanne," Cherisse said, turning to regard Susanne.

Susanne smiled. "Of course it is. I've never been able to interest them in skiing. Maybe you'll have some luck."

She and Cherisse watched the girls leave. "She's a sweetie, your Danielle," Susanne said. She looked serious. "Do you mind if I ask you a very personal question?"

Cherisse hoped it wasn't something about Charlie. Charlie was the unknown quantity in tonight's equation. She didn't know how he was going to react when she and Harry made their announcement. She hoped he remained as unobtrusive as possible, but didn't hold out much hope of that.

She smiled at Susanne. "No, I don't mind."

"How old were you when you had Danielle? You look so young!"

"I was only twenty when Danielle was born," Cherisse said. "I'm thirty-seven now."

Susanne looked flabbergasted. "I'm thirty seven, too! When's your birthday?"

"January seventeenth."

"Mine was December tenth!" Susanne exclaimed. "I'm a little over a month older than you are. What else do we have in common? Did you pledge a sorority in college?"

"No," said Cherisse. "I just didn't have the time. I was already a mother of a seven-year-old and that sort of thing seemed like a luxury to me."

"I went to college under different circumstances," Susanne said. "Right after high school, and I was tempted to pledge but didn't because my curriculum counselor said it would take too much time from my schoolwork. So I didn't pledge a sorority, either."

Cherisse saw Harry making his way toward her and Susanne. There was a serious expression on his face. He took her by the arm when he got to her, and said to Susanne, "Excuse us, Suse, I need to speak with Cherisse in private."

Then he grabbed Cherisse by the hand and led her away.

Chapter 16

When she and Harry hit the stairs running, Cherisse asked, "Harry, what's the matter with you? Where are you taking me with such a serious look on your face?"

"I've got serious business to discuss with you, Ms. Washington," Harry said grimly. He opened her bedroom door, pushed her inside then peered both ways down the hallway before shutting and locking the door behind them.

"Serious business," he repeated as he bent his head and kissed her with such longing that it took Cherisse's breath away.

Raising his head, he said, "Good God, woman, don't you realize it's been twenty-four hours since we kissed? And four days since we made love? That's serious business to me!"

Cherisse laughed. "Then kiss me, you fool, but don't even *think* about making love to me here and now, not with sixty people downstairs!"

Harry smiled contentedly and did just that. He kissed her

until they were melting in each other's arms. Until Cherisse fell against him with a sigh, and said, "Maybe we can get away with it if we're quiet."

Harry laughed softly. "We could never get away with it. You're a screamer."

Cherisse punched him on the arm. "I am not. You're the shouter."

"Okay, we're both loud," Harry conceded. He gave her a peck on the cheek. "Come on, let's go downstairs and tell everybody the good news."

Cherisse was glad to. She had been on pins and needles all evening, worrying about how Charlie was going to react to their engagement.

She took Harry's hand. "I'm a little nervous."

"So am I," Harry said. "I don't think Charlie is going to take it well."

"Well, there's no getting around the fact that he's going to be a part of our family. He's Danielle's father, after all. He's going to have to get used to you and I being together."

"Forever," said Harry as he opened the door and let her precede him.

Cherisse walked into the hallway and said, "Wait a minute, I want to get Danielle."

She walked a few feet to Danielle's bedroom door and knocked.

"Who is it?" she heard Danielle call.

"Danielle, please come downstairs right away. Harry and I are going to make an announcement."

Danielle opened the door in a matter of seconds. Grinning, she called to her mother's retreating back, "We'll be right down!"

When Cherisse and Harry reached the bottom of the stairs, Harry spotted Echo and called, "Echo!"

Echo hurried over.

Harry said, "Would you turn the music off? Cherisse and I want to say something to everybody."

"Sure!" Echo replied and went to do as he was asked.

Harry and Cherisse moved to the center of the room. Danielle and her soon-to-be cousins by marriage came running down the stairs.

As soon as the music was cut off, the guests looked around expectantly. Jo looked up and saw Cherisse and Harry standing in the center of the room and said to Mildred, "Something's up." She turned to the two gentlemen she and Mildred had been chatting with. "Please excuse us, professor, reverend."

In the back of the room, Charlie was still engaged in conversation with Kendall and Kendall, Jr., Susanne had joined their group when Harry had dragged Cherisse away but she hadn't contributed much to the conversation, choosing to sample the fare on the buffet table instead.

Charlie also looked up when the music stopped and, spotting Cherisse and Harry obviously about to say something to the guests, got a terrible feeling in the pit of his stomach.

Kendall, stating the obvious, said, "Looks like Harry and Cherisse are about to make an announcement."

"Everybody gather 'round!" Harry said in a loud voice. "Cherisse and I want to say something to you."

Once the group had moved in closer and the murmuring had died down, Harry said while putting his arm around Cherisse's waist, "As you know, Cherisse and I have been seeing each other exclusively for a while now."

"Oh, yeah, we're aware of that," Charlie muttered under his breath. Kendall, Kendall, Jr. and Susanne looked at him strangely but he didn't care.

Gazing into Cherisse's upturned face, Harry continued.

"We fell in love almost instantly and four nights ago I asked her to marry me."

"And I said yes!" Cherisse said to a group of people who stood stunned, yet happy to be privy to their friends' happiness.

Clapping, whistling and shouts of "congratulations" filled the room.

"Wait, that's not all," said Harry. "Since we see no reason for a long engagement we're getting married at the resort next Thursday, January first. You're all invited."

Gasps arose among those present and everybody started talking at once.

"No!" Cherisse shouted above the din. "I'm not expecting. We just didn't want to wait."

Dead silence.

"That *is* what you were thinking, right?" she asked, grinning.

Some nodded, embarrassed. Others laughed uproariously. Then she and Harry were rushed by friends and family, being hugged within an inch of their lives. Afterward, the guests parted to let Mildred and Jo through.

Mildred grabbed Harry and hugged him. "Well, I didn't expect this, but I'll take it!"

Jo squeezed Cherisse tightly. "Do you love him, baby?"

"Ma, I love him to death!"

"Okay, then. I'm happy for you. I just don't see why you can't get married in the church, though. Reverend McLeod is right here, we could ask him now."

"That's fine, Ma. He can marry us at the resort. There isn't enough time to prepare the church for the ceremony but Harry has it all worked out at Karibu."

Jo sniffed back tears. "Okay, just so you're married by a man of God."

Cherisse kissed her cheek. "Then it's settled."

Mildred tapped Jo on the shoulder. "May I hug my soon-to-be daughter-in-law?"

Jo relinquished Cherisse and as if they'd choreographed it, Cherisse hugged Mildred while Jo accepted a warm hug from Harry.

"Welcome to the family," said Jo.

"I knew you were the one when Harry told me you loved my quilt," Mildred said in Cherisse's ear.

Cherisse had tears in her eyes, otherwise she would have seen Charlie when he came barreling through the guests, eyes flashing fury and hands balled into fists.

"You son of a bitch!" he yelled just before he hit Harry right in the mouth.

Harry was nearly knocked down by the punch. Jo stumbled backward out of his embrace. Mildred and Cherisse both gave gasps of surprise and horror at the attack. Only Harry maintained a clear head. Relying on his honed reflexes, he immediately went on the defense and stepped backward, got his bearings and let loose with a right cross that sent Charlie sprawling onto the floor on his back.

"My mother's standing right there!"

Charlie, dazed, slowly got to his feet. At this point the other guests had formed a circle around Harry and Charlie. Cherisse had to push her way into that inner circle.

"Harry, Charlie, stop this! No more fighting!"

Charlie, rubbing his jaw, glaring at Harry, ignored Cherisse. "You had to tell her, didn't you? You couldn't play fair. You had to deal dirty with me."

"You're wrong, as usual," said Harry menacingly. He was bleeding from the corner of his mouth where his lip had been split.

Charlie growled and launched himself at Harry but was prevented from doing so by Gerald Cramer, who put him in an unbreakable headlock. Taz Coffman stood on the sidelines, ready to step in if further assistance was needed.

"Cheri, what do you want me to do with him?" Gerald asked calmly.

Cherisse was confused. What had Charlie been accusing Harry of telling her, some seedy secret from the past that Harry was aware of but she wasn't? That didn't make any sense to her.

"Charlie, if Gerry lets you go, will you go somewhere and talk with me and Harry rationally? No more fighting?"

Charlie grunted, "Yeah."

"Let him go, Gerry," said Cherisse.

She looked at Harry. She wasn't too happy with him at this moment, keeping secrets from her. Then she regarded Charlie. "I want to see both of you in the kitchen, now!"

"Handle your business, girlfriend!" Susanne called out.

"Susanne, please!" said Kendall, aghast at his wife's outburst.

"Loosen up, dentist-man," said Susanne. She turned to eye the buffet table. There was a piece of pecan pie with her name on it. A good fistfight always made her ravenous.

Mildred and Jo comforted each other. "I'm sure they'll work it out," said Jo.

"I'm not worried at all," Mildred lied. She *was* worried. Harry had been so close to becoming a husband and, hopefully, a father. It was obvious that Charlie Washington was still in love with Cherisse. What if when the three of them came out of that kitchen something will have been revealed to Cherisse to make her choose Charlie Washington over Harry? She had never known Harry to love a woman the way he loved Cherisse.

She felt like crying.

A few feet away, Danielle *was* crying. Echo, Sandrene and Sage tried to comfort her with softly spoken assurances that everything would be all right. But Danielle couldn't shake the feeling that all of this was her fault. If she hadn't insisted that her dad come stay with them until he found a place to live maybe he wouldn't have started fantasizing about getting back together with her mom. And when he had come to her to recruit her help in his mission, maybe she should have warned her mother about what he was up to. Instead she had chosen to remain silent, hoping that her dad would come to his senses on his own. She would never understand the workings of her parents' minds. Sometimes they behaved more like children than children!

"Echo," she said through her tears, "please go turn the music back on, maybe everybody would stop standing around gossiping about my parents!"

Echo was happy to do her bidding.

Sandrene and Sage led her over to the bottom step of the stairs and they made her sit down. They flanked her.

"Parents can be buttheads sometimes," Sandrene said. "But they usually figure things out in the end."

"Yeah," Sage said, smiling at Danielle, whom she liked a great deal after knowing her less than two hours. "Our parents argue all the time and they've been married forever."

Their brother walked up and cleared his throat. They moved aside and he went and sat down on a stair above them. "Mom and Dad are arguing," he said.

"See what I mean?" said Sage to Danielle.

When the music came back on, Danielle saw that Echo had decided to switch up and eliminate the Christmas music. He'd put on a Ben Harper and the Innocent Criminals CD.

He knew she loved Ben Harper's music. She smiled.

In the kitchen, Cherisse paced the floor alternately glaring at Harry and Charlie, both of whom looked uncomfortable under her scrutiny. Harry leaned against the kitchen sink.

Charlie was sitting at the table with one leg crossed defiantly over the other.

Cherisse didn't feel calm enough to start asking questions. She thought she would end up shouting at them if she didn't first control her temper. Charlie and Harry trading punches, on Christmas Eve! In front of everybody!

She truly could not believe it. She had never seen Charlie hit anybody except on the football field. As for Harry, she never would have thought he had it in him. He seemed so together all the time.

She took a deep breath and slowly released it. Looking at Charlie, she said, "Let's start with you, shall we? First of all, Harry hasn't told me anything about you."

"Told you so," said Harry.

Cherisse shot him a silencing glare.

Harry crossed his arms over his chest and fumed.

Turning back to Charlie, Cherisse said, "What was it you didn't want me to know, Charlie?"

Charlie looked away. His back stiffened. His lips tightened and Cherisse knew he was going into a pout. Oh, she hated it when he would pout like a spoiled child. It was one of the things she certainly didn't miss about their marriage.

"I hate you, you know that!" she shouted. "At this moment I hate you with a passion. I was beginning to consider telling you I forgive you for the past. I forgive you for not loving me enough to fight your addiction, because that's what it amounted to, Charlie. You just didn't love me enough to sacrifice your pleasure for me!"

Charlie looked at her with a hurt expression. "Pleasure?" he asked plaintively. "I got no pleasure from gambling. Do you get pleasure out of something you hate but can't quit doing? Gambling was destroying our marriage. Gambling made me do things I would never have done if I were not addicted."

He paused, taking a deep breath. "Okay. You want to know what I begged Harry to keep his mouth shut about? One night, a long time ago, when we were still playing ball we wound up at the same house party in Philly. And the owner of the house, a big-time sports agent, hired prostitutes to keep the guests, mostly professional football players, happy. But I was there for the high-stakes poker. Not the prostitutes. And Harry left once he found out that there were prostitutes servicing guys in the back rooms. He left and I should have left but I had a great hand and I wanted to play it out."

Cherisse's legs suddenly felt weak. She sat down at the table.

Looking at Harry, she said, "And you didn't want me to know because you figured I wouldn't understand?"

"I was embarrassed," said Harry simply. "No, I didn't want you to know any more than Charlie did. If some reporter had caught us there it could have ruined our careers. Our families would have gone through the embarrassment right alongside us. I started being very careful about whom I associated with after that."

"If either of you macho men had thought for a second you would have realized that football wives, any woman married to a celebrity, know what kind of things go on at parties! I'm not shocked. I'm disappointed that neither of you thought you could confide in me. It makes me wonder about other things that haven't been said."

She regarded Charlie. "I do forgive you for everything. I'm tired of carrying around the anger. You're Danielle's father and therefore you're a part of this family. But you've got to admit that you really didn't want me back, Charlie. You were simply afraid of starting over, afraid of being alone."

Charlie hung his head. "You're wrong. I do love you, Cheri. I'll always love you." He met her gaze. "But I guess you're right about one thing. I was afraid of being alone and, maybe, I saw you, Danielle and me being a family again as the perfect solution to that loneliness. I do want you to be happy. That's all I've ever wanted. You don't know how much the divorce affected me. I felt like such a loser. I thought getting you back would make me a winner again."

"Things are never that simple, Charlie. Like I've told you, I've moved on. And no matter how hard you tried, I would never feel the longing for you that I used to. That part's over with. But, yes, I will always have a soft spot for you somewhere deep in my heart. Just not close to the surface because, after all, you were my first love and you're the father of my child. So, can we bury the past here and now? Can we go forward and be friends? Be the parents that Danielle needs now that she's practically a grown-up? She must have been terribly upset by what happened here tonight!"

Charlie smiled. "Yeah, I did make an ass of myself." He looked over at Harry.

"I'm sorry for slugging you."

Harry hesitated. "I'm sorry for knocking you on your ass, too."

Cherisse got up and went to Harry. He pulled her into his arms. Looking at Charlie, she said, "You want to make this up to me, Charlie?"

"How?" asked Charlie with real sincerity.

"You're going to give me away at our wedding next Thursday," Cherisse shocked both of them by saying.

"What?!" both of them cried at once.

Cherisse smiled. "That's right. To demonstrate your willingness to move on with your life, and your happiness at our union, you're going to give me away to Harry. After that, no one can say there is any animosity left between the three of us."

Charlie sighed. "My friends will think I'm a punk!"

"Do you care more about what your friends think or what your *family* thinks?" asked Cherisse, eyes narrowed.

Charlie gave up. He had rarely been able to win an argument with her when he had been married to her, he didn't see why things had to change now. "Okay, okay, I'll do it."

Cherisse peered up at Harry. "Is that satisfactory with you?"

Harry just wanted to get married. "I can live with it."

The three of them returned to the party to find Danielle and Echo dancing, Jo and Mildred chatting up their gentlemen friends, Sandrene, Sage and Kendall, Jr. also dancing, and Susanne and Kendall in the corner kissing under the mistletoe.

Cherisse was immediately set upon by Sonia and Mary, who wanted to know if she was all right. She assured them that everything was all right, and that Charlie had agreed to give her away at the wedding on Thursday. Whereupon Sonia placed her hand on Cherisse's forehead and said, "She doesn't have a fever, Mary. Something else must be making her talk crazy."

Later, after everyone had gone home except for Harry and his family they all sat in the family room quietly drinking coffee and eating what was left of the ice-cream pound cake.

"You all certainly know how to show your guests a good time," Susanne joked. "I haven't had this much fun in years."

Harry laughed. "Wait until the wedding. I'm sure we can come up with something to keep you entertained."

Cherisse hoped his words were not prophetic.

Christmas fell on a Thursday. And Cherisse had to work the next day plus the following week on Monday, Tuesday and Wednesday. David was kind enough to let her leave early on Wednesday.

* * *

On the day of the wedding, it snowed in Vail, thankfully not so heavy that the roads were impassable. The two families had spent the previous night at the resort, occupying two of the new condominiums.

Cherisse and Harry hadn't gotten the chance to be alone in days. In fact they had not had a chance to make love since their night in the Hotel Teatro. A memory Harry thought of fondly, and Cherisse felt had been a dream at this point.

So they looked forward to their wedding night in Harry's suite with great expectation.

The wedding was to take place in the ballroom. The high-ceilinged room had been furnished with a hundred gold straight-back chairs with beige striped seats. Down the aisle ran a red carpet. Orchids, rare at this time of the year, were in the centerpiece on the stage where the minister's podium stood ready.

The bride wore a simple sleeveless white tea-length gown by Carolina Herrera that complemented her lovely arms and legs. The groom wore a Hugo Boss tuxedo with a red cummerbund. Cherisse chose Sonia as her maid of honor. Harry asked Kendall to be his best man.

Danielle, Sandrene and Sage made lovely bridesmaids.

The guests sighed when Charlie escorted Cherisse down the aisle. And when Reverend McLeod asked, "Who gives this woman to this man?" Charlie said in a clear voice, "I do."

He then placed Cherisse's hand in Harry's and went and sat down in the front row beside Jo, who was silently weeping. She took his hand in hers.

Reverend McLeod cleared his throat. "We are gathered here today in the sight of God to unite this man and this woman in holy matrimony." On Harry and Cherisse's advice, he skipped the part where he might have asked if anyone objected to the union. "Do you, Harrison Walker Payne, take this woman, Cherisse Patterson, as your lawfully wedded wife? Do you promise to love and cherish her until death do you part?"

Harry gave an emphatic, "Yes, I definitely do!"

"And do you, Cherisse Patterson, take this man, Harrison Walker Payne, to be your lawfully wedded husband. Do you promise to love and cherish him until death do you part?"

"Yes, I do!" said Cherisse, smiling up at Harry.

"Wonderful!" intoned Reverend McLeod. "Then with the power vested in me by the Lord God above and the state of Colorado, I now pronounce that you are husband and wife. You may kiss your bride, Harry!"

Harry did so with a great deal of enthusiasm, so much so that the guests started clapping loudly and two minutes later started laughing because it didn't appear as if he was going to let go of her anytime soon.

As it turned out, it was a three-minute kiss, after which Harry picked up his bride and carried her back up the aisle to the song "Bring It On Home to Me" by Sam Cooke, the very song that Cherisse had sung in his ear the night of the red-and-white ball.

The song selection was a surprise to Cherisse. She smiled into the face of her new husband and whispered in his ear while he swept her up the aisle, "You actually remembered that song?"

"Baby, how could I forget?" Harry asked, grinning.

The wedding photographer snapped photos of them as they passed him. The guests were on their feet applauding the happy couple, and when they disappeared out the entrance, they began filing out of the room and making their way to Solomon's, where the reception would be held.

Harry and Cherisse were applauded by guests of the resort

as they moved through the lobby to the elevators. "Are you going to put me down anytime soon?"

"Not until I carry you over the threshold of our suite," Harry said.

Cherisse held a small bouquet of white orchids in her right hand and was grateful that the length of the dress afforded her a modicum of modesty since Harry was adamant about not putting her down.

A couple was standing in front of the bank of elevators when they reached it.

"Where're you taking her, Harry?" the middle-aged black woman dressed in bright blue ski togs teasingly asked.

Her husband laughed. "Where did I take you the moment we got married, Bernice?"

Bernice suddenly laughed and clasped her cheeks as though they'd grown hot with embarrassment. "Oh, my, then we must not hold you up!"

"Jack, Bernice, meet my new wife, Cherisse," Harry said.

"Delighted to meet you," said Bernice.

"Likewise," said Cherisse feeling kind of awkward sitting in Harry's arms.

When the elevator arrived, Bernice and her husband stepped aside. "Go for it, Harry," said Jack, gesturing toward the open elevator doors. "Bernice and I will wait."

"Thanks, Jack, Bernice," Harry said as he stepped into the empty conveyance.

Cherisse pressed the button for Harry's floor, and the elevator doors slowly slid closed. Alone at last, she kissed Harry's mouth softly and looking deeply in his eyes said, "I love you so much, Harry Payne."

"I hope so," Harry said, smiling, "because you're stuck with me now. I don't ever plan to let you go."

In the suite, Harry put her down and kissed her again.

Raising his head, he said, "The staff has instructions to begin serving even if we don't show up for a while."

Cherisse was way ahead of him. She had already put her flowers down and was unbuttoning his shirt. "Listen, Harry, we can save time if we don't talk, just make love."

Harry liked the sound of that, and turned her around and unzipped her dress. In less than two minutes they were both completely nude, and falling onto the bed in each other's arms.

In Solomon's the wedding guests were being entertained by jazz vocalist Cassandra Wilson. Her deep, soulful voice was in fine form this evening, and the audience sat rapt. With her signature dreadlocks she was also a physical presence to be reckoned with.

Echo couldn't take his eyes off her. Sitting across from him, Danielle wondered what it was that Cassandra Wilson had that made her so magnetic to him. "Echo," she said softly.

He didn't seem to hear her.

"Echo!" she said in a louder voice.

Echo turned to look at her. "Did you say something?"

Irritated, Danielle asked, "Why are you staring at her?"

"It's her sound," Echo said. "I never knew jazz could be that good. I'm going to have to sample more jazz artists."

Danielle smiled. It was true. Echo was a diehard fan of rap and hip-hop music. He would tease her because she liked a wide range of musical styles. She guessed it was because when she was a kid her mother exposed her to so many kinds of music. She had grown up listening to Motown, opera, jazz and the blues. She loved some of today's hip-hop artists, as well, but she had to admit that some of her favorite musicians—like Nina Simone, Fats Waller and Carmen McRae, who had the smoothest voice she'd ever heard—were long dead.

"You can borrow all the CDs you want from me," she said.

Echo smiled at her. "You wanna dance?"

Danielle grinned. Usually, Echo didn't like to dance. But maybe he was trying to compromise. He'd danced with her on Christmas Eve and, now, he wanted to dance with her again.

"Sure," she said.

As they rose their eyes met and held. "You're the prettiest woman here," he told her.

Danielle blushed. He'd called her a woman!

At the bar in the front of the restaurant, Charlie had ordered his second gin and tonic.

He was trying to stop thinking about where Cherisse and Harry were. Okay, he'd agreed to give Cherisse away at their wedding but only under duress. His participation didn't mean he had stopped loving her or that he didn't harbor ill feelings toward Harry Payne. Maybe one day he would be able to look at him and not wish he'd step in front of a speeding bus, but not today.

A woman with short dark brown hair and a black dress sat down on the bar stool next to his. Charlie saw her only peripherally. He had no interest in striking up a conversation with anyone. When he finished this drink he planned to leave, whether or not the happy couple had returned from lovemaking by then. He knew that's what they were doing. *Let's face it,* he thought, *that's exactly what I would be doing if she'd picked me.*

The bartender placed the drink in front of him and Charlie immediately picked it up and drank deeply.

"Whoa," said the woman, "what are you trying to do, get loaded then pass out right here with your face in the peanuts?"

Charlie merely grunted and set the glass down. He didn't say a word, just looked at his reflection in the mirror behind the bar. What was wrong with him? Why couldn't he find some balance in his life? For once he'd like to have every aspect of his life in sync.

Now that he had a good job and had some control over his gambling, and was enjoying being back in his daughter's life, why couldn't his love life fall into place? He wasn't a bad guy. He wasn't bad-looking, either. Didn't have a paunch, still looked good in his clothes and his breath didn't stink. Yet, after his last relationship with a woman who left him because he wasn't making the big bucks, he had somehow lost his confidence.

Frowning, he picked up the glass again. He hated it when Cherisse was right! She had told him he was just lonely and was grasping for the familiar, hoping to revisit a time when he'd been happy. That she was simply convenient.

And it was true. Cherisse had been the only woman who had ever loved him for himself, and he'd ruined it.

He took a large swig of his drink and set the glass back down, still deep in thought. He had to do something to break the cycle. If he didn't he would wind up another bitter divorced guy who no longer believed there was a woman out there who could love him.

"You don't look like you want to be bothered, but I'm going to hate myself in the morning if I don't say what I came over here to say," said the woman in the black dress.

Charlie now turned to look at her. She was around five-six, a little plump, with beautiful brown skin and compelling dark brown eyes. She looked vaguely familiar.

She smiled nervously. "You don't remember me, do you?"

Charlie smiled. *You don't remember me, do you?* If he had a nickel for every time somebody had said that to him he'd be as rich as Harry Payne. "I'm sorry, no, I don't."

He said it matter-of-factly, not derisively.

She visibly relaxed and said, "I'm your ex-wife's best friend's sister, Gracie Lopez."

The fog lifted a little from Charlie's brain. "Sonia's sister. You were three or four grades behind us in school."

She smiled more broadly, dimples appearing in both cheeks. "Yeah, I was in ninth grade when you all were seniors. I used to follow you around like a puppy."

Charlie laughed, remembering a chubby little girl who ran her mouth constantly. And who never had any money when they went to McDonald's. He must have bought her a hundred hamburgers and Cokes his senior year. "All those burgers I bought you, you owe me dinner at least," he told her, smiling.

"Honey, I will *make* you dinner any night you want," Gracie told him.

Charlie looked at her. If she were four years younger than he was that made her thirty-four. She appeared younger, or maybe that was because she had such a vivacious air about her. Fully alive and ready for whatever life threw her way.

Like a lonely divorced guy trying to get on with life.

"I'll tell you what, Gracie. I'll accept a dance for now."

Gracie stepped off her bar stool and turned around in her little black dress. Plump or not, she had a fit body and killer legs. "Let's go. I hope you can keep up with me!"

Charlie hoped so, too.

Chapter 17

"Damn, baby, I can't believe I don't have any condoms here. I took them to the Denver house, hoping to get you alone at some point and never got lucky," Harry said just as he had Cherisse panting on her back, quite ready for penetration.

"Harry, how cheap can you be?" said Cherisse. "You can't afford condoms for your suite *and* your house?!"

Laughing, Harry said, "I'm sorry!"

Sitting up in bed, Cherisse narrowed her eyes at him. "You ought to be, getting me all hot and bothered for nothing."

"What are you complaining about, you've already come once," Harry pointed out.

"Yeah, but I wanted to feel you inside of me, Harry. That's the best part of sex with you, feeling your belly rubbing against mine. All of you inside of me."

Harry's penis got even harder at her description. He looked

down at it and back up at Cherisse. "How soon do you want to have a baby?"

Cherisse smiled. "The sooner, the better," she told him.

"It would be funny if you got pregnant on our wedding night," Harry said as he pushed her back onto the bed, and straddled her. He bent and kissed her deeply, savoring the warmth of her mouth while his penis found the opening of her sex.

Pushing, he moaned as she pushed back and then he was easing inside of her and the sensation was so delicious he felt like crying.

About an hour later, showered and dressed in more casual clothing, they finally put in an appearance at the reception. Mildred walked up to them, her index finger pointed at Harry. "Where have you been? I had Susanne spread the lie that you had gotten stuck in the elevator!"

Unapologetic, Harry bent and kissed his mother's cheek. "We were making you a grandchild."

Mildred put her hand over her heart and smiled. "You're forgiven."

Ignoring Harry, now she took Cherisse by the arm. "Darlin', the guests have all eaten and we were just waiting on you and Harry to cut the cake so we can wish you well."

The cake was a three-tiered work of art—white, trimmed in pale yellow. It had three different flavors of cake: vanilla, chocolate and lemon. The icing was vanilla cream.

Harry and Cherisse made the ceremonial cut while the photographer took several photographs to document the occasion. Cherisse picked up a piece and fed it to Harry and, seeing the mischievous intent in his eyes, she warned, "Do it and die!"

Harry grinned and fed her a piece of the cake. "I don't know what you're referring to, darling girl."

They kissed briefly, after which they got separated,

Cherisse being pulled away by Sonia and her friends and colleagues from the hospital's staff and Harry dragged off by some of his football buddies.

"So, how're you holding up, girlfriend?" asked Sonia. Her date was Ken Kesey who seemed, to Cherisse, to be in it for the long haul.

"Doing great," said Cherisse, looking at Sonia keenly. There was something different about her today. Her skin was flushed and she looked as if she had gained weight around her middle. It might not be noticeable to someone who didn't know her well, but Cherisse saw her practically every day. She could tell there was a thickening there.

She grabbed Sonia by the arm and pulled her aside. "What's going on with you? You look three months pregnant! That's why you've been wearing those loose tops, isn't it?"

"Will you keep your voice down?" Sonia said. "My mom's here. She came with Gracie. Okay, I lied about meeting Ken for the first time at Karibu. I'm ashamed to say I met him about three months ago and, loose woman that I am, I slept with him the night I met him. Obviously the condom broke! I didn't expect to see him again and I ran in to him at Karibu and he confessed that he really liked me but he didn't think I was into him. We started dating again and the rest is history."

"Well, thank goodness you ran into him again since you're about to make him a father!"

Tears came to Sonia's eyes. "He wants to marry me."

"Do it before you give birth," Cherisse advised.

Sonia laughed. "Yeah, I suppose I should." She wiped her tears away with a finger. "That's enough about me, kiddo. Where are you and Harry going on your honeymoon?"

"He's taking me to a ski resort in the Alps," Cherisse said.

"You don't ski," said Sonia.

"I'm sure the beds will be nice and comfortable," said Cherisse.

* * *

The beds were nice and comfortable. Their first day in Zurich was spent mostly in bed. The trip had been exhausting, hours on the plane, then more time on the train.

Zurich was known for its transportation system and they took the train from Zurich Kloten Airport. Called the S-Bahn, the rapid transit train got them to Zurich in about fifteen minutes. From the train station they got a taxi to the resort, a huge complex perhaps twice as large as Karibu.

The town of Zurich was the largest city in Switzerland yet it had a small town feel with quaint houses and shops. It was a walking city; pedestrians leisurely strolled the streets. In fact the whole place took on a fairy-tale appearance. There were snow-covered chalets, wonderful old churches like St. Peter's Church that had the largest clock dials in Europe and the Fraumünster, famous because of the wonderful stained-glass windows by artist Marc Chagall.

On the morning of the second day, Harry awakened her with a cup of coffee underneath her nose. "Wake up, sleepy-head. It's time for your ski lesson."

Cherisse dug deeper into the lovely bed. She slowly opened her eyes and sniffed, smelling the coffee. Debating whether it would be more advantageous to stay in bed or take the coffee, she opted for the coffee.

Sitting up in bed, naked, she took the cup from Harry. Last night she'd put her hair in a single braid before getting into bed, now it was loose and hanging down her back. Meeting Harry's eyes, she said, between sips, "Good morning, Mr. Payne."

"Good morning, Mrs. Payne," said Harry. He took every opportunity to call her that.

He'd never been happier in his life. Not when he'd been drafted by his first professional football team. Not when he made his first million. Not when he got that Super Bowl ring. They all paled in comparison to one little woman with frizzy hair.

She blinked at him now. "Who said anything about my taking ski lessons? I certainly didn't. I don't like the snow, Harry. I thought you knew that. I don't like it because it's cold and it's wet and it's deep, I'm scared of drowning in snow should I fall. I'm terrified of the possibility of an avalanche. I don't want to end up like the Donner party. A reference I'm not making to be funny but to express to you just how serious I am about never going on a slope with you."

Harry sat on the side of the bed and looked at her with a puppy dog, pleading expression in his eyes. "But you weren't the owner of a ski resort then, darling girl. How is it going to look to our guests when they learn you can't ski?"

"Don't take this the wrong way, Harry, darling boy, but I don't care! You're not getting me on a snow-covered rock to schuss down it like a maniac on nothing but two pieces of wood and holding steel poles that can impale you if you fall on them the right way! I pass."

"Your daughter does it all the time."

"Oh, so now you're going to appeal to the mother in me? That's dirty pool, Harry Payne. Are you saying I don't have the guts to try skiing?"

"I didn't say it, you did," said Harry.

"But you were thinking it!"

"I most certainly was not," Harry denied. "I think you're one of the bravest women I've ever known, even if you *are* afraid of a little snow."

Cherisse put her coffee cup on the night table beside the bed and pushed Harry off the bed. Rising, she said, "I'm going to need a good, fortifying breakfast, oatmeal and scrambled eggs. You order it for me while I shower." She looked back at him. "Oh, and Harry, if you let me die out there today, I'm going to haunt you for the rest of your life."

"Yes, ma'am," he said, smiling. He didn't tell her that she wouldn't be able to haunt him because if anything happened to her he wouldn't want to live and would take his life so he could be with her again. He didn't think she'd appreciate that kind of morbid talk when she was getting ready to risk her life.

A few minutes later they were taking the lift to the part of the mountain that was shaped like two large bowls. Two thousand vertical feet were served by lifts and the area offered open terrain, glades and chutes from which beginning skiers and intermediate skiers could launch themselves down the mountain.

When they reached the top and got off the lift, Cherisse quipped, "Well, it's all downhill from here."

Harry laughed shortly. "You're going to be a natural. Surely Danielle didn't get all her talent from Charlie."

"Don't bet on that," said Cherisse, eyeing the steep slopes. At least it wasn't snowing.

When she'd read in the brochure that Switzerland had as many sunny days a year as Denver enjoyed, she had been skeptical, but the sky was a beautiful cerulean blue.

Too bad there was all of this snow on the ground!

"Okay," said Harry, coming to stand behind her. "We're going to take it slowly. First I want you to learn how to control the poles and how to turn in order to stop yourself from going forward."

"Yes, that's a good skill to learn," Cherisse agreed. She could see her breath on the air and thought she might be about to hyperventilate.

"I brought you down here," Harry was telling her, "because we're going to practice your cross-country skiing technique first. It's all a matter of coordinating your leg and arm movements. You thrust out one leg while gliding forward on the other. It's easy."

"Okay," Cherise said.

Harry bent and kissed her cheek. It was about twenty degrees out today so they were both dressed warmly in layered ski clothing. Harry had advised her that if she got warm, she could always take something off but if she didn't bring adequate protection from the cold there was no getting warmer.

Plus, they were wearing goggles to prevent snow blindness since the day was sunny and bright.

He showed her the basic move called the snowplow. It was a turn designed to help a skier slow down or stop. Cherisse learned it in a matter of minutes and felt more confident about the rest of the lesson. So far, she'd stayed on her feet, so that was saying something.

Soon, Harry was teaching her how to move atop the snow using cross-country techniques. Cherisse found this a simple maneuver and thanked her lucky stars that she was a runner. She imagined the movement was hell on her thigh muscles and she would feel it in the morning.

"Okay," Harry said after a while, "you're doing well. Now, let's see if you can go downhill for a short distance and stop using the snowplow move."

At the top of a not very steep hill, Cherisse stood poised, nervously chewing on her bottom lip. Harry was beside her. "Whenever you're ready," he encouraged her.

Cherisse pushed off on her ski poles and soon she was moving down at a slow pace at first, then she hit a mogul, or a bump in the terrain. She went up and over the mogul and suddenly she was launched into the air and onto another, steeper course. She started moving down at a faster pace, then faster and faster. Her heart raced. Everything Harry had taught her flew from her panicked brain and all she could think about was that there was a tree down there and she was going to hit it and break every bone in her body.

Harry was right behind her yelling, "Turn, Cheri, turn like I taught you and go into the snowplow!"

Cherisse closed her eyes and twisted her body as he'd taught her then pointed her toes inward. She immediately began slowing, and finally, about five feet away from the spruce tree that she had been sure was going to be the death of her, she stopped.

Harry schussed to a stop beside her. "Baby, that was great!"

Cherisse burst into tears. "That wasn't great! I thought I was going to get creamed by that tree!"

"But you didn't, you stopped in time."

"By the grace of God," she said.

Harry sighed but did not push her to admit that for a split second there she had been enjoying herself. Yes, she'd been terrified, but flying down that hill had also been an exhilarating experience for her. He felt it in his bones.

"Okay, sweetheart," he said. "There's a lift down there. We'll take it and go back to the resort."

Cherisse took a deep breath. Her face was colder now due to the stupid tears. And she'd just been scared out of ten years of life, but she was no quitter. "I'm not ready to go until I can go down a hill better than that," she said.

She began walking back up the hill. Harry followed her, a smile on his face. "If you insist," was all he said.

Cherisse spent another hour going down the hill and practicing the snowplow. She got better with each try, and only when they started losing daylight did she say, "All right, I'm cold and hungry now, it's time to go."

Harry was impressed with his new wife. Impressed and

falling deeper in love with her every minute he spent in her presence.

Back in their suite, he washed her back, lifted her from the tub, dried her off then carried her to the bed, where he gave her a massage with warm scented oil.

While she was in the tub he had taken a quick shower in the other bathroom and ordered them meals from room service. He didn't want to go anywhere tonight. He was going to pamper his woman.

Now, Cherisse gave a satisfied sigh and turned over to gaze up at him. Her body glistened from the oil he'd used, and she was so relaxed from the massage that she could do nothing but smile. "That wasn't so bad."

"What wasn't so bad?" asked Harry. He was wearing one of the hotel's robes and he looked very handsome in it.

"Don't pretend you don't know what I'm talking about."

"I told you that you would be a natural," he said, running his hand along her shapely thigh. "Now, what do you say we have something to eat and then go to bed? You have a long day tomorrow on the slopes."

Cherisse nudged his robe open with her foot. "What do you say you make love to me before we eat? Your hands on my body left me wanting to feel more of you."

Harry stood up and doffed the robe, revealing his already semi-erect penis. He had been hoping she was in the mood, although he wouldn't have suggested it because she'd had a rough day on the slopes.

He stretched the length of his body over hers. Cherisse opened her legs and welcomed him into her arms. Warm brown bodies pressed closer, chest to breasts, groin to groin, mouth to mouth.

Cherisse felt so full, completely happy. She realized that in Harry she had the passion that had at first been in her relationship with Charlie plus the bonus of a reliable man who adored her as in her relationship with Neil. She had the best of both worlds and didn't know how she'd gotten so lucky.

Harry entered her and his thrusts were powerful, purposeful, it seemed. When his seed spilled into her she felt warm and satisfied. This moment felt perfect. She came, and her vaginal walls convulsed around his still-hard penis.

Harry trembled. Her name was on his lips as he whispered again and again, "Cheri, my sweet Cheri."

Cherisse merely smiled. He lay his head on her chest and they held each other until they both came down from the most wonderful high they had yet shared.

In the morning they were on a slope designed for intermediate skiers. Harry had to warn her about avoiding other skiers as this area was more populated. The beginning area had not been so busy because most of the skiers who came to this premier resort were either intermediate skiers or experts.

Today, Cherisse was wearing blue. Yesterday she'd been in bright yellow. She looked up at Harry after he had told her to watch out for other skiers and said, "You don't think I wore this color for my health, do you? I wore it so that I would be seen a mile away by anyone else who happened to be in my path. If they can't see me, then they are truly snow-blind."

Harry did think she resembled the Michelin man in that getup. He was all seriousness now, though, because what she'd learned yesterday would be child's play compared to what she had to learn today.

Yesterday the cross-country techniques were easy to learn—they had required endurance, which she had plenty of. Today would require skill and balance which Harry thought she might be lacking in.

He was slightly worried.

Cherisse smiled up at him. "Get on with it, Harry."

"All right, then," said Harry. "You have to know a few basic things in order to ski downhill without hurting yourself. You've already learned how to stop, that's the most important thing. Next you'll learn how more effectively to change the direction in which you're skiing. You do this by learning how to shift your weight. Forward, backward, to the side, when to shift it to one leg or the other. After a time it comes as naturally as breathing, that's why you see Danielle going downhill with such abandon. She's done it so often that it's second nature to her."

Cherisse was nodding. She understood. She was glad she was learning more about what her baby girl was so in love with. Now, she could empathize with her, know how she's feeling when she's competing.

Harry saw how intently Cherisse was listening to him and felt a surge of pride swell his chest. She was really getting it.

An hour later, after intense instruction on the proper form for schussing and traversing down the slopes, Harry took her to the top of the hill.

Cherisse once again felt a sick feeling in the pit of her stomach, but she was determined to take the slopes today and she wasn't going to forget everything Harry had taught her today like she had in a panic yesterday.

Therefore she regarded her course with steely determination and pushed off. Harry followed two lengths behind her, observing her form, which was surprisingly good for a beginner.

She began picking up speed, in true schuss form, but then she felt the need to slow down a bit and Harry watched her tilt the lower part of her body toward the slope so that her skis would get a better grip on the snow. She slowed a bit, gained more control and toward the bottom of the slope began to gradually go into the snowplow. Then she came to a complete stop without incident.

Harry schussed to a stop beside her and whooped. "I knew Danielle didn't get all her talent from her dad. Her mom's got mad skills!"

Cherisse laughed, thrilled with her performance. She wanted to go again and they did, two more times, but after that Harry told her she'd done quite enough for one day and Zurich had so much more to offer than skiing. Tonight, he was taking her out on the town. For that, she required time to get all dolled up.

But first they went shopping in an exclusive dress shop. Harry sat down in a spindly antique chair he feared might not be able to hold his bulk while Cherisse modeled designer dresses for him.

The proprietor of the shop, a sharp-nosed blonde with too-red lipstick and a permanent grimace on her pinched face, treated them like royalty. Cherisse didn't know why the woman looked as if she smelled something bad, but her service was definitely among the finest she had ever gotten. A speed demon, the woman fetched shoes and dresses at a breakneck pace and offered suggestions here and there. "With your coloring," she said when Cherisse picked up a white dress, "you can pull off the richer shades, something in a deep red or a deep purple." She had a German accent and when she said something it came out sounding like *zumzing*.

Cherisse and Harry finally decided on a strapless deep purple sheath that displayed her breasts to perfection and cinched her waist, flaring out at the hips. It was a creation that reminded Cherisse of those tailored dresses fifties stars like Bette Davis and Joan Crawford wore in movies. She knew just how she was going to style her hair, in a French twist. Harry told her that since the dress was strapless, she required something fabulous to keep her lovely shoulders warm, and told the proprietor he wanted to see his wife in the sable in the window.

To which Cherisse immediately protested, "Harry, you've already spent a fortune on this beautiful dress. Besides, I don't want to wear dead animal carcasses on my body."

"Darling," said Harry, "you're married to a very rich man, and those animals took their own lives."

"Yes," said the proprietor, "they all committed suicide."

But Cherisse was adamant. "Don't you have something warm but that doesn't have the blood of dead animals on it?"

So it was decided that she would wear a lovely floor-length black wool parka with a hood. It was sufficiently elegant and warm enough for the cold winds off the Alps.

Harry resigned himself to the fact that his wife wasn't a fur-wearing woman.

He would have to find other ways to spoil her.

They went to a five-star restaurant near the river Limmat and afterward went to a jazz club. The city had nightclubs to please every taste and budget. The club they chose turned out to be in the seedier range and they wound up laughing about it in the cab on the way back to the resort. "Imagine," Cherisse said, cozying up to Harry in the back of the cab, "if I had walked in there in my sable. We might not have gotten out alive."

"The way those hard-looking dudes at the table across from ours were looking at you, I feared for my life and your virtue. They couldn't keep their eyes off you."

"I don't see why not," said Cherisse. "I've noticed a few other black women since we've been here."

"Yes, a few, *few* being the operative word. They're not used to the beauty of our Nubian queens."

"It's true," said the cabdriver in perfect English. "You're a lucky man."

Cherisse had to put her hand over her mouth to keep from guffawing. She had assumed that the driver did not understand English very well, he'd had such a thick accent when they'd hired him. Perhaps he affected that accent to please gullible tourists who came to Zurich for the full effect of being in a Swiss town.

"I am," said Harry to the driver, "the luckiest of men. Thank you."

In their suite, Harry slowly undressed her as he gazed into her eyes. "So, Mrs. Payne, are you enjoying yourself so far?"

Cherisse smiled indulgently. That beauty mark next to her luscious mouth beckoned him and he kissed her there before she could reply. His mouth was still there when she said, "Harry, I've never had such a good…" She didn't get to finish because he'd found her warm breath wafting up his nostrils too much of a temptation and covered her mouth with his in a searing kiss.

God, she was sweet and he was a sugar addict. He couldn't get enough of her.

Cherisse's body sang with his touch. Each kiss was like a lifeline. She wondered how she had managed to exist for thirty-seven years without him. Why had it taken her so long to find him?

Harry's hands cupped her buttocks, drawing her closer to his hard body. Cherisse sighed into his mouth. Her ripening female center craved his touch, wanted it so badly that she was in pain.

Good Lord, had she turned into a raving sex maniac in the space of two months with Harry? Had she locked away these desires all for the express purpose of unleashing them on one man? It would seem so because, suddenly, she was insatiable.

Twisting her head to the side, she broke off the kiss and pleaded, "Harry, now, I can't wait any longer."

Harry ripped off her silky white bikinis, picked her up and tossed her butt-first onto the bed. Then he had to get out of his slacks, but didn't fare well because he ripped the seat of them in his haste. He rid himself of his boxers and tossed them behind him. Where they landed, he didn't know.

All he cared about at this moment was melding his body with Cherisse's, and her eagerness only fueled his passion. He was so hard with need by the time he placed his penis at the opening of her sex that any touch was exquisite pain.

Harry paused. If he entered her right now, he knew he would hurt her. His need was so urgent, so frantic. So he slowed down. He bent and licked her nipples, stayed a while, then moved downward to her flat stomach and licked around her belly button.

Moving farther down, his tongue licked her clitoris and he felt her writhe with pleasure.

He could tell by how erect her clitoris was that she was more than ready for him. She was begging him to take her. He raised his head and positioned his penis at her vagina once more. Upon entering her, he felt her come just that quickly. And while she bucked against him he took his pleasure, took it for all that it was worth. She answered his passion with her own, never the shy retiring miss, she loved it. Loved it, and that fact was gratifying to him, to know that he was pleasing her, made her melt beneath him, made her yearn for his touch. That she needed him as much as he needed her.

He came with a growl deep in his throat.

Collapsing onto his side next to her, he said, "You're insatiable."

Cherisse laughed softly because that's exactly what she'd been thinking a minute ago.

Kissing his mouth, she said, "Yes, so get your rest because you're on again in a few hours."

Chapter 18

Harry and Cherisse spent an idyllic ten days in Zurich, but like all good things their honeymoon had to come to an end. They returned to Denver on January 11th and went straight to the Patterson house from the airport.

It was six o'clock in the evening. Danielle and Jo met them at the door and it seemed to Harry that they hadn't seen each other in years. There were so many hugs and happy tears.

Charlie wasn't there, a fact that he appreciated. He didn't think seeing another man returning from a honeymoon with his ex-wife would be something Charlie could stomach. He knew he wouldn't have been able to take it if Charlie had been on a romantic holiday with Cherisse for ten days.

Danielle exclaimed, "How was Switzerland?"

"It was gorgeous," said Cherisse. She wore a smart black pantsuit with comfortable pumps and she glowed in the presence of her daughter and mother. "We've got pictures that need to be developed."

"Ma, it's a digital camera," Danielle said, smiling. She always had to explain any sort of electronic device to her mother. "We can look at them on the computer."

Cherisse reached into her shoulder bag and handed the camera to Danielle. "Here it is, then." She looked around. "Is your dad here?"

"Nah, he moved out while you were gone," said Danielle. "And guess what? He's dating Gracie Lopez."

Cherisse smiled. She liked Gracie. Gracie wasn't aware of it, but Cherisse had known that she had had a crush on Charlie when they were in school. "That's great," she said. "Gracie's a good woman. She's just who Charlie needs in his life."

"I couldn't agree more," said Jo. Then, turning to Harry, she said, "Are you hungry, baby?"

"Starving," said Harry.

She took him by the arm, leaving Danielle and Cherisse in the foyer.

"Danielle," Cherisse said excitedly in her mother and Harry's absence, "Harry gave me ski lessons."

Danielle screamed and hugged her mother again. For years she'd been trying to get her mother interested in the sport. "Don't you just love it?"

"I do," said Cherisse.

Danielle let go of her mother and looked into her eyes. "And married life? How is that?"

"I highly recommend it," said Cherisse.

Danielle beamed. "I knew hooking you up with Daddy Harry was a good idea."

"Daddy Harry?" asked Cherisse.

"That's what I'm calling him this week. I may decide on something else next week," said her daughter.

Cherisse laughed, put her arm about her daughter's waist and they went to join Harry and her mother in the kitchen.

Harry protested mightily when the next day, Monday, January 12, Cherisse had to go into work. They had spent the night in the Denver house. Harry wanted to go check on things at the resort. However, as he explained to Cherisse, he was taking the full month of January off to be with her. Besides, he had a general manager who handled things in his absence. He didn't need to be at the resort 24/7.

Cherisse didn't spend much time vindicating her actions. She simply told him over breakfast that, "I'm a nurse, Harry. I have an obligation to my patients. I've agreed to give them six weeks' notice and that's what I'm going to do. After that, I'm all yours."

"So, I can just like it or lump it?" he asked, brows drawn together in a frown.

"You don't have to like it, Harry," Cherisse said sweetly. "But I'm still going to do it whether you like it or not." She rose and kissed his forehead. "Have a nice day, sweetie."

Harry blew air between his lips and simmered for a good half hour after she had left him high and dry. Then he stopped pouting and got on with his day. He had to make some compromises. That's what marriage was about. He would phone her later and tell her he was sorry for acting like a big baby.

At work, Cherisse was met with applause when she stepped off the elevator onto the pediatrics floor. The gang was all there: Gerald, Sonia, Katy and other nurses and nurses' aides who were not always on their shift.

When she reached the nurses' station, Sonia grabbed her and hugged her. "How was the honeymoon, you lucky, lucky girl?"

"Everything I imagined and more," Cherisse said. "It was

a long plane ride but once we got to Zurich traveling became more enjoyable. I really liked the trains."

"How romantic," Katy said. "I love trains."

"I do, too, now," said Cherisse. "It was the first time I'd ever been on a train." Her Granddaddy Patterson, the Pullman porter, would be aghast.

She got down to business after that and asked, "Who's been filling in for me since I've been gone?"

"David Pedersen," said Gerald.

"David?" cried Cherisse.

"I know it's hard to believe," said Sonia, "but he came down here, went through the charts, advised us on schedules, congratulated us on jobs well done and left in about an hour or so every single day while you were gone. I tell you, we didn't know whether we were going or coming, wondering when he was going to lower the boom. All that niceness coming from him gave me chills, girl!"

Cherisse laughed delightedly. David was keeping his word and trying not to be such a tight-ass. She wondered if he had gotten his wife to come back to him. He had not come to the wedding. She assumed he hadn't had any success.

"He can change, he's human," she said.

"Mark my words," Sonia said, "he's going to change all right, into a worse monster than he already is."

Cherisse sighed. She wanted to ask Sonia if David had spoken to her about taking the head nurse position. But she couldn't because she hadn't even told Sonia she'd suggested her to David. Now with Sonia expecting, she didn't even know if she wanted the added responsibility.

So she didn't say anything about it.

"I'd better get to work," she said and everyone else, taking their cues from her, went back to what they'd been doing before her arrival.

Cherisse went to her office to put her coat and shoulder bag in the closet. Afterward she returned to the nurses' station and began perusing the charts. She would go over the schedule after lunch.

While studying the charts she learned that while she had been gone three patients had been released. A couple had been upgraded from critical care to the general population. And four new patients had been admitted. One little boy was HIV positive.

He'd been admitted with respiratory failure but was holding on.

Cherisse made a note on his chart to pay him a visit. By the time she'd gone through the charts, she'd added ten other patients she wanted to personally check up on.

Getting up from her swivel chair, she realized that while she'd been engrossed with the charts all of the other nurses had left. She stepped out from behind the circular counter and headed down to the HIV-positive boy's room.

He was sleeping peacefully when she entered. She walked over and observed his monitors, making sure they were operating at maximum proficiency. Satisfied that they were, she watched him breathe for a few minutes. His chest rose and fell in a steady rhythm, his heartbeat, as seen in his skinny little neck, strong.

She said a silent prayer for him, and left.

She hated to see any child suffer, but the ones who only suffered for a short time due to the fact that they had a malady that was curable didn't bother her nearly as much as those who were not going to get better. On these children's behalf she railed against God in his sky. Asked Him why? Why must the children suffer? In her opinion she never got an answer. It just made her love them more. Love them because they needed all the love they could get.

She went on to visit the other ten children on her list, walking in cheerful in spite of the depressing emotions she was feeling at the moment. Some of them were awake and smiled at her. Others were in too much pain to smile and she did what she could to comfort them.

When she had visited each child and determined that they were all receiving the best possible care, she went to her office to work on next week's schedule. As she was working there came a knock on her door.

"Come in," she called.

David Pedersen strode in, looking much more rested than he had the last time she'd seen him. His crisp scrubs fit him well, and his white lab coat didn't have a spot on it. He was sharp in appearance and in demeanor.

"You're back," he said and sat down in the chair directly in front of her desk.

Cherisse eyed him suspiciously. He looked like the old David, the arrogant, unforgiving David who was not lamenting the loss of his wife. "Indeed, as promised, I have returned to serve out my sentence of six weeks since you were kind enough to grant me a ten-day leave."

He smiled. "Still with the caustic tongue, I see. I was hoping marriage would have mellowed you."

"Speaking of marriage, how is yours?" Cherisse asked. Her brows arched questioningly.

"She came back to me," David stated simply. "And we couldn't be happier. Threat of divorce is a surprisingly effective salve for a failing marriage."

"Then you agree that you could have been a better husband?"

"A better husband, better father, better human being, Mrs. Payne," David said. He got up. "I just wanted to welcome you back and tell you that I've spoken with the board and they've agreed to give Sonia Lopez a try. I'm going to tell her now."

Cherisse was out of her chair and hugging him before she could weigh the pros and cons of her actions.

David laughed as he set her away from him. "Now, now, Mrs. Payne, anyone coming in here would think you have a thing for me. I'm a married man!"

"So sorry, Dr. Pedersen," Cherisse said, laughing softly.

David actually winked at her. "And I would appreciate it if you wouldn't tell the others I've softened. I like having them fear me. I don't get invited to all those endless birthday parties they're always throwing throughout the place. Any excuse to have cake." With that, he left.

Cherisse sat back down.

She phoned Harry at lunch and found out that he was in Vail. "I'll be back before you get home," he told her. "I'll cook for you and rub your feet."

"This doesn't sound like the same Harry I left this morning," Cherisse said.

"That Harry was a horse's ass," said Harry with a chuckle. "This Harry knows you were right. It's your career and you mean to end it on a positive note. You have integrity. I admire that in you."

"Thank you," Cherisse said. She then went on to tell him about her day so far. Harry asked her if the little boy with HIV had family or if he were alone in the world.

"His chart shows that he has family," she told him.

"Good," said Harry. "I would hate for him to be alone."

By the time February 26 rolled around, Cherisse's official last day at work, Harry had gotten a good taste of what it was like to be married to a nurse. He'd listened to her days, held her at night and comforted her when the little boy with HIV died in his sleep. She'd cried herself to sleep that night, and he'd lain awake watching her face in repose.

He didn't understand why she'd put herself through such agony, because that's what her job was in his opinion—sheer agony. He wouldn't have lasted a month, let alone eight years.

The next morning when he'd asked her why she had stayed for so long, she had answered rather glibly, "Somebody's gotta do it." But one look in her eyes told him she was not nearly as detached as she pretended to be. He saw pain in her aspect, pain and a kind of helplessness that clutched at his heart.

But that morning, she had had to go to work and he hadn't had the time to pursue it.

At work on her last day, everyone gathered in the employee lounge to give her a send-off. David was there in spite of his dislike of such gatherings. And he ate cake alongside the rest of them.

Sonia got up and made a short speech. She was definitely showing by then, her smock unable to hide her baby bump. But she had accepted David's offer of the head nurse job after he had promised her a sufficiently long maternity leave.

"I'm a little biased," she said, "because Cheri has been my BFF, best friend forever, since we were in second grade. You all know her history, she married her childhood sweetheart and moved to Philadelphia but wound up coming back home. I was the one who told her she should try nursing. I had been a practical nurse for years. Then she came home, got into nursing school, became an RN then had the nerve to go for her master's degree, leaving me in the dust. So, jealous heifer that I am, I went back and got my bachelor's degree. A few years later she goaded me into going for my master's. So, thank you, you interfering busybody. Because of you I've nearly got my master's degree and that crazy man over there—" she pointed to David "—has offered me your job, which I took in a moment of madness. I'll never be able to replace you, but I'll do my best."

Cherisse got up and hugged her. "Girl, you're gonna set this place on fire."

"Before it's over, she might try to out of frustration," David said. "But I won't let her."

Everybody laughed. Cherisse believed that was the first time any of them had laughed at something David had said.

He didn't take it well. Not used to their benevolence, more used to their acrimony, he looked slightly embarrassed and beat a hasty retreat after telling her, "You were an excellent head nurse, Mrs. Payne."

"Thank you, David," she called to him before he disappeared into the corridor.

So she left Mercy Hospital unbowed and with her dignity intact as she'd promised David Pedersen she would.

About three weeks after becoming a woman of leisure, Cherisse awoke after three in the morning, her breasts throbbing painfully. She had noticed some tenderness in them perhaps two weeks ago, but had not thought anything of it because she and Harry were sometimes overly enthusiastic when they made love. This morning, however, she was certain that she was experiencing pregnancy symptoms.

She climbed out of bed. Harry's big hand felt for her as soon as she got up. He could detect her absence even in his sleep.

The urge to go to the bathroom had struck her upon awakening, and she had to go.

He was wide-awake when she walked back into the room. "Is something the matter?"

She started to say she'd only had to go to the bathroom but thought better of it. "My breasts are really sore. The pain woke me."

Instantly concerned, Harry's first thought was cancer

because his mother had recently fought the disease. He leaped from bed and pulled her into his arms. "Who's your doctor? Oh, hell, I don't even know my wife's doctor's name!"

"Harry, calm down," Cherisse said, smiling up at him. "I don't think it's anything you need to be worried about. I'm pretty sure I'm just pregnant."

Harry was floored. He had to sit down. After sitting on the bed, he peered up at her with a confused expression in his dark brown depths, and said, "You think you might be pregnant?"

Cherisse sat on his lap. "It's a distinct possibility," she said. "We have been making love practically every day for weeks now, without birth control."

Harry hugged her tightly. "Let's not guess. I want to know for sure. Can you get an appointment with your doctor for today?"

"Probably not," said Cherisse truthfully, "but over-the-counter pregnancy tests are about ninety-seven percent accurate. We can buy one of those and find out. I can make an appointment to see my doctor later. I'm a nurse, Harry, I know these things."

Harry grinned broadly. "I'll go buy a couple right now."

He got up, nearly dropping Cherisse onto the floor in his eagerness to get dressed and find an all-night pharmacy.

"It's three-thirty in the morning, Harry!"

Harry was in his closet pulling a pair of jeans from a drawer. "I think there's a Walgreens near here that stays open twenty-four hours a day," he said, not hearing anything she had to say about it being pitch-black outside.

"Harry, it can wait until daylight."

He already had one leg in the jeans. "It's only a few miles from here," he said.

Jeans and sweatshirt on, he wiggled his feet into athletic

shoes sans socks and went to plant a kiss on her cheek. "Lie down, baby, I'll be back in no time."

Cherisse got back into bed. Let him go out there if he wanted to. It was probably thirty degrees with the wind chill factor off the scales. "Harry," she called, "don't forget your coat."

"Okay, sweetheart," she heard him say. Then she didn't hear anything else in the big house on the hill. In the Patterson house she could always hear doors closing. She knew where every creak was on the stairs. This house was like a mausoleum, deathly quiet. No creaks in its stairs or hardwood floors. Everything looked new and perfect. Eventually, she knew she and Harry would turn it into a home, but for now it was just an expensive place where she could lay her head.

Lying on her back, she placed her hand on her stomach. "What will you be?" She didn't need a home pregnancy test to tell her that Harry's child was growing in her womb. She knew it with her heart.

Soon, she drifted to sleep. The next thing she knew, Harry was back and sitting on the bed, waking her. He had a huge bag with him. Sitting up, she said, "What did you do, buy every kit on the shelf?"

"I got different kinds," Harry explained, "in case we get fuzzy results."

"Fuzzy results?" asked Cherisse.

"I stood there and read the instructions on the boxes. Sometimes results can be inconclusive." He emptied the bag's contents onto the bed.

"I see," said Cherisse, reaching for one of the boxes. She quickly read the instructions, which basically said all she had to do was pee on the strip provided.

"This one looks simple enough."

She got up. Harry got up. She turned. "If you don't mind, I'd like to do this in private."

"But, baby, I was there at conception, I want to be there every step in the process."

"No!" said Cherisse. "Now stay here and read some more boxes and I'll be back as soon as I get the results on this little strip."

Harry acquiesced, but unwillingly.

In about five minutes, Cherisse returned with the strip held aloft. "Okay, now we wait."

It was the longest wait in the history of waiting. Harry nervously paced. Cherisse tried to lie down and close her eyes, but Harry's constant pacing was getting on her nerves.

She was relieved when the timer went off and they could read the results. She read the instructions again to make sure she hadn't misread it before. She peered at the strip. If she was reading it correctly, she was definitely pregnant, although the instructions said to make an appointment with her doctor as soon as possible.

"We're pregnant," she told Harry.

Harry yelled, picked her up and spun her round and round until he got dizzy and had to stop, then he got nauseous and had to run to the bathroom where he threw up.

"Oh, God," Cherisse said to herself as he left the room in a hurry, "looks like I won't be the one in the family to have morning sickness." Her stomach felt just fine. Her breasts were still aching, but that was something she'd experienced with Danielle. It wasn't hard to get used to. Vomiting, on the other hand, was something she had always avoided if she could. When she was pregnant with Danielle she hadn't had it. She hoped she'd be as blessed with this pregnancy. Harry could have it for her. She thought that was fair seeing as how she was going to be the one to push the baby from her body when the time came.

She stood at the bathroom door. Harry was at the sink, rinsing his mouth out.

"What was that?" he asked, seeking her medical opinion.

"Excitement," she said, smiling. "Don't worry, Harry, you're going to be a wonderful father."

She went to him and hugged him. "I'll phone my doctor's office in the morning. Maybe you should see yours, too, just in case. He can tell you more about why some men have sympathy symptoms when their wives are pregnant. It's a stressful time. A happy time for the most part, but it does make you worry about whether or not you're going to step up to the plate when the time comes and be a good father and a supportive husband. Some men worry about that."

Harry suddenly got a whiff of his breath and turned around to go brush his teeth. "Go to bed, sweetheart," he said. "I'll be there in a minute."

In her fifth month, Cherisse was having a routine sonogram when her doctor, Edie Warren, a young black woman who wore her black natural hair in a short afro, said excitedly, "Did you see that?"

Cherisse was lying flat on her back. She had difficulty seeing the screen. You could barely make out the images on the screen anyway. Cherisse sometimes thought Dr. Warren didn't know what she was talking about when she pointed out the baby's heartbeat or when she said the baby was sucking its thumb. Cherisse just saw dark globs on the screen.

"What!" she said, just as excitedly as her doctor.

Dr. Warren laughed. "Cheri, it looks like you're having twins."

Cherisse sat up. "Twins?!" she shouted.

"Well, because of your age," explained the twenty-seven year-old, "you are more likely to have twins."

"I understand that," Cherisse said testily. "And thanks for calling me an old crone."

Dr. Warren continued to laugh. "I didn't call you an old crone, my dear," said Dr. Warren, in her clipped British accent.

"Would you take another look?" Cherisse asked. "Harry's going to faint when I tell him. I'd like to be positive I'm delivering the right news."

"Very well," said Dr. Warren. "Lie back down."

Cherisse lay down and Dr. Warren once again ran the cold instrument over the surface of her distended belly. "Mmm, huh, twins," the doctor confirmed. "Do you want a second opinion? I can get one of the nurses to come in and have a look."

"No, that's all right, thank you," Cherisse said as she sat up on the examination table.

"Did you see any interesting appendages while you were looking?"

"I can't tell whether they're male or female at this point," said Dr. Warren.

Cherisse pulled the paper gown as far over her belly as it would go, which wasn't very far. Her body was getting rounder every day. Thank God, she hadn't experienced morning sickness. But her ankles were swollen half the time and she was already having back pain. No wonder since she was carrying twins!

Harry was waiting for her outside the examining room. He grinned when he saw her. Cherisse grimaced. The man thought she was a goddess. He loved her blossoming body. He doted on her. If she weren't careful she could easily turn into a beached whale, as much as he waited on her hand and foot.

Sometimes she went to bed early just to give him a rest from his constant vigilance to make sure her feet were raised, or her back was rubbed. She would tell him to stop, but she was afraid she would hurt his feelings.

"Well, how is our little one?" he asked expectantly.

Because Cherisse thought it might be unsafe to spring the news on Harry when he was behind the wheel of their car, she thought she should tell him here in the office.

"Honey, maybe you ought to sit back down," she said, taking him by the arm and gently prodding him toward the dark purple upholstered chair he'd gotten out of a minute ago.

He hadn't had any more sympathy symptoms since the night he'd thrown up, so Cherisse didn't think he was going to react in a similar fashion here in Dr. Warren's waiting room.

She sat down beside him and took his hand in hers. Taking a deep breath, she said, "You know those twin brothers who were professional football players at the same time? I can't think of their names."

"You're talking about the Barbers," Harry said.

"Yeah, the Barbers. Um, baby, we're going to either have a couple of football players or a couple of skiers. Dr. Warren can't tell the sex just yet but we're definitely having twins."

Harry didn't say anything for a solid two minutes. He sat there staring into space.

Cherisse squeezed his hand. "It could be worse, it could be triplets."

Harry focused in on her again. He smiled. "I wanted two kids, so this is perfect. You'll have both at the same time."

"They usually come out one at a time," Cherisse pointed out, making sure he knew she was in for double the labor, double the pain. She had a mind to make him work extra hard today to pay for that comment.

But she couldn't look at that happy expression on his handsome face without loving him a little more.

"Come on, big daddy," she said as she took his hand, "let's go home."

* * *

The projected due date of the twins came and went. Dr. Warren had told Cherisse that it was difficult to predict with any accuracy when a woman of her age would give birth, especially if she was carrying twins. The babies might come early or they might come late, although if the due date had come and gone, it was important to monitor the mother closely for signs of fetal distress.

It had been more than a week since she was due to deliver and Cherisse was at her mother's house helping cook for the family reunion that was going to be held that weekend. Everyone was coming here this year.

Harry had decided not to go to his family's reunion in Kentucky to be near Cherisse's side so close to her giving birth. But he was driving her crazy with his constant pampering, both at the resort and at the house in Denver. Cherisse needed a calming influence and there was only one place she could get it—at her mother's house.

Sonia was there with her three-month-old baby, Joy Renee. Harry and Ken were outside getting the grill started because they were going to barbecue some chicken and ribs for dinner.

Cherisse was standing at the sink washing red potatoes in preparation for peeling them with a potato peeler. Her mother liked to add them to the pole beans, a big pot of which was simmering on the stove.

Suddenly, her water broke. It gushed down her legs, wetting the floor and forming a puddle around her feet.

She surprised herself with the calmness she demonstrated when she turned to her mother, who was taking something out of the refrigerator, and said, "Ma, would you go tell Harry my water just broke and the babies are on the way?"

Jo screamed and ran out the back door to the yard.

Danielle came running downstairs and straight to the kitchen when she'd heard her grandmother's blood-curdling screams.

When she got to the kitchen, her mother was standing wide-legged at the sink, holding on to it. Danielle ran to her.

Cherisse forced a smile, although right after her water had broken, she'd been hit by a hell of a contraction that was twisting her up inside. "Sonia went to my old room to put Joy Renee down for her nap," she said. "Would you get her for me, baby?"

She didn't have to because Sonia had also heard Miss Jo's screams and had stood stock-still for a moment, afraid that the sound would awaken Joy Renee. When Joy Renee did not move an inch, she made sure the sides of the portable crib were secure, then she left the room, pulled the door closed behind her and hurried downstairs.

She entered the kitchen now and quickly assessed the situation. To Danielle, she said, "Help me get her to the couch in the living room. She needs to lie down where her head can be raised and her feet lowered."

They were headed in that direction when Harry burst through the back door, followed by Ken and Miss Jo.

"Has anybody called nine-one-one!" he yelled.

No one had. Danielle took care of that and afterward went to her grandmother, who was looking quite pale, and made her sit down on a chair at the kitchen table. The action was in the living room and she didn't think her grandmother needed to be in the thick of it.

Harry sat behind Cherisse on the couch so that she reclined on him. Sonia was busy removing Cherisse's underwear. Ken, who was quite queasy in these kinds of situations—he'd fainted when Sonia had given birth—retreated to the kitchen to wait with Miss Jo and Danielle.

Sonia was squatting at the foot of the couch with a bird's-eye-view of the crowning of one of the twins' heads while Harry was holding Cherisse, and whispering, "It's gonna be all right," over and over again.

"It won't be long now," Sonia cried. "When I tell you, I want you to push, sis, but not too hard, okay?"

Cherisse let out a groan. "Okay!"

"Push," said Sonia.

The baby's head emerged and soon the body followed. Sonia held the little boy in her arms with his head pointed downward. The baby began to cry and Cherisse breathed a deep sigh of relief. He was okay!

Sonia promptly placed the baby on her chest and went back to her post at the foot of the couch. The other baby's head was crowning.

Sonia counted silently, wanting to be able to say how many seconds or minutes the twins had been born apart.

Eighty counts later, she cried to Cherisse, "Push!"

Cherisse pushed and soon another little boy came into the world bawling. Sonia also placed this child in his mother's arms. Harry was holding all three of them with a thankful smile on his face.

He had two sons, both healthy, both with strong lungs and all their limbs, and his beautiful wife worn out but very much alive, in his arms.

Life was good.

REQUEST YOUR FREE BOOKS!

2 FREE NOVELS
PLUS 2 FREE GIFTS!

KIMANI™ ROMANCE

Love's ultimate destination!

YES! Please send me 2 FREE Kimani™ Romance novels and my 2 FREE gifts (gifts are worth about $10). After receiving them, if I don't wish to receive any more books, I can return the shipping statement marked "cancel." If I don't cancel, I will receive 4 brand-new novels every month and be billed just $4.69 per book in the U.S. or $5.24 per book in Canada, plus 25¢ shipping and handling per book and applicable taxes, if any*. That's a savings of over 20% off the cover price! I understand that accepting the 2 free books and gifts places me under no obligation to buy anything. I can always return a shipment and cancel at any time. Even if I never buy another book from Kimani Press, the two free books and gifts are mine to keep forever.

168 XDN EF2D   368 XDN EF3T

Name	(PLEASE PRINT)	
Address		Apt. #
City	State/Prov.	Zip/Postal Code

Signature (if under 18, a parent or guardian must sign)

Mail to **The Reader Service:**
IN U.S.A.: P.O. Box 1867, Buffalo, NY 14240-1867
IN CANADA: P.O. Box 609, Fort Erie, Ontario L2A 5X3

Not valid to current subscribers of Kimani Romance books.

Want to try two free books from another line?
Call 1-800-873-8635 or visit www.morefreebooks.com.

* Terms and prices subject to change without notice. N.Y. residents add applicable sales tax. Canadian residents will be charged applicable provincial taxes and GST. Offer not valid in Quebec. This offer is limited to one order per household. All orders subject to approval. Credit or debit balances in a customer's account(s) may be offset by any other outstanding balance owed by or to the customer. Please allow 4 to 6 weeks for delivery. Offer available while quantities last.

Your Privacy: Kimani Press is committed to protecting your privacy. Our Privacy Policy is available online at www.eHarlequin.com or upon request from the Reader Service. From time to time we make our lists of customers available to reputable third parties who may have a product or service of interest to you. If you would prefer we not share your name and address, please check here. ☐

KROM08R

Love, honor and cherish…

i promise

NATIONAL BESTSELLING AUTHOR

ADRIANNE byrd

Beautiful, brilliant Christian McKinley could set the world afire. Instead, she dreams of returning to her family's Texas ranch. But Malcolm Williams has other plans for her, publicly proposing to Christian at the social event of the year. So how can she tactfully turn down a proposal from this gorgeous, well-connected, obscenely rich suitor? By inadvertently falling in love with his twin brother, Jordan!

"Byrd proves once again that she's a wonderful storyteller."—*Romantic Times BOOKreviews* on *The Beautiful Ones*

Coming the first wefi of December wherever books are sold.

ARABESQUE®

www.kimanipress.com

KPAB1151208

Should she believe the facts?

Essence bestselling author

DONNA HILL

SEDUCTION AND LIES

Book 2 of the TLC miniseries

Hawking body products for Tender Loving Care is just a
cover. The real deal? They're undercover operatives for a
covert organization. Newest member Danielle Holloway's first
assignment is to infiltrate an identity-theft ring. But when the
clues lead to her charismatic beau, Nick Mateo, Danielle has
more problems than she thought.

TLC—There's more to these ladies than Tender Loving Care!

Coming the first week of December wherever books are sold.

KIMANI™
ROMANCE

www.kimanipress.com

KPDH0921208

*They had nothing in common—
except red-hot desire!*

National bestselling author

Marcia King-Gamble

TEMPTING
M O G U L
the

Life coach Kennedy Fitzgerald's assignment
grooming unconventional, sexy Salim Washington
to take over as TV studio head has become a little
too pleasurable. For both of them. But shady
motivations and drama threaten to stall this
merger before the ink's even dry!

*Coming the first week of December
wherever books are sold.*

KIMANI
ROMANCE ™

www.kimanipress.com   KPMKG0931208

Too close for comfort...

National bestselling author

Gwyneth Bolton

THE LAW

OF DESIRE

Book #3 in Hightower Honors

Detective Lawrence Hightower's stakeout is
compromised by a beautiful, suspicious stranger.
Minerva Jones needs his protection—but he's not
so sure he can trust her. Minerva is intensely
attracted to the sexy cop, but she's got secrets...
and trouble is closing in.

HIGHTOWER HONORS

FOUR BROTHERS ON A MISSION TO PROTECT, SERVE AND LOVE...

*Coming the first week of December
wherever books are sold.*

KIMANI™
ROMANCE

www.kimanipress.com   KPGB0941208

Will she let her past decide her future?

NATIONAL BESTSELLING AUTHOR
Melanie Schuster

trust
IN
Me

Playboy Lucien Deveraux is ready to settle
down and be a one-woman man. Trouble is,
Nicole Argonne has no time for "pretty boys"—
especially the reformed-player type. If Lucien
wants her, he needs to prove himself...and
Nicole's not going to make it easy.

"A richly satisfying love story."
—*Romantic Times BOOKreviews* on *Let It Be Me*

*Coming the first week of December
wherever books are sold.*

KIMANI™
ROMANCE

www.kimanipress.com   KPMS0951208

*Their marriages were shams,
but their payback will be real....*

Counterfeit
Wives

Fan-favorite author
PHILLIP THOMAS DUCK

Todd Darling was the perfect husband...to three
women. Seduced and betrayed, Nikki, Jacqueline
and Dawn learned too late their dream marriage
was an illusion. Struggling to rebuild their lives,
they're each invited by a mysterious woman to
learn more about the husband they thought they
knew. But on a journey filled with surprises, the
greatest revelations will be the truths they learn
about themselves....

*Coming the first week of December
wherever books are sold.*

sepia™

www.kimanipress.com   KPPTD1291208